HIDDEN DESTINATION

A True Romanian Adventure: Escape, Revolution, and a Story of Compassion

by

R. Lee Brennan

ACW Press
5501 N. 7th Ave. #502
Phoenix, AZ 85013

Scripture quotations unless otherwise noted are taken from the *Holy Bible*, King James
Version.
Scripture quotations marked Jerusalem Bible are from *The Jerusalem Bible*, copyright ©
1966 by Darton, Longman & Todd Ltd and Doubleday & Company., Inc. Used by permis-
sion.
Scripture quotations marked TEV are from *The Good News Bible, The Bible in Today's
English Version*, copyright © 1966, 1971, 1976 by the American Bible Society.

Publisher's Cataloging-in-Publication
(Provided by Quality Books, Inc.)

Brennan, R. Lee.
    Hidden destination: a true Romanian adventure :
escape, revolution, and a story of compassion / by R. Lee
Brennan. — 1st ed.
    p. cm.
    Includes bibliographical references.
    ISBN 1-89252-500-3

    1. Olari, Mike. 2. Romania--Biography. 3. Romania--
History--Revolution, 1989 4. Christianity and politics
--Romania   I. Title

DK267.5.O53B74 1998   943.8'05'092 [B]
                            QBI98-1147

To my sons
Andrew and Noah,
for patiently accepting a preoccupied
father during the writing of this book

Contents

Part 1: Into The Unknown 9

Part 2: Revolution! 183

Part 3: To Heal a Wounded Land 221

"I assure you that unless you change and become like children you will never enter the kingdom of God."

Jesus Christ

"Every Communist must grasp the truth: Political power grows out of the barrel of a gun."

Mao Tse-Tung

PREFACE

This book is a contradiction. Amazing things happen, but few notice. God answers prayers miraculously, but more needs to be done. This account is true, but can easily be seen as naive exaggeration.

Christ told his followers to be as wise as serpents and as harmless as doves. Healthy skepticism is necessary as some people will believe anything. Their imaginations are titillated by the very mention of the word miracle, and they can be easily exploited. Yet miracles do happen, and to believe otherwise is to embrace a lie.

I cannot prove the miracles recorded here. However, I have come to know Mike Olari, and have found him to be an honest man. I have checked his references. Without exception his sincerity has been endorsed. Those who know him will corroborate these accounts. I have documented my sources, except for when Mike has provided information. There is also one source who wished to remain anonymous.

Mike Olari, his wife Ana, and their children are average people, and writing this book runs contrary to their cultural values. They come from a society where virtue and low profile coexist, this account seems to be a brash and garish glorification of self. However, the objective of this book is to show what can happen when one steps out in childlike faith. It is meant to encourage others to do the same, and watch God act.

Divine intervention is what kept the church alive and growing during Romania's dark years. Communist authorities forced Christians' backs to the wall, with no place to turn except God. And God was there, in an amazing way.

His miracles were experienced by many, and Mike's story is not unusual.

This is Mike Olari's story, not mine. Mike asks God for signs in ways I would not feel comfortable. Mike asked in simple childlike faith, was prepared to obey, and God answered.

Miracles are interesting. Many can easily be explained away by a nonbeliever. But as one opens up to the supernatural moves of God, the miracles become more remarkable. It is important to give God the credit for each miracle, and not the recipient of the gift.

I would also like to thank the following for their voluntary editorial assistance and constructive criticism: Aretta Loving, Ernie Haas, Ted Thomas, Linda Zaccone, Nancy Pruett-Williams, Karen Olson, Andrea Wallach, and Sylvia Hughes.

Read with caution and an open mind.

R. Lee Brennan

Phoenix 1998

INTO THE UNKNOWN

PART 1

*"None who have always been free can understand
the terrible fascinating power of the hope of
freedom to those who are not free."*
Pearl Buck 1892-1973

CHAPTER 1

Panic surged upward through Mike's chest, lodged in his throat, and began to swell. His heart thumped wildly as he hugged the damp earth. He yearned to melt into the soil, like a disappearing raindrop.

All had heard it—the crisp sound of a snapped twig shooting through the trees. Pressed low, breath held, they strained their ears for the next sound. It came, a soft footstep on the fallen leaves, followed shortly by another crunch and rustle of underbrush.

Could it be a soldier without a dog? Perhaps he would unwittingly walk by. Maybe he would not notice, if everyone stayed calm, if no one ran in blind fear. All remained frozen, as tense seconds dragged into minutes. Minutes crept by. Slowly the steps drew closer. With a final crunch of leaves a deer stepped into view. The animal sniffed the air, paused for a moment, turned, and bolted though the woods.

A rush of giddy relief washed over them. Briefly. A dozen dirty and fatigued refugees lay scattered about. Prostrated in silent supplication, they begged the God of nature to breathe their scent on a gentle breeze, away from any soldier's dog. Sometimes patrols walked the road just below them. Other times they stalked these woods near the Romanian border.

Thirst once again seeped into Mike's consciousness and gripped it. Choked in stillness, they lay hushed for hours. Late summer sun heated the high forest foliage and blanketed them in heavy humidity as they lay hidden in underbrush and tall weeds. Their last drink had been skimmed from lonely puddles, deeper in the Transylvanian woods. That was yesterday. A few meters away the Danube slipped silently past. No one dared cross the road and drop down the steep bank for a drink in the dirty river. That would put everyone at risk. Guards hunted them and any like them. They could be shot then and there, or face the uncertainty of capture. It had happened before. If taken prisoner, they would face the whim of their captors; they could be put on trial, sentenced to prison, or beaten. Some died from the beatings.

In the distance the sound of an automobile engine gradually became louder. Was it actually slowing down? Time again slowed into forever. The car finally passed, and left the fugitives in silence once again. Why was it moving so slowly? Were they looking for something, or someone? Mike preferred vehicles that traveled faster, the driver was more apt to concentrate on the road, and less likely to stop.

"I'm too jumpy," he thought. "The worst thing is to be frightened at nothing. I've got to pray, trust God." He glanced at his hand and noticed a mosquito, as it drilled its long stinger into his flesh. Silently he smeared blood and insect parts across his skin. Now all his bites itched.

No matter what the danger, or how thirsty and hungry Mike had become, a separate concern floated continually through his brain. This was a concern, not a worry, for Mike knew that all was in God's hands, and he trusted his Maker, as a child would trust his parent. Still, he wondered how Ana, his young pregnant wife, was coping back home. Would the police harass her when they discovered he was gone? She could be arrested for his escape, taken in and interrogated under bright lights. Sometimes they commanded spouses of escapees to sign papers. But the authorities never allowed them to read these texts. These documents could be anything from a divorce to a confession of crimes. That is the way things worked in Romania during the early 1980s when communism gripped the land.

And what about his young son, just over a year old? When would he see him again? Was Ana right? Her idea was to keep applying for emigration papers, no matter how many times they had been turned down.

Mike turned his mind from his family, only to have thirst again seize his thoughts. Even still, the water that flowed in the nearby Danube did not tempt him, at least not for now. The river was filthy, oil floated on the surface. Many nations did their commerce on this waterway. Most boats and barges constantly leaked petroleum and dumped waste anywhere in the river. These same countries also pumped their industrial refuse into the once fresh water.

Hunger held Mike's stomach, but he was too parched to eat his few pieces of bread and chocolate. In a plastic bag a small quantity of sugar waited to replenish a weak body's ebbing strength. His mouth felt as if it were swabbed with a sticky-dry cotton ball, and eating sugar would make him sick.

Mike remained confident in spite of hunger, thirst, danger, and the mighty Danube they had yet to cross. He had no comprehension of what he was in for, no concept of what lay before him. But memories of past escape attempts built his courage. He had tried to flee Romania before. Once he was even caught along with his brother-in-law, Mircea. His captors seemed unaware of what was going on, almost as if they were blind to the reality. They did not notice those telltale items any self-respecting guard looks for. Mike's bag contained the basic quick-energy staples of sugar and chocolate. Most importantly, Mike had U.S. dollars. It was illegal for a Romanian to posses United States currency. American money was a quick passport to prison.*

Now, as he lay in wait, Mike's mind replayed that earlier escape with Mircea. They had been dropped off near the border. Supposedly, this would be a short hike overland into Yugoslavia, not far from the Hungarian border. However, in the darkness of night with no compass to guide them, the two quickly became disoriented. They headed in the opposite direction, away from freedom; many miles were covered before the sun came up. In a forest they found a set of train tracks and followed them until a station came into sight. Here in the early morning rays they read a sign giving destinations, departure, and arrival times. Mike and Mircea quickly learned that they were still in Romania near the city of Timişoara. From there they could take a train back north to Arad; however, the next train was not due for several hours.

A road intersected the tracks near the station. Perhaps it would be a better idea to catch a bus than to wait for a train. The two would-be refugees headed off down the country highway at a brisk pace. The quicker they could get to Timişoara the better. They looked suspect. Dirty, hot, sweaty, and carrying handbags, they fit the profile of those on the run.

---

*The maximum sentence for possession of foreign currency was seven years. However, on certain holidays the dictator Nicolae Ceauşescu would release prisoners halfway through their terms. Ceauşescu thought he would gain political support through those early releases. Only rarely did one serve a full sentence for this "crime." Possession of American currency was usually dealt with more harshly than possession of other currencies.

Mike remembered how they approached one of Romania's many small villages where two soldiers on patrol spotted them and signaled them to stop. As they approached the soldiers, an unusual boldness came over them.

"We are lost. Where are we?" Mike's question was firm, his earnest blue eyes pierced the soldier's concentration.

"Who are you?" the second soldier demanded. "Are you from around here? You don't look familiar. Let's see your papers."

Mike and Mircea quickly produced their documentation.

"Where is the nearest train station?" asked Mike. "We're late and I've got business to tend to!"

The guards sorted through the papers as Mike continued his questioning, "How much does a train ticket cost?"

"Can we get a bus around here?" Mircea interrupted.

Mike and Mircea continued the questions, and did not give the guards time to think.

"Wait a minute! Quiet! How did you two get to this part of the country?" Perhaps the soldier was on to them. "You are from Arad!"

In exasperation Mike explained, "We got a ride with some guy who dropped us off in the wilderness."

"Look, we are Romanians. We can go anywhere we want in this country. That's the law!" Mircea reminded them.

"He is right! We are Rom..."

Mircea interrupted again, "We have been walking all night, we're tired, and we're in no mood for this."

"We got lost cutting through the woods," Mike chimed in.

"Do you have any idea what it's like to be lost in a dark woods at night?" complained Mircea.

"Where are we anyway?" Mike's query sounded sincere.

"You're about an hour out of Timişoara...."

"Which way are we out of Timişoara, north or south?" Mircea demanded.

The soldiers eyed the two. They didn't act like refugees on the run. "Let's see what's in your bags."

Inwardly Mike and Mircea prayed, while outwardly their mouths were in full operation.

"You never told us how far it was to the train station," Mike reminded the guard.

"Where is the train station anyway?" Mircea continued his relentless questioning.

The guard looked up, while his fingers dug down through the contents of one bag. At the same time he tried to give directions. His hands went right past the chocolate and sugar.

"Which is cheaper, a bus or a train?" asked Mike. "Can we get a bus to Arad from here?"

The soldiers conferred between themselves, not really paying attention to their bag search. "From the next village I think you can get a bus to Arad but it will go down to Timişoara first," the first soldier said, trying to be helpful.

"We must search you," said the other. "Lean forward, put your hands on the tree, and spread your legs."

Mike and Mircea complied, still asking questions. "What time does the next bus come by."

"I think...about ten this morning." It was obvious the soldier was guessing. Frisking the two suspects had been reduced to a mere formality. Neither trooper noticed Mike had American currency in his possession.

"You are free to go now. If you hurry you can catch the bus!" The soldiers handed Mike and Mircea their bags.

"Good-bye. Thanks for your help!" Mike was more grateful than the guards would ever know.

"You have been of great assistance!" Mircea called back over his shoulder as he cheerfully waved. Both hustled down the road praising God. To them it was clear He had protected them, sending His angels to distract the guards.

Mike's mind was instantly jerked into the present, as a bird fluttered in the branches above. He was back in the grass stifled in stillness. Yet the memory of their attempted escape brought a smile to him as he now lay hidden, waiting for darkness, waiting to attempt another escape. Fortunately this time of rest was necessary for Mike and the others. The last two days had been grueling. All were exhausted, to the point of wanting to give up. A dangerous and difficult swim lay ahead of them when night fell.

Eyes always turned toward the road. They scrutinized what was ahead. Ears strained for strange new sounds, but they heard only silence. No one wanted to hear anything new. No one needed more excitement. Then, as if from nowhere, a woman appeared on the road, walking steadily, silently in a northerly direction. Again all became breathless, motionless. Nothing could be heard but a faint zephyr in the trees and a mosquito's high squeal in the ear. It was unlikely she had seen them. There was a preoccupied manner in her stride. No doubt her course led towards a nearby village. These villagers were paid a bounty by the government for any refugees caught. One could not be too careful. No one relaxed until she was well down the road.

Again Mike's mind wandered back, and he pondered the wisdom of this whole adventure. A man—with a family depending on him—was now jeopardizing all for freedom. Then again, what security existed here for him? He could lose his job at any time if the government decided.

Or he could be jailed tomorrow for no reason. For him the real question was: where does God want me? Mike felt quite confident that God was leading him out of Romania. He felt a quiet peace about this. Closer to the surface, other emotions were present, including doubt and fear. But in the deepness of his soul, Mike tried to listen to what God was saying. He was willing to stay in Romania, if that was what God wanted and he prayed that God would stop him if he was not supposed to go. He also prayed that his escape would help him grow — grow in knowledge and sensitivity to God's nudging on his spirit. Finally, Mike wanted to help the people of Romania, but he had no idea how. There was an inkling in his soul that things were going to get worse for those he left behind.

To build and bolster his courage, Mike spent the long afternoon hours replaying events of the last three months, as if they were there for him to review and reconsider. For the past three months this plot had built to a climax, a climax that would play out in a few more hours. Why had so many escape attempts failed? Even though he failed, why hadn't he been caught? Mike had few answers, but careful reassessment of events showed God's hand, protecting and guiding.

The occurrences of the last ninety days had fallen into place like a row of tumbling dominoes. In retrospect each event was linked to the one before it. Yet as Mike progressed along the line of falling pieces, he had no idea, not the slightest comprehension, of what would happen next.

The trigger domino had been an elementary plan of escape: put a driver in Mike's cramped Dacia,* add four refugees, and drive to a spot close to the border. The driver

---

*A Dacia is a Romanian version of a Renault.

would stop, everyone would pile out and make a run for it. The driver would return to Arad. Simple.

That night was cloudy and dark. The plan worked perfectly, with one small problem. When the car came to a stop, Mike could not get out. The door was open, but he could not move. The others ran across the highway and into the woods. Mike was stuck in the back seat! Immobile!

"Go! Get out! Run!" hissed the driver.

"I can't move!" Mike was desperately bewildered.

"We can't stay here, get out of the car!"

Mike remained frozen.

"Soldiers will see the car! I've got to go." The driver pulled away.

Once they were down the road Mike was able to move again. He sat stewing in frustration. He even thought of going back and catching up with his companions, but it was too risky and would only increase the chance of everyone getting caught.

A few days later, his friends made a quick phone call back to Romania. They had successfully made it through Yugoslavia into Italy. While Mike was happy for them, at the same time he was crestfallen. He should have been in Italy too!

A growing state of confusion and depression lay hold of him. Finally Mike came to the realization that he must retreat and seek the counsel of God. Needing a place away from the city, he returned to the village of his childhood. Heading east from Arad, about fifty miles, Mike found solitude in the village of Chisindia. He walked the nearby fields and forests venting frustration to his Maker. At first his words were swift and angry, but as his disappointment was expunged, he felt the quiet love of God ebbing upwards in his soul. God was illustrating, giving Mike a new message, showing him something else to do. Desire shifted from freedom, to making himself sensitive to the impulse of the Holy Spirit. Emotional quiescence reigned as an image materialized in his mind. First he saw a woman named Ana, then her husband Ioan, then their children. Ioan and Ana Sopţ were tireless workers. Their older boys worked neighboring fields for wages. Every member of the family did their share, yet the fruits of their labors were lacking. They knew what it was like to go to bed hungry.

In the past Mike had taken it upon himself to supplement the family's income with bags of groceries. He did this simply as a favor, never thinking the family was his responsibility. Realization dawned upon him: he had not arranged for the provision of the Sopţs. Once he left the country, who would help them? The fact that Mike was "his brother's keeper" now became very clear to him. He needed someone else to be committed to this family's well being.

With this new awareness, he hopped into his car and drove back to Arad. There he bought bags of groceries, selecting items from sparsely stocked shelves. Hurrying, he made it to the village of Drauţ before dark and found Ana home. At the door she told him that her sons would be returning from work in the fields shortly, but she had nothing to feed them. Mike took Ana out to his Dacia, and showed her the food in his trunk. Ana cried.

Within the next few weeks Mike found another believer to help the family. He then ran down a mental checklist. It seemed he had covered all his responsibilities. He was free to plan another escape. This time he felt it was wise to ask for help. However, that would be risky also. Guides could not always be trusted. If they took your money and did not provide reliable service, who could you go to?

About three months after Mike delivered the groceries, another chance to escape presented itself. A guide had been recommended; a man who lived to the south in a village outside Timişoara was reported to be trustworthy. His job was to safely guide his clients to the border and see that they made a successful escape. His fee was 10,000 lei* per person. Mike and three of his relatives gambled and hired the man.

Once again, they were driven to a location close to the border where the guide pointed to a line of trees faintly illuminated in the moonlight. Not willing to personally take them to the border, he merely pointed and said, "Cross that field, and you will leave Romania in a couple of miles."

No one felt comfortable with the way things had developed, but what other choices did they have? After a heart pounding sprint across the open field, the party plunged into a dark woods. At first, they covered much ground. Then someone caught a trip-wire with his foot. The wire was connected to a small explosive charge designed to make noise rather than injure a person. Shortly after the first charge went off, another was triggered, then another. Guard dogs barked in the distance.

In darkness each fugitive fumbled to cover themselves in foliage. Guards and their leashed dogs edged closer. Breathlessly, they listened. It became obvious someone else was in the woods too! Another escape party and the soldiers were after them. After a long wait, Mike and his relatives slipped out of the woods. By the time the sun came up they were far away from their scheduled escape point, and still in Romania.

----

*In 1982 eighteen lei were equal to one U.S. dollar. 10,000 lei was worth about $550.

"Thou strange seducer, Opportunity."
Dryden 1672

Chapter 2

Their clothes were caked with dirt, filthy from hiding and crawling through the moist debris of the woods. They looked out of place, suspicious, since most Romanians are clean people in spite of their poverty. Their problem now was getting back to Arad without attracting attention. A train or bus was out of the question. Someone would definitely report them. Calling family in Arad was also impossible, since few owned a telephone. There was no one they trusted enough to relay a message. In the end they decided to hire a taxi. Their cash reserve would be drained, but this was their only option. The cabby would remain silent, grateful for the large fare.

Their guide had not delivered. Quite the contrary, he had sent them into a trap. Mike wanted his money back! After a few days his brother Ted drove him to the guide's house south of Timişoara.

"He's on vacation," a neighbor told them. Mike and Ted knew where he got his money for the trip. Both drove back to Arad in discouraged silence, pondering their next move. Ahead of them on the edge of the road stood a hitchhiker. As they drove past, Ted recognized him. Quickly he swerved to the shoulder and swung the door open. A fellow believer climbed in. His name was Mitaru from a church in Arad.

After a brief greeting Mitaru asked, "So are you guys going to escape tonight?"

Mike chuckled, "We weren't planning on it."

"I saw Ted's name on the list."

"What list?" Mike asked.

It was time for Ted to explain, "Well I didn't know anything was in writing, but I heard about this guide named Mihai who can be trusted."

"But after yesterday, who can we trust?" Mike looked bewildered.

"See, Mihai doesn't get paid until you are safely inside Yugoslavia." Mitaru appeared confident.

"How does that work?"

"Well there is this family in Timişoara. You pay that family, then one of them pays Mihai when he does his job."

"What about this family, can they be trusted?" Mike asked.

"I know them, they are members of the church in Timişoara," Mitaru assured him. "I would trust them."

"But still," the picture didn't seem clear to Mike, "How does the family in Arad know Mihai does the job? I mean Mihai could say we're safe in Yugoslavia, and we're really just sitting in jail, right here in Romania. How is the family to know any better? And then this Mihai just walks away with the money."

"OK, we've got that covered. See, one of the refugees carries a watch, and only when everyone is safe in Yugoslavia will the watch be handed over to Mihai. Then Mihai takes the watch back to the family in Timişoara and collects. Simple," Mitaru smiled.

Satisfied, Mike turned to Ted, "Are you going?"

Ted hesitated, a hint of frustration passed over his face. "I haven't sold the house yet. I really need the money.... I don't see how I can."

"Well, Mike, do you want to go?" Mitaru asked.

"Tonight?" Mike thought a minute, then committed himself. "OK, I'll do it." As an afterthought Mike asked, "What about Mihai? What kind of guy is he?"

"I think he's OK." Mitaru paused then continued, "He comes from a Christian family."

Mike mulled over this new scenario of escape. It was good he did not own a house. His equity was more liquid as cash easily converted on the black market. He would need dinars to make it through Yugoslavia. Also it was good that he and Ana still lived with his family. Commonly, newly married Romanians lived with their relatives for a few years. Mike felt better knowing his wife and baby son would be with his parents until they could get out of the country.

At home Ana helped her husband pack. She knew he had been planning another "trip," but had not expected it to come so soon. She tried to persuade Mike to stay, to keep applying for an exit permit. However, she knew once Mike got an idea in his head, it was hard to talk him out of it, impossible once he had prayed and believed in his heart he was right. Her only sane option was to leave Mike in God's hands. In the meantime she would keep applying for an exit permit for herself.

Mike knew he had to travel light. He slipped on a pair of dark slacks. Jeans would have been better but were almost impossible to purchase. Then he buttoned his forest green shirt. After he laced his tennis shoes, he stuffed a change of clothes, windbreaker, water bottle, and some food into a small backpack. For nourishment he took a round loaf of bread, a stick of salami, sugar, and chocolate. He wrapped his Yugoslavian dinars in plastic, then crammed the wad deep into his pants pocket. Dinars were also illegal to own, but penalties were not as severe as possession of U.S. dollars.

It was time to go and there was not much to say. Mike lightly kissed his sleeping son on the forehead. Then he held his wife and kissed her for the last time. Ana was the only one who knew of his escape. He had not told his parents who slept in the next room. It was two a.m. Ted now waited outside. Mike slipped out of the house and quietly into the car. As he got in he noticed another familiar face in the back seat. "Bembea, what are you doing here?"

"I'm going to escape with you guys."

Mike raised his eyebrows. "How old are you."

"Nineteen."

"Do your parents know about this?"

"Yes."

"Good, I hope we make it this time."

Mike did not know Bembea well. He had seen him at church and was acquainted with his parents. He hoped the teenager had the stamina for the midnight run.

The silent streets took away their desire to speak — streets lit only by a nearly full moon and an occasional streetlight. They drove quietly past familiar land marks that were somehow changing. They were landmarks of an ended phase of life, reminding Mike of good times and hard times, but mostly of lessons he had learned. Despite government repression, he had made the most of life and God had protected. He loved his countrymen, but now it was time to move on. New landmarks would be erected in the next chapter of life.

Miles outside the city Ted finally spoke, "I understand you two will be crossing the Danube."

"You know I really don't like the water...," Mike spoke euphemistically, suppressing his fear. Turning, he faced Bembea in the back seat, "How good a swimmer are you?"

"OK, I guess."

Ted looked at his brother. "Well Mike, we were hoping you could help Bembea if he got into trouble on the river."

Mike said nothing. He felt he was being put in the most helpless of situations. A water crossing confirmed the worst of his phobias. He had to depend on God totally.

"Anyway," Ted continued, "I heard there is a rope tied across the river, so you can pull yourself across."

Mike hoped that was the case, as they drove in silence for the next hour. When they arrived in Timişoara everything was quiet. It was too early for many to be out of bed.

The meeting spot was a second story apartment, inconspicuously planted on a street heavy with dark shadows. Ted drove Mike and Bembea a couple blocks past their destination and dropped them off. Then he drove on in an opposite direction, while Mike and Bembea doubled back. Quickly they stepped inside the apartment's entryway. An elevator was at the far side of a broad hall. They walked silently past first floor apartments, and entered a tiny metal cubicle. Mike manually fastened the elevator's flimsy doors and pressed the button for the second floor. Four stories above, the elevator's motor groaned loudly as it pulled them upward. Both realized that it would have been quieter to take the stairs.

Moments later they were at the second floor, where they found the correctly numbered door in the half-lit hallway. Mike pressed the doorbell and almost immediately the door partly opened and a figure motioned them inside. Quickly Mike and Bembea crossed the threshold, stepping into a dimly lit room with several other people.

Mike recognized no one. Two women talked quietly in the center of the room. All around them others milled about, or attended to last details of packing. Not all had backpacks or even a handbag. Some carried their belongings in plastic garbage bags. Proper hiking equipment was almost impossible to acquire. No one was well prepared. The man at the door briefed them on the situation. Mihai, the guide, was asleep. He also explained that he would hold Mike's money until all had escaped into Yugoslavia.

Mike already knew how payment was to be made, but asked, "Who is carrying the watch to the border?"

"See that man by the light?"

An inconspicuous man stood by the lamp. He used its light to rifle through belongings in a plastic bag.

"He's the one."

Two more people arrived, and the man went over to talk to them. At the same time, the lady of the house came into the room with a tray of cups filled with steaming coffee. Coffee was a rare commodity, seldom seen in the stores, usually served at special occasions or celebrations.

Mike unloaded several spoonfuls of sugar into his coffee before he stirred it. As he sipped his overly sweetened beverage, he wondered if Americans could get coffee more easily. As people finished their hot drink, Mihai was awakened. Mike watched two men enter the room. The first was short. Powerful muscles rippled beneath his T-shirt. The second man was taller and leaner.

"Gather 'round me, I have a few instructions." The smaller man stepped to the center of the room while the other waited in the entryway. Quietly everyone crowded around the short man.

"My name is Mihai, you must trust us." Mihai glanced at his partner in the doorway. "Dinu will assist me. You must do what we say. We will get you to the border safely." His voice was firm and businesslike, yet quiet enough not to be heard beyond the circle. "The first leg of our journey will take us about 100 miles south to Băiile Herculane.

We will go out of the way — less chance of being detected. You will leave the house individually or in groups of two. No more. Quietly use the stairs, that elevator makes too much noise. Take different routes to the train station. There you will buy a ticket to Băiile Herculane. Scatter yourselves about the train station. Don't talk to anyone. When on the train, spread yourselves around, look straight ahead or out the window. Meet me in the station at Băiile Herculane. From there I will tell you where to go."

All were silent for a moment, as the dangers and implications of this trip soaked in. Mike spoke up, "I think we should pray for God to protect us." Everyone agreed and knelt in the living room, acutely aware of their need. They were helpless as children. But a child could succeed under the cover of God's hand, and without God's help the craftiest would fail.

Over the next half hour people left the apartment by the single front entry, one by one or in pairs. Never more than two. Mihai and Dinu stayed behind. They would drive to Băiile Herculane. Mike left with Bembea about midway through the exodus.

As Mike and Bembea stepped into the morning darkness, all was quiet as moonlight on the pavement. Their footfalls could be faintly heard on the silent street. Lights of the train station soon glimmered in the distance. Quickly they crossed the small parking lot and passed through two large doors.

Brighter lights glared in the station's clean interior. A few people sat dispersed throughout the depot waiting for a late night train to somewhere. Some read a book or the state newspaper: *Flacăra Roșie.** Others slept hunched over, most just blankly stared ahead. Mike uneventfully purchased his ticket and took his place with the others. He too stared ahead.

Flacăra Roșie means the Red Flame.

The train pulled into the station shortly before four a.m. A few passengers disembarked. After giving the conductor their tickets, Mike and Bembea found a seat and began to chat about nothing in particular. Soon the train pulled out of Timişoara and took a southeasterly passage, only to swing back towards Băiile Herculane. On the way it stopped at every small village.

Mike and Bembea eventually sat in silence and stared blankly at the worn royal blue upholstery covering the seat in front of them. They did not look out their large window for inky blackness had swallowed the countryside. Clouds blocked the moon's soft light. Soon the sun would rise.

As the train's wheels rhythmically clicked along the steel track, Mike began to reconsider. His mind reviewed the man with whom they had entrusted their lives. Mike's brother had actually made the contacts. This guide could be trusted, or so sources said. He had helped others escape, and the price was right.

Mihai, the short powerfully built man, took great pride in his physical agility. Rumor had it that he himself had fled from Romania for disturbing the peace. They say he needed to prove himself, and he liked to drink. When he drank, he wound up in a fight. When alcohol was out of his system, he was a quiet, cautious man, keeping to himself.

As the story went, once in Yugoslavia, Mihai began to think. It dawned on him that he could make good money helping other people escape. If he charged less than others, a steady stream of clients would be guaranteed. Each escape could be different, never the same route, always a separate crossing point. As Mihai began to act on his plan, he became more and more shadowy, never living in the same place for more than a few months. However, he ate in the finest restaurants and drank the best liquor. Consequently, there were the fights, always the fights.

With the earnings of this single trip Mihai could buy a used car — a cramped, five passenger Dacia. A car would be a great status symbol for Mihai. It would also make him conspicuous.

Years later the Securitate, or secret police, would catch up with Mihai. His broken body was found on the pavement four stories below a shattered apartment window. It was assumed that Mihai had jumped to his death to avoid capture. But he could have been thrown out.

Mihai's fate was unknown to Mike now. Today Mike's only question was: can Mihai do his job well?

A couple hours passed. The train no longer pierced the silent night. The sun had risen as they slowed for Băiile Herculane, a scenic mountain resort with hot springs that attracted visitors year around. In the winter the wealthy came to ski the nearby slopes. The train station sits on the edge of town, nestled against a steep mountain.

Mihai and Dinu had arrived and sat in the shadows of the depot lobby. People milled about preoccupied with daily cares. Mike and Bembea walked casually through the activity. Almost immediately Mihai met them.

"See that mountain through the doors?" Mihai pointed with a diverted glance. "Tell the others to meet me at the top." Mihai spoke to a couple of others then evaporated into the crowd.

Abandoned, they were on their own for now. All tried to look casual as they regrouped. With natural stride and conversation they quickly exited the station. Briefly, in the bright morning light, they gazed up the steep slope just across the road. Here in open view the mountain's full height was evaluated.

How could eleven adults, with baggage, ever look natural ascending this rocky mass? Yet Mihai's directions must be followed. Obediently all crossed the road with no more hesitation, feeling fully exposed as the climb began. They wished for vegetation to hide them, but only loose rocks and scrubby brush rose above them. Each clutched their possessions, and hoped they were inconspicuous.

One man muttered, "This is nuts!" All agreed, but said nothing. They focused on the climb, as their breathing became labored under the exertion.

When they had climbed about 200 meters, a man called out from the small train station below. "Hey! What are you doing?" His voice rolled up the mountainside loud and clear, ripping composure from everyone. Panic and adrenaline surged through their bodies.

"He is gone, he has fled,
he has eluded our vigilance,
he has broken though our guards."
Cicero, 63 B.C.

CHAPTER 3

Reflexively all sprang into a panicked primal scramble. Hunched over, each used their free hand to help pull themselves up and ahead, and grasped their belongings with the other. Rocks kicked loose by their rapid maneuvers, tumbled and spun downwards.

One man carried a round loaf of shepherd's bread under his arm. In the rush he stumbled and lost his sustenance. The loaf spun like a little wheel, bouncing off rocks, and hit the road below. The image froze in Mike's mind, as he prayed none of them would lose their footing, and start a similar descent.

Breathlessly they surged up and on, occasionally looking back to see if the police pursued. It seemed they would never get to the top. Suddenly they leveled off, but to their dismay the summit lay farther on and higher. A few effortless strides were taken across flat soil, then instantly the steep assent began again. No one dared rest, no matter how limbs ached and lungs heaved. With sheer dogged determination, they crested the ridge to see Mihai and Dinu down the opposite slope, a short distance away, resting under a tree.

In a few seconds the whole group collapsed in the shade. Here they spent the next several minutes catching their wind. Mihai seemed unconcerned about any observers from below. In his opinion, they were so far from the border no one would suspect an escape. After a few swallows of water, he gave the next segment of instructions.

Below them were smaller mountains and valleys. Mihai pointed to a distant peak that rose above the others. "I will meet you on the high mountain. Stay in the woods, and don't cross any open fields."

The escape party gathered their few belongings and headed down the slope. Going down was easier. Before long they were at the mountain's foot, in a narrow valley. Through the trees they could see a nearby farm. Staying clear of fields and buildings, they were soon climbing their second mountain.

On the second slope they became separated in the woods. Mike and Bembea stuck together, and a third man fell in with them. Others could be seen or heard ahead or behind. Each knew they must keep up, because Mihai would not wait. The sun burned hot, and each consumed more water than expected. At this rate it would not last until noon.

Mike and Bembea strode through the woods with excitement. The dream of freedom was soon to be fulfilled. However, the third man expressed doubts, questioning Mihai's ability to lead. He claimed they would not make it to Yugoslavia that night. He suspected Mihai was not with the group because he was looking out for his own skin. If they were caught, Mihai could make a clean getaway. Fear edged his voice as he spoke of prison. Still, for now, they pushed ahead.

In late morning the entire escape party straggled to the crest of a high ridge where they could see the destination peak in the distance. Their goal was closer, again they pushed on. Around noon Mihai met them in the woods.

"Hurry!" he urged them. "We're almost there, we have to keep going."

The sun beat down from the afternoon sky, as the refugees trudged up the slope of that distant peak. At the summit more mountains spread before them. Again in the distance was the hue of another dominant mountain whose elevation rose above the rest. Mihai pointed and gave his instructions, "We will meet on that mountain, Yugoslavia is not far beyond."

Each groaned inwardly. In minutes they again headed down the far side of a mountain, towards their next rendezvous. It was decided they would eat lunch when they got to the bottom. This time Mihai stayed with the group for awhile.

In the valley they found a dried stream bed where water had recently flowed, perhaps in the last of couple days. Upon investigation, they discovered a large pool, not yet soaked into the earth. Quickly all fell to their knees and slurped water into parched mouths. With thirsts satisfied, they filled empty water containers and extra plastic bags. By hanging filled bags from their belts, some managed to carry water a considerable distance.

Once water containers were filled, they hastily consumed their lunch. At this point many decided to bathe in the pool. Deodorant was unavailable in Romania. Washing was not only refreshing but a good idea as all felt grimy and uncomfortable.

The fugitives did not dare indulge in the luxury of a long rest. Again they set off through the forest, avoiding open spaces, only seeing their goal from hill or mountaintop. This time, the fearful man chose not to accompany Mike and Bembea. He was now with someone else, seeding doubt with them.

That afternoon the sun beat down unmercifully as the string of refugees toiled on. All kept up the grueling pace. Now the question was not, "Will we make it to Yugoslavia tonight?" but rather, "Will we make it to the second high mountain tonight?" With maximum exertion placed on sore and aching muscles the escape party straggled into the vicinity of the higher mountain's base. Evening shadows now began their extension.

Mihai met them again at the foot of the rendezvous mountain and joined them in their immediate assent. About halfway up, the evening shadows swallowed them in murky darkness. The moon had not yet risen and mountain climbing in this blackness was hazardous. They came to a level spot in a large stand of trees, and there Mihai decided to set up camp. They had traveled in wilderness for a long while, miles removed from the most remote farm. In their dark isolation the team felt they could relax for the time. Mihai assured them things would go better tomorrow.

The day had been hot. The clear mountain sky allowed atmospheric chill to quickly descend upon the Transylvanian Alps. The entourage had not brought much in the way of warm clothing. Mike put on his windbreaker. It offered little warmth. Along with the crisp night came mosquitos.

Clothes soaked from perspiration by the day's exertion now chilled the body even more. All huddled close and shivered. "Can we build a fire?" someone asked Mihai. With brief consideration he gave his consent. Hands immediately groped about, searching for dry wood. Sticks, twigs, fallen branches, anything dry would do. Soon a considerable pile of fuel was accumulated. They could keep a small fire lit for several hours.

In no time Mihai ignited a small, dancing light. The band of refugees crowded around its warmth. It was now supper time. Each produced their bread and consumed it in the flickering firelight. Some, like Mike, had salami with their bread. Sugar and chocolate would be saved for the next day. Everyone was careful not to drink too much water. Each hoped they would come to a stream or spring sometime tomorrow, before it got too late in the day.

The long exhausting day provided no energy for worry about tomorrow's travels. No one was in the mood for conversation. Soon all had found a way to lay down so that at least part of their body could be warmed by the flames. As the night wore on, positions changed, allowing different sections of the body to be warmed. Occasionally someone threw on another stick. The smoke chased the mosquitos away.

In the wee hours of the morning, before the sun came up, their fuel ran out. The fire flickered into extinction, and with no smoke, thirsty mosquitos closed in. Sleep was now out of the question. Mike was cold, his summer clothes offered little insulation. In fact, they were still damp in places not toasted by the fire.

By dawn all were awake, and gathered their few possessions for another day's journey. Some tried to comb their hair and look their best, but nothing could be done about the layered odor from the day before. For breakfast it was bread and salami again, washed down with a little water. By this time tomorrow they would be out of Romania. All could taste freedom.

On the second day of their trek Mihai stayed with the group. Today he would encourage them, trying to give them confidence to make it to the border, assuring them they would make it by nightfall. He also warned them about farmers in this area with dogs trained to sniff down potential refugees. A handsome bounty was paid for any caught. Some farmers even had two-way radios to contact police. Others simply rode horseback to the nearest village to notify law enforcement.

It seemed Mihai never tired. While others in the party grew weary as they climbed up and down countless mountains, Mihai effortlessly floated along these slopes. He needed his fit body, for today he would do more than double the work of the others.

Sometimes the escape party hid and waited for Mihai to reconnoiter the surrounding countryside. Sometimes he went ahead for just a few hundred yards, then he returned and led them to the next point of seclusion. Or he would scout ahead for miles then double back to lead the escapees on an extended detour.

Some hikers recognized landmarks and talked about where they were. This recognition brought about curious behavior on the part of Mihai. It appeared that he now led them in circles, as if to confuse them. Mike estimated they were somewhere in the vicinity of Turnu Severin or Orşova. If they were in fact near Turnu Severin, the Danube was not far off. He said nothing about this in the presence of Mihai or Dinu.

Mike surmised that Mihai had tricked them so they would lose their orientation. Apparently, he wanted this route of escape to remain confidential, a protected trade secret. If just one of their party gave information to the wrong person once outside the country, Mihai could be captured.

As afternoon grew late, it was obvious they would not make it to the banks of the Danube that night. Somewhere along the way they lost one of their party — the fearful man. No one knew when he slipped away. They thought it must have happened during a time of separation in the woods. The common consensus said he was not lost, rather he simply dropped out. But even if he was lost, it was out of the question to wait for him. That would put all at risk.

Mike wondered if this man might work for the secret police. Sometimes an agent would actually escape from Romania only to return later. The agent would now have the name of the guide, a list of any people who assisted in the escape, and knowledge of the escape route. But more likely, the fearful man was simply who he appeared to be — one who lost his nerve in the exhaustion of flight.

All in the escape party could sympathize, for they knew the power of the government. People had been put into prison for years, just for thinking about fleeing this terrible yet beautiful land. Sometimes people were arrested, then tortured until they were no longer of sound mind. In this condition, they confessed to the crime of "contemplating escape." No plans were made, no contacts, no supplies gathered. Just the thought of freedom, the simple thought, was enough to sentence one to prison.

By noon everyone had consumed their last water. Of greater concern, however, was the populated region they had just entered. They crouched at the edge of a large wheat field. This time the field could not be skirted. Houses, farms, and more fields lay in either direction. To avoid detection they had to crawl through the field on their elbows and knees. Mike did not find this difficult because he had practiced this exercise in basic training. But the women and young teens found it cumbersome and exhausting. Close to the earth the refugees scurried in suffocating closeness, frantically trailing Mihai like a pack of panicked rats. A few feet above them a gentle breeze blew, but none of them could feel it.

Holes appeared in their pants from crawling. Elbows and knees were skinned and ground with dirt. Finally a line of weary, soil-streaked faces poked from the standing wheat stalks on the far side of the field. Here the field was bounded by a small woods. All quickly scrambled into the trees.

By now everyone doubted Mihai and Dinu's ability to lead. Exhaustion, thirst, and hunger twisted everyone's perception. Their bodies rebelled. Some in the group had reached a critical point — they did not care if they were caught. Freedom seemed unattainable. Now reality was defined by each aching and depleted muscle. The ravenous fatigue made danger seem far away.

Bembea, the young nineteen year old, was the first to speak once they were in the woods. "I'm never doing that again! This is stupid! We are better off just running through the fields. Nobody is watching."

Mihai overheard the grumbling and strode back to Bembea. Extending his forefinger he thumped Bembea in the chest. With icy tone he spoke, "You're talking like a fool! You want to put everyone in danger?" Then Mihai turned to Mike. "He is your friend. You make sure he crawls when he's supposed to crawl."

Mike was not happy with his new responsibility, but the next time they needed to crawl, Bembea crawled. He crawled and complained, but he crawled.

Mihai realized that his biggest enemy was the growing discouragement, so he tried to give the fugitives hope. "We are almost there," he would say. "See how the mountains are not so high. They are more like big hills. This means we are close to the Danube."

Still they hiked on through the day. More fields, more forests, more farms, and more crawling. All landmarks blurred together. The only perception that stood out in their mind was the bodily craving for water. The inhabited countryside was drier and well drained. They gave up hope of stumbling onto another puddle of water.

———

Mihai rapidly continued to lose what credibility he had. At one point he had them all stop and listen. "If you are quiet, you can hear the Danube."

Mike could only hear the breeze in the trees.

Again afternoon light gave way to evening shadows. All moved with quickened pace, to cover as much ground as possible before twilight turned into total darkness. Suddenly their worst fears were realized. Lights moved and flickered through the trees. Each reflexively scrambled into the underbrush and burrowed beneath leaves and small branches.

In deafening stillness they watched the lights come to a halt. A vehicle door opened, seconds later it slammed. Silence. Then a dog barked; a breeze drifted their scent away from the soldiers. Frozen motionless, all knew the dog could still spot movement. Faint voices were carried toward them. More barking; maybe there was more than one dog.

Guards routinely patrolled this area, but they were unaware of the refugees hidden nearby. Everything was now on hold. Again complete darkness filled the forest before the moon came up. The patrol lingered in the distance, blocking the exhausted, hungry escapees.

Finally, the soldiers moved on into the night. No one was sure when they left, because exhaustion had given way to slumber. Hours later the nip of dark morning chill woke them. Moonbeams had broken through the canopy of branches giving an eerie calm to the forest.

Before long everyone was huddled together in the darkness, rubbing sore muscles. Waiting for morning light, each slowly chewed bits of bread. Slowly was the only way they could eat, mixing dried bread with saliva in dry mouths that craved a few drops of water.

Again Mihai claimed, "We are very close. We will be to the Danube in a couple hours."

No one believed him. But this time Mihai was right. The patrol last night must have been a routine border precaution. Soon the dark blue waters of the Danube could be seen through the trees. Now they searched the trees for a suitable place to hide for the rest of the day. The river crossing would be attempted later that night.

The dozen dirty refugees lay hidden in the bushes and tall grass. Mentally, Mike mulled over the remarkable events of the last few days. He sensed God was moving him safely down the razor's edge of danger to a whole new existence. But the danger was not over yet. The Danube lay ahead. Normally, Mike would be terrified of the water, but now he rested in God's hand.

In this location the broad Danube was forced between two opposing mountains. Upstream it twisted around a bend made sharper by a ridged, mountainous arm jutting into the river. This broken dam of solid rock caused the water to churn and swirl as it passed. The downstream volume of water cut deep, still churning and swirling but under a placid liquid veneer. Whirlpools formed in the depths of the river. The downward suck of the spiral drew water in over the top, making the whirlpool invisible from the surface. Yet water was continually drawn down and could take a person with it.

Mike was unaware of the currents; however, a separate realization emerged in his mind. The rope they had brought to stretch across the river was too short, far too short. Not even close to the necessary length. There would be nothing to hang on to during the crossing. He would have to swim!

As their final evening in Romania drew on, three of the travelers produced deflated inner tubes from their bags. Someone else unveiled a hand air pump. Soon all took a turn filling the tubes. Excitement built. Escape was close!

In the darkness Mihai led them though the woods to a location where a drainage culvert passed under the road. On the way Mike noticed a plastic bag caught in a tree. He stepped over to investigate and discovered about a liter of rain water trapped inside.

"Hey, look what I found!" Mike whispered loudly. "Water!"

With much crunching of leaves, everyone crowded around asking for a swallow. It did not go far, split twelve ways, but it was a nice reminder of how water tasted. Immediately Mihai led them on to a circular culvert. All crouched low as Mihai crossed the road. He tied his rope to a reflector post then motioned for them to follow. The guide disappeared down the steep, rocky slope using the rope to steady himself at the water's edge.

Dinu then led the entire group across the road en masse. One by one they descended the steep bank, using the rope to steady themselves. Suddenly they heard the sound they least wanted to hear — an approaching car. Several began to descend, one after the other. Mike was last, still standing on the road. The car's beams swung around the bend, now visible on the pavement. Mike dove down the slope like a great tumbling bowling ball, toppling all that were ahead of him. Everyone sprawled into the water. Fortunately, the river was only waist deep at this location, and no one was hurt.

Each waded back to the bank and stripped wet clothes from their bodies. Swimming in underwear would be easier. Some stuffed their wet clothing in their packs and began to swim almost immediately. Others neatly piled their clothes on the bank. Mihai said he would bring their clothes across later. Some baggage was attached to a couple of the inner tubes and pushed across the Danube by swimmers.

Mihai had contracted to help the two women cross. They hung on to one inner tube, and he pulled them while they kicked from behind.

Another complicating factor now surfaced at water's edge. A teen, younger than Bembea, neared collapse. He would never make it on his own. Mihai agreed to pull him across with the women. Later all agreed that Mihai saved the boy's life.

As Mihai launched the first two tubes, Mike and Bembea pushed into deep water. As Mike fought the water's current, expending valuable strength, he had no idea how he would help Bembea if he got into trouble. It rapidly became apparent that Bembea was a much better swimmer. Mike, now worried that he would actually endanger Bembea, commanded the young man, "Go on! Save yourself! I can't make it, I'm going back."

Just as Mike arrived back at the Romanian shore, Mihai was leaving with the women and the boy in the last inner tube. "Wait here," he told Mike. "I'll help you cross when I come back for their clothes." Mike noticed a large heap of clothes on the rocks. Up the bank he spotted a large bush and decided to wait in its cover.

Mike sat hidden, the water that passed by pulled at his rancorous thirst. "Why not try some of this water?" he thought. "Maybe the water below the surface is cleaner." Silently he slipped into the Danube. With his hands he pushed floating pollutants aside. He put his lips to the cleared surface between his hands, and sucked water into his mouth. Immediately he spat it out. He had never tasted anything so awful.

On the other side Mihai received the watch as token for successfully delivering the refugees. However, it was a long time before he returned from the Yugoslavian bank, physically drained. "I can't help you Mike," Mihai panted between breaths of air. "I brought this inner tube back for you."

Mike lay in the tube belly up, and faced the midnight sky. Mihai piled the wet clothes on Mike's chest. The inner tube floated low in the water.

With strong arms Mike then pulled himself backwards into the river. Glancing up over his shoulder, he located a tall tree on the Yugoslavian bank. This tree was his marker and he pulled himself towards it. Long powerful strokes caused him to glide backward towards freedom. Keeping a rigorous pace, he made rapid progress. With each stroke he put more distance between himself and any Romanian gun. On the water he was a bobbing target in the moonlight should a patrol spot him.

Somewhere over the deep water Mike's progress slowed to a standstill. Caught on an eddy or current he could not break free to the Yugoslavian bank. He exerted more energy, and pulled harder and faster, kicking as best he could. Yet he was held stationary in a river that flowed.

Deliberate, powerful strokes that should have propelled him feet at a time across the river's surface were rendered useless. Glancing over his shoulder he checked his mark. He was not going downstream with the current, so he increased his pace, rapidly pulling at the water. All was in vain. His inner tube sunk low in the water which churned downwards, pulling at his backside. The tube strained to maintain buoyancy.

Mike had no conception of time. In these conditions, his mind's ability to measure minutes was overruled by breathless heaving of his lungs, and by arms and legs wearied by the threat of extinction. Cramping seized his muscles as the water tightened its grip.

The weight of wet clothes pushed down on Mike. In his mind he knew it would be wise to let them drift with the currents. Yet the picture of his comrades escaping through Yugoslavia in their underwear forced him to reconsider in a visceral irrational way.

Adrenalin played out its last benefits, but panic never took hold. For all of Mike's young life he had in some way struggled against godless powers in a desire to be free. Now even the forces ruling nature beckoned with a dark downward draw, proving to be a great anti-climax. Death, somewhere in the Danube's depths, desired to pull him into its murky bowels. The air inside the thin inner tube walls was now the only thing that held Mike in the realm of the living. Captured like a ball at the end of a vacuum hose, his final effort to break away was futile.

"God!" Mike's soul cried out. "I give up! I have no strength! Help me!"

"Instruct a child in the way he should go,
(according to his disposition)
and when he grows old he will not leave it."
Proverbs 22: 6 (Jerusalem Bible)

CHAPTER 4

Mike's mind and body told him life was over. But sometimes God waits. He leaves us exhausted like limp rags, waiting for our last weak cry of help. This was Mike's condition. Held helpless. Depleted on the Danube, he called out to his Creator, "God I give up! I can't go any more...."

It was then that the push came, as though a hand covered his body and inner tube then gently, but firmly, pushed him out of the downward draw. This was not a dragging from underneath by some countercurrent, but a definite perceptible force that intervened to push Mike out of danger. Delighted, energy surged through his listless body. With this wave of vigor he made it to the Yugoslavian bank where his comrades pulled him from the water.

Exhaustion had carved itself into their faces, but excitement shone through in their eyes. Mike looked back over the river, his friends' clothes held in his arms. In a tone of awe-filled reverence Mike murmured, "We've gotta thank God for getting us across that!" All agreed. They knelt, and thanked God. It was a strange sight, a moonlight prayer meeting — half-naked figures praising their Maker on the Danube's bank.

Soon after, plastic bags were ripped opened and dry clothes removed. Shivering bodies eagerly received their long awaited protection from the night chill. As a sense of warmth returned, they discussed where they should go from here. Uncertainty stepped in. Mihai was not there to guide them.

"We should all get some rest. We'll do better in the light," someone suggested.

"No!" Mike insisted. "We need to get as far into the country as possible! We can't stop now!" His voice was labored with urgency.

"Whatever we do, we have to get away from this river!" another interrupted. "A border patrol could be through here at any time."

This made sense to everyone. Immediately they began to climb the mountain slope ascending from the Danube. The way was steep and difficult. After a couple hundred yards one refugee stumbled on a small pipe protruding from the mountainside. A slow but steady trickle of water drizzled down.

"Water!" a muffled call went out. A half second later the discoverer was on his knees, lips to the metal, filling his mouth with cool refreshment. Quickly a line formed in back of him. After a few swallows he was pushed out of the way so the next person could drink. The discoverer went to the back of the line and slowly worked his way forward. Each person was pushed away from the pipe after just a few swallows. Everyone passed through the line several times before they were filled and their thirst satisfied. No one really cared if the water was pure. It tasted clean and their long thirst was finally quenched.

The brief rest here at the waterpipe caused their bodies to cry out for sleep. "I think we should hide here, and sleep till morning," one tired refugee groaned. The idea was tempting and sounded good.

Mike felt danger. "We've got to keep going. Soldiers could be close!"

Someone persisted, "Our bodies need rest; we will do better in a couple hours when it is light."

Weariness took its toll, and most agreed that sleep sounded like the best idea. But Mike was determined to go on. Bembea agreed to go with Mike. He suggested that the married couple accompany them, since they were friends of his. So the party split, six stayed to sleep and four pushed on deeper into Yugoslavia.

Both groups wished each other well, then Mike and his three companions headed on up the mountain. Shortly after the rise was crested, they stepped onto a road. The first gray streaks of dawn lit the sky as they ventured down the pavement. Their goal now was to head west by north-west, hoping to find a road leading to Belgrade where Mike had a contact who agreed to drive him to the Austrian boarder. Once in that country they would truly be safe because Austria did not return refugees. On the other hand Yugoslavia might return a refugee to Romania.

In the wee hours of the morning they walked on, this time staying on the road. They were able to gain a few miles in the early morning twilight. By the time the sun had fully risen, Yugoslavian farmers were going about their business. There were few cars on the road, since most people walked to their destinations. Occasionally a wagon pulled by a plodding horse passed by.

The farmers did not pay attention to the westward bound refugees, who didn't look much different from the Yugoslavians. There was, however, one man who came up to them and attempted a conversation in some unknown Yugoslavian tongue. No one knew how to respond. It was obvious they were foreigners. The man said a few more words then walked on in the opposite direction.

Mike glanced back over his shoulder just in time to see him slip into an automobile. "I don't like this! He's going to get the police!"

"What makes you think so?" Bembea asked.

"Did you see his car? It was a Mercedes." Mike knew that Yugoslavia was not that different from Romania in certain ways. "I'll bet he got that car with Party help."

"Besides, they probably pay people to report refugees," another added.

Mike scanned the landscape, and pointed to a nearby wood. "Let's hide up there! Stay on the road till we're almost to the trees, there where the forest comes down to the road."

It was their only plan. All quickened their pace until they reached long morning shadows thrown by tall trees. A hasty check forward then back revealed no one in sight. Instantly the four disappeared into the forest. They penetrated the woods a good distance and found a dense growth of underbrush and brambles. Having also gone uphill they were able to view sections of the road. They hid and waited awhile to see what transpired on the road below, then fatigue overtook them and they all fell into a deep sleep.

Hours later they awoke. Now police cars patrolled the road below. More time passed, the mood of those who hid with Mike began to shift. They talked of surrending to the authorities, further flight appeared futile. Yet Mike held out and tried to convince them to remain hidden or run.

Exhaustion and hunger took their toll on Mike's three friends. Their resolve weakened rapidly. To run from the Yugoslavian authorities seemed hopeless. They had been on the run for days. Discouragement was in every aching muscle. It was easy for a tired mind to rationalize. Feeling that the Yugoslavians would treat them fairly, the others decided to turn themselves in. Mike alone stayed behind.

From Mike's perspective he had gone through too much to get this far. It was simply too risky to put himself at the mercy of unknown authorities in a communist land. He would find a new place to conceal himself once his friends were out of sight.

Once Mike's friends descended the slope to the road, Mike emerged and followed at a distance, then doubled back across the road. He hoped the police would expect him to run deeper into the countryside while he neared the Danube and hid.

Time dragged by. Mike was concerned for his friends. Much later there was movement in his area and the sound of people calling out. Mike thought he recognized his name mixed in the strange syllables. Then clearly he heard, "Mike, where are you?" It was Bembea!

His three friends were looking for him! Mike knew they wouldn't betray him... unless coerced. It didn't sound like they were forced to look for him. Perhaps they had cut a deal with someone. Maybe this person could drive them to Austria for American dollars.

That must be it! They must have found someone to take them to Austria, maybe just to Belgrade. But what if it was a trap? Mike cleared his mind and tried to think logically. He prayed for wisdom, and hesitated. In the end he decided to turn himself in, and hoped this was the right thing to do.

Mike stepped from his seclusion and called out. Almost immediately he was surrounded by his friends and strangers who led him down to the road. Word was spread that the search was over. Soon dozens of police and soldiers swarmed the refugees.

Mike had a panicky feeling as he was loaded into a transport vehicle. This was too much like Romania. All were taken to a nearby town to be "booked." The weary refugees were unloaded at a jail, only to find the other six there ahead of them. The police had found them asleep by the waterpipe.

An officer, who spoke Romanian, tried to explain that their cases would be considered individually. " We don't know if you are criminals or spies, so we need to search your records. We are going to have to put you in jail for the night."

In spite of the dismal implications, there were two advantages to being in jail. First, the refugees could take a shower, and second they were fed well. This good treatment was a hopeful sign. The rest of the day and that night passed quickly in deep, weary sleep.

The following day all were brought into court where the magistrate informed them that more research needed to be done and they would be detained for another fifteen days. Mike's heart sank as the official lectured about how it was necessary to protect the people of Yugoslavia from criminal elements that might cross their borders. In a way, what the magistrate said made sense. On the other hand, these words sounded too much like the rhetoric Mike had heard in Romania.

Mike was led back to his cell and locked into uncertainty. His thoughts returned to his pregnant wife. He knew she was a strong woman of great faith, but he missed her. He had no idea that a false rumor had reached Ana that her husband had been shot and killed as he attempted to cross the Danube. His body had not been recovered. It was unclear if soldiers had dumped his body in the river, or if they shot him from the shore, only to watch him disappear beneath the water. But Ana did not believe the story. Her intuition told her that her husband was still alive.

Then there was the report that Mihai had returned with the watch. Before Mike left he had explained the plan to her. Mihai would be paid only if he returned with the watch. He would be given the watch at water's edge by one of the refugees when all were across safely. What's more, Mihai had not spoken of a shooting. Still she wondered. Was there room for confusion? Had Mihai left out some of the story? Was he wanting to maintain a good safe reputation as a guide? Had there been fatalities before, and Mihai not reported them? Questions at a time like this can rattle one's faith, so Ana could only leave Mike in God's hands.*

In prison Mike prayed for his wife and his son. Still the limbo of his own position weighed upon him. He recalled miracles and the leading of God in his life. As far back as he could remember God had protected him. There was never any lingering doubt about His care and power. The faith needed while locked in a Yugoslavian jail had been bred in the back hills of Romania. A godly family scratched subsistence from the soil; they depended on God for every drop of rain and every crust of bread. God had met Mike as a young child, on Mike's level — answering childish prayers, disciplining childish transgressions. Incidents that would bring a smile to an adult were used to forge spiritual character.

When the cold prison door slammed, Mike's mind returned to the warm memories of the past. His recollection began with a small one room house, shared with ten brothers and sisters. It was a life of hard work and communal effort. The cramped chatter and commotion of such a small place rushed back to him. He could almost smell the chickens and pigs in pens butted against his home, and the earth odor mixed with sweat in clothing — all the things that delight a young boy.

---

*Actually what happened was this: an acquaintance of Mike's was killed the night after Mike crossed. This happened in the same area of the river front. The details of the mix-up would not be straightened out until some time later.

This cottage was built on the site of the old Olari home-
stead. It is similar in structure and size. Note the animal
shed butted against the house. Electricity has not yet made
it to this hamlet, and is still an hour's hike from the nearest
dirt road.

Mike remembered his small mountain hamlet. Hidden along a shallow valley at the base of two gentle slopes,
four simple houses — widely separated from the next —
formed a line. Here the wells were shallow and the water
sweet. Mike recalled how he was lowered into them, selected because he was small. In the cool damp shadows
he twisted and turned in cramped confinement as he
scrubbed the well's wall, ensuring a fresh water supply.

In little Mike's mind, the main attraction of the week
happened on Saturday night. With the day's work done
and chores out of the way, Mom and a couple of the older
sisters baked for the week. All baking was done in an iron
oven fueled by wood. It sat just outside the door. Dis-
tracted by games, children eagerly waited for the oven

door to squeak open. Country bread, golden and steaming, was cut and divided among them. Hurriedly the hot slices were covered with soft butter that quickly soaked in. For the children there was nothing better than this fresh treat washed down with a glass of warm sheep's milk.

During winter's Saturday nights, while the children waited for bread to bake, they sanded and polished long strips of wood cut from trees. Each child fashioned their own pair of skis. With these homemade skis they went cross country or downhill on the many low mountains near their home. Winter was their favorite season, not as much work had to be done so there was plenty of time to play. New skis and sleds were continually designed and crafted, then taken out for test runs.

Mike spent countless hours outside in the snow, usually clad in his summer shoes. Winter boots were hard to come by. His feet were always wet and cold. He just got used to it. For some reason the children rarely got sick.

All eleven children felt needed. Each had their separate tasks, which in warmer weather required every daylight hour. The younger children's chores consisted mainly of taking care of animals. The older children did heavier work in the fields. There were no machines. All work was done by hand and horse. Electricity never made its way to this rural location. With sundown all work ceased, and they gathered to eat dinner by the light of a kerosene lamp.

When it was time to put up hay, Mike joined the rest of his family in the fields. With their pitchforks they tossed hay up onto a horsedrawn wagon. When the wagon was piled high, the hay was taken back to their small barn. Here it was unloaded into the mow, one pitchfork at a time. The family started at dawn. All day the wagon was loaded and unloaded under the summer sun. Once the mow was full, extra hay was heaped in huge piles. By hand, they placed hay around a large inverted sapling with branches still attached. The sapling stabilized the pile keeping its slopes steep to shed rain. Rain could mold a crop that lay open in the field, so all worked long hours to stay ahead of the next cloudburst.

This field, a short distance from the house, was one the Olari family worked. Note the haystack in the distance. Plum trees, common in the region, are in the foreground.

Usually Mike's work was not difficult. Since he was third from the youngest he often got the easier job and herded sheep. Sometimes the herd got up to one hundred head. The sheep were very useful. The family ate the meat, used the wool for clothing, and drank the nutritious milk. In Mike's opinion, sheep's milk was even better than goat's milk.

Pete was Mike's younger brother and best friend. Sometimes they would herd sheep together, leaving their mountain farm and driving the sheep through the woods to patches of deep grass.* To a child, leaving home for the day with a small bottle of water, a chunk of bread, and sheep cheese meant total freedom. And the responsibility of tending the sheep only served to make the boys feel important.

The boys herded the sheep home before nightfall, allowing time for evening chores. If the moon was full, dinner was wolfed down. A full moon meant there was enough light to play soccer. Children from three other village houses joined in and formed two teams. Running with friends, kicking a ball through pale moonbeams and shadows created sheer pleasure. Screaming, laughing, pushing, sprinting ahead of the others to receive a pass — it seemed that energy knew no bounds.

On hot summer nights, Mike's parents let the children sleep in the barn. Crawling into the loft, their bodies sprawled on the fresh hay, the youngsters giggled and talked about anything and everything. Slowly one by one they drifted off to sleep.

One day as Mike and Pete walked down the road, Pete cried out in amazement, "A watch." He bolted ahead, bent down, and picked up his prize. No one in the family owned a watch — not the older brothers or sisters, not even Mom or Dad. Now only Pete had one. Mike was excited too, but thought Pete was too young to really appreciate the value of his find.

---

*In this region of Romania the communists had taken fertile flat land that had been owned by families for centuries, and collectivized it into state run frms. A fertile plain extends across Hungary into western Romania and has functioned historically as a bread basket for this part of Europe. Private land could be had on the nearby mountain slopes. Here many, including the Olari family, operated small subsistence farms. Mountain collectivization was not profitable for the government.

When the excitement cooled, Mike suggested, "Pete, this is a really nice watch, and it would be bad if you lost it. Why don't you give it to me? I won't lose it."

Pete thought for a minute. To his childish mind, Mike made sense. "Okay, here take it." As suddenly as he had found it, Pete was resigned to the fact that the watch was Mike's.

Mike was thrilled. He looked at his new watch constantly. A sudden time consciousness descended upon him. He was the envy of the village, all four households. Best of all, no one ever came to claim the watch.

Sometime later, while working in a cornfield with his grandfather, Mike paused to check the time. His wrist was bare! The watch was lost! Panic surged up in his little chest. On the verge of tears he searched everywhere. Grandpa helped, but to no avail. The watch was truly gone! Mike was devastated.

When Sunday came around, the weather was good, so the entire family decided to go to church. It was a five-mile walk from Ciolt—the village where Mike lived—to Chisindia, where a small body of believers met. A sort of unwritten agreement existed. Christians could meet twice a week, anytime on Sunday and Thursday evenings. If they did not attract attention, these unofficial meetings would be allowed to continue at the edge of town. Government officials for this region perceived these poor ignorant farmers to be of little threat to the state. Their superstitious behavior would disappear in time — they thought.

Occasionally the church was fined for meeting on the wrong night. Sometimes special prayer was needed, so believers would slip into a residence and lock the doors. Pillows were put in the windows to block sound. These people were Pentecostal, so volume during prayer tended to rise on most occasions. Intercession from this small body of the faithful would touch the heart of God, and He answered in wonderful ways.

On this particular Sunday, as Mike walked the five miles with his family, he had one thing on his mind: the watch. In this small home church they set aside a long time for prayer. During this time little Mike pleaded with God to help him find his watch. He was not sure how long the prayers had gone on when a mental image clearly came to his mind: a tall tree stood by the corn field. Under the tree, on a stalk of corn, hung his watch. Mike, in his childish mind, was sure God had answered his prayer. He could hardly wait for Monday, to go back out to the field. The next day Mike went directly to where he had pictured his watch. It was there! Thrilled, he thanked and praised God just as he had seen the adults do.

For these poor, uneducated Romanian farmers, accused of superstition, events of this sort were not uncommon. God was their help in a thousand substantial ways when the communist state was of little assistance.

Summer gave way to fall. Now it was time for Mike to go to school. With the nearest one in Chisindia, a village of about 450 families, it was decided that Pete and Mike should live with their grandparents in town. On weekends they returned to the farm to be with the family.

School was a strange and exciting place with much going on. Mike was in a class with twenty other students; first and third grade were taught in one classroom. The teacher taught first grade for about thirty minutes, then gave them work to do while she taught third grade. Mike always found it difficult to do his work because he found the third grade lesson more interesting.

Mike and Pete liked school and did well. They loved to play soccer. Everyone wanted them both on their teams. On Friday afternoon they left Chisindia and walked the five miles back to Ciolt. It was always good to be back with the family. It was even better when they had time for soccer.

One Friday afternoon when the boys came back from Chisindia, something was different. The house was quiet. Soon they learned their mother was sick. Blood came from her nose and mouth, and she could hardly sit up. In the past when someone was sick, the family prayed. Sometimes prayer lasted a few hours. Sometimes their dad would pray for several hours a day for a few days. Prayer was not stopped till the sick had recovered.

This time, no matter how much they prayed, his mom only got worse. It was unheard of to take someone to the doctor. Mike was born at home, as were his ten brothers and sisters. The midwife was untrained; she was simply Mike's aunt. The unthinkable was considered after Mom's condition continued to decline. His dad decided to take her to the clinic. The horses were hitched to the wagon, padding placed on the bare boards and Mom was wrapped in blankets.

The clinic in Chisindia was simple. It did not take the doctor long to see that the condition was serious, and he told Mike's father that Mrs. Olari needed to be hospitalized. The nearest hospital was several miles away in the village of Sebiş. Again they loaded Mike's mother back into the horse-drawn wagon for the trek. After a brief stay and a few tests, the doctors concluded there was no hope. Their advice was to take her home, where she could spend her last few days with her family. Despair settled in.

Mrs. Olari was not taken all the way back home, only to Mike's grandparents in Chisindia. Friends and relatives came to pay their last respects and sit quietly in the presence of the dying woman. The house was always full. Mrs Olari was loved by many. One evening Mike felt he must go outside to get away from the gloom and despair. He wandered a short distance, then began to quietly and desperately beg God to spare his mother. He was small and helpless. The only thing he could do was pray. He could not imagine what life would be like without Mom.

He paused, afraid the neighbors might have heard him, and listened, then he heard others praying too. All his brothers and sisters had at some time left the house. Each had found their own separate place and each pled to God for their mother's life.

A day or two later an acquaintance, from some distance away, showed up at the door with a message. He said the Holy Spirit had spoken to him. He claimed to know what would happen.

"It was God's plan to take Mrs. Olari home to be with Him. She was to die. However, God has heard the children. The children needed a mother, so God is going to extend her life." In a quiet way the man appeared confident that he spoke the truth.

Family and friends accepted this as a revelation from God Himself. Again all knelt and prayed for Mrs. Olari. Then the children watched their mom make a rapid recovery. Within days she resumed her normal duties, and lived another twenty years.

In 1965, Mike was in the third grade. This was an important year. Electricity came to the village where he attended school. One by one households saved their lei, wired their houses, and paid the hookup fee. Within two years all villagers had set their dim kerosene lamps on the shelf, and enjoyed the wizardry of electricity. Not only did the houses now have electric lights, but a few families purchased televisions.

There was much excitement over the TVs. Just down the road and across the street lived Mike's good friend, George. George's family had just purchased one of these fascinating boxes. Pete and Mike were drawn to this new TV. It was so delightful! They would have watched it all the time. However, there was not enough programming to fill the day, and work had to be done.

Another factor complicated Mike and Pete's viewing pleasure. Grandma and Grandpa said TV was a sin. Actually, with severe state censorship, entertainment was good natured and innocent. The government saw television as a way to get their propaganda out. It was also a way to pacify a needy people with a morsel of frivolous amusement. No one took the propaganda seriously. The shows were family oriented and captivated Mike and his friends. Yet Grandma and Grandpa maintained the box could corrupt a young boy's mind. End of discussion.

If Mike or Pete were caught watching this worldly contraption, it would be a whipping for sure. Both were frustrated. They stayed home while friends went to George's house and watched. Thus the forbidden device became more appealing. Then an idea popped into young Mike's mind. Why not sneak out after both grandparents went to bed? Most movies started at nine, a time when Grandma and Grandpa slept soundly with their encrusted ideas.

Pete embraced the scheme enthusiastically. So the boys set about to put their plan in motion. Earlier that afternoon Pete went around and unlocked the window to their room. Windows locked from the outside (crime wasn't a problem in rural Romania). As evening drew on the boys went to bed. When they heard Grandpa snore, pillows were stuffed under their blankets. If Grandma checked on them it would look like someone was there. With their plan in place, and their pillows in position, they cracked the window open. Two small figures slipped silently under the opened pane and down the wall, then scampered across the yard. In seconds they were down the street for their evening of excitement.

The movie was a comedy and everyone laughed a lot. Mike felt good and planned to do it again. Everything seemed safe because George's parents thought Grandpa was a little too strict, and there was little chance they would tell. Grandpa would remain uninformed.

Silently the boys stole back to the window they had left ajar. They had not been missed. After climbing into bed Pete immediately fell asleep. Mike, on the other hand, found himself consumed with overwhelming fear and dread. When he finally did drift off to sleep, he had nightmares of someone trying to kill him. In the dark he could not distinguish dreams from childish fears. It was so real, he could almost see the man with a pitchfork trying to kill him. Real or imagined, Mike was in a desperate struggle.

He looked over and saw Pete sleeping soundly. This was not fair! Didn't Pete feel guilty about sneaking out on Grandpa and Grandma? Mike woke him up. Pete was groggy, but not irritated.

"Pete! Pete! We have to pray! I don't think we should have tricked Grandpa. I think God is mad at us."

"What?" Pete tried to focus his eyes on Mike. "I don't feel bad."

"No, really, we have to ask God to forgive us."

So Pete prayed with his brother, then rolled over and went to sleep. Still Mike lay awake filled with dread.

Eventually morning came and everything was fine. The night before seemed like a confused memory from the distant past. However, when evening came again Mike was filled with fear. The internal struggle and fear continued to haunt him at night for almost a year.

<hr />

Now, years later, sitting in a Yugoslavian jail cell, Mike had plenty of time to reflect and muse over this incident. Why had he felt such fear as a child? With jeopardized fate, why did he feel no fear now? Still more puzzling, why had he felt so guilty over something so innocent?

As he pondered, a significant answer began to emerge. The issue was not watching a movie or watching TV. This issue was rebellion. Somehow the seed of revolt had been planted in the desire to see what his grandparents had forbidden. His revolt was not only against their strict standards, but was generalized against Grandma and Grandpa. The seed of revolt, if allowed to grow, would eventually bear the fruit of turning against Grandma's and Grandpa's God. It was as if God were trying to wrench this rebel sprout out, with all those nights of fear.

Adults could easily justify the revolt, for Christianity had nothing to do with watching an innocent family comedy on television. In fact, such rules cause children to become discouraged with the Gospel, and encourage rebellion. However, young Mike didn't know this. All he knew was that his grandparents were godly. He had seen the power of God work through them, and to disobey them was generalized into disobedience to God.

Conversely, Mike wondered if the issue for Pete was entirely different. It seemed Pete approached the situation as a boy who followed the example of his big brother. There was no rebellion for him, he was just having fun with his brother. Consequently, Pete could sleep at night.

Now, housed in cement walls and iron bars, Mike awaited the dawn and actually felt grateful for this incident from his childhood, certain God had allowed this to happen. It inoculated him against later opportunities to rebel during adolescence. As a teen he did not rebel as many do. Somehow the issue had been settled long before with a seemingly insignificant event, a lesson his Father in heaven had patiently taught him in his childhood. Once it was learned, he could now sit peacefully in his jail cell with no fear.

"I admire the serene assurance of those who have religious faith. It is wonderful to observe the calm confidence of a Christian with four aces."
Mark Twain

CHAPTER 5

On this night Mike could not sleep. Fear was not his companion, but contemplation was. Fourteen other men in the cell were deep in slumber. Insomnia and evening chill did not bother Mike because he felt the nearness of his Maker and wanted to enjoy Him. He warmly recalled the past as he reviewed how God had uniquely prepared him for this struggle. Each lesson of life was molded for his individual needs like a customized tutorial service. A sense of privilege filled him as he sat in jail.

As a boy, Mike's family was fortunate. They had a Bible. Some pages were lost, but enough remained to teach the principles of Christian faith. The Bible came into the Olari family's possession well before World War II. When Russian troops pushed Hitler's forces out of Southeast Europe spiritual darkness settled even deeper. Evil had a new national label, yet a few candles of righteousness flickered in the gathering gloom. Under Hitler there was hypocrisy. One could worship at church so long as the Reich and its horrible ethnic cleansing were not challenged.

Under communism virtually any pretense of godliness was attacked. Ironically the communist government gave the appearance of religious freedom by permitting some churches a limited function. An increasing number of

Catholic and Protestant churches were closed, but many Orthodox churches were allowed to stay open, even thought the Orthodox priests were under tight state control. The government steadily increased pressure to wring all religion from the people.

Despite this environment, Mike's parents continually sought to raise their children in the ways of the Lord. They knew those outside the faith could make little sense of it. They also knew the ironies of the faith; that young minds and hearts more quickly grasp the baffling mysteries of spirituality.

Mike tried hard to please his parents, especially after the TV incident. But he was not above mischief. He liked to sneak off and roll homemade cigarettes with his buddies. Still, by today's standards, Mike would be considered a good boy; nonetheless, he was taught there is a root of evil in every human being, a root that inevitably grows into a toxic plant. This toxicity, in turn, separates a person from God. This plant is known as sin — simply doing something in one's own way, instead of God's way. His parents taught him that this sinful behavior can be seen in everyone, from two-year-olds, to teenagers, to cranky old men.

Sometimes the plant's toxicity is mild, and a person can be very respectable by society's standards. Other times a person can become a crazed killer like Hitler or Stalin. However, the question is not how much of the plant's poison exists, but whether the poison exists at all. Mike was taught that any amount is spiritually fatal. A small dose just takes longer to corrupt. The problem of the human race is not that there are nice people or not so nice people. The problem is that we are all separated from God. Even though all humans are toxic, Mike was taught that there was one cure - the blood of Jesus Christ. For some strange, loving reason Jesus offered Himself as a sacrifice. He suffered the consequence of our poison, which was death. By faith, any person can ask Jesus to clean up the toxin of sin. The cleaning is not something anyone can do by themselves. The cleaning is done freely by Jesus, unconditionally. He simply waits politely for the invitation.

In jail, Mike contemplated these great mysteries: first, that the problems of humanity can be solved by a blood sacrifice. Second, that God would offer the life of His Son for mortal humanity. Third, that this Son would rise victorious over death three days later to sit at the right hand of His Father. And finally, that He will physically return to rule all humanity with peace and justice.

These mysteries are a stumbling block to the educated of secular society — mere foolishness and superstition. However, the Christian begins to realize that a true mystery is not an absence of truth, but more truth than one can comprehend. Here is a mystery so profound that the angels themselves desire to look into it.

One day Jesus set a child on His knee, and said, "Unless you become as one of these you will in no way enter the Kingdom of Heaven."

Children have the advantage over adults. They have little problem accepting this mystery by faith. A child leaves the mystery untampered, undissected; he just believes. The mystery's truth is living and cannot be torn apart by secular analyses; just as a flower cannot be dissected and still keep its beauty. At the age of nine or ten Mike began to consciously accept the mystery. He was born again into the kingdom of God.

When a person becomes one of God's children, it does not mean all developmental struggles are over. Each day was a new learning experience as Mike discovered what it meant to follow Christ. Living in poverty, his parents taught their children to depend on God alone. The

Bible stories they read to them became examples of how God works in the lives of His children.

The story of Joseph lodged in Mike's mind, and became his favorite. Joseph, exploited, sold as a slave, and sexually harassed, remained true to God, and God always turned evil into good. Joseph never took revenge. In fact he saved the lives of those who conspired against him. To Mike this seemed to be the way to live.

In school Mike continued to do well. His elementary years passed uneventfully, except for one incident when he was twelve or thirteen. One weekend at home in Ciolt, he played hide and seek with his brothers and friends. He had been running hard, and it was his turn to hide. He sprinted to the barn, then climbed into the mow to hide in the straw. As he burrowed down, still out of breath, he inhaled a small fragment. Instantly it was in his throat. Violently he coughed and choked, unable to dislodge the particle.

In time Mike steadied his breath, but there was still something wrong. He felt an obstruction in his left lung that burned. It hurt to breathe, but breathing was possible. He tried to force it out of his mind and he continued to play. He just figured he would get better. He always got better when he was hurt before. To ask his parents to take him to the doctor never entered his mind. No one went to the doctor. In fact he decided not to complain to his parents. What could they do anyway? Besides, they were so busy. Mike decided to pray about it and he would be okay.

The next week at school Mike found it difficult to play soccer. When he ran, unbearable pain stabbed his chest. In his mind he pictured the little piece of straw in his heart.

Weeks turned into months, and Mike's chest hurt with every breath of air. Soccer was a thing of the past. Still he did not complain. With independent determination he did his best to appear normal. His overworked parents never noticed he was not himself. Even though he was young, he vowed to confront this malady with adult stamina. The only solution Mike knew was prayer, and it did not seem to be working.

Finally on a rainy Saturday, out in the barn, Mike began to pray. "God I hate this pain! It hurts to breathe, I can't play soccer. I don't want to live when I hurt like this, so I want to die. If You won't make me well, then let me die. Besides, dying wouldn't be so bad, I would get to be with you." Mike was not being melodramatic, this was simply the way he saw the issue.

Even though he was a boy, Mike meant what he said to God. He felt that all would be well. An awareness of contentment grew, but he still had pain. Now, since the pain remained and God seemed so near, he naturally assumed God was not going to heal him and would let him die. It was as simple as that. This did not frighten Mike. He actually felt fortunate about this new development. The rest of the day he went about his work singing and praising God.

When evening came, Mike was still alive, but the pain still stabbed his chest. God must have decided to take him in the night, he reasoned. Night was good. So he went to bed with a sense of excitement. The next morning Mike did not wake up dead, but he did wake absent of pain. He was never bothered by the splinter of straw again.

Mike always looked back on this experience as the most significant event of his adolescence. Later, when he was in his twenties, he told his mom about it. She cried, and asked Mike why he had not told her what he was going through. She could have at least prayed for him. Mike explained that he hadn't wanted to worry her.

Mike's days in rural Romania approached an end. His parents saw the value of an education beyond the eighth grade. Farming was difficult, and there was not enough land for all the children to make a living from the soil. The government was making it more and more difficult to own a farm, and encouraged people to move to the city. Mike heard talk among the adults; they whispered suspicion that the government desired the masses in the city, to control them more easily.

Mrs. Olari made trips to Arad in an effort to seek out a school suitable for Mike. In Romania only the wealthy went to high school. Ninth grade began career training for most. Each school was designed to teach a specific occupation. In her search, Mrs. Olari found a slot open at Câi Ferate Române school. Here Mike could learn engineering and be trained to work on the railway system in Romania. He would attend this trade school for three years. After his studies he was virtually guaranteed a job with the country's transit system.

By this time Mike's parents and brothers had built a small three room house in Arad. One bedroom belonged to Mike's oldest brother John and his wife Maria. The second bedroom was for Mike and his two brothers Ted and Ilie. Everyone shared the third room which functioned as a living room and kitchen. Things were cozy, but there was more room here than back on the farm.

Mike was jolted by city life. Fields and forests were gone, replaced with parks, overgrown with tall grass and wild Queen Ann's Lace. Isolated rural homes were a memory. Now Mike saw endless rows of apartments. Later he learned these tall concrete gray structures were the legacy of the communist world. Yet when Mike walked the streets of Arad he discovered evidence of a more stately past. Dwellings and business built under the Hapsburgs still remained. While repairs were needed, these structures spoke silently of a more prosperous time.

Arad had a numbing effect on Mike. There were so many people everywhere. All buses and trains were packed full of passengers. People crowded onto steps of buses, with only a toehold and hands that clasped anything that protruded from the vehicle. Occasionally a person would slip and tumble from the moving bus to the pavement below.

Here everyone was a stranger. Mike didn't have the identity he once held in Chisindia. No one knew him. Of those that knew him, not all liked him. At school his classmates noticed he was different and often challenged him.

"Mike, you don't swear and you don't fight. What's the matter with you? Are you one of those stupid Christians?"

"I am," was Mike's simple reply.

With that, all kept their distance. Not only was it not cool to be a Christian, a person could get in trouble. Mike didn't like being by himself, but he had made up his mind to be loyal to his Christ. Jesus was too real for Mike to turn his back on Him. Being small and shy, Mike headed home from school every day when classes were out.

At first Mike's refuge was found in his brothers and sister-in-law. They all crowded around a small table early in the evening. Simple Romanian meals were eaten under the dim glow of a bare light bulb that dangled from the ceiling. Conversation flowed freely as the little family bonded closer. Virtually every topic was covered, and here Mike's older brothers gave advice on how to flow with city life.

On Mike's first weekend in Arad, late Saturday evening, the five of them ate dinner together. The meal consisted of potatoes in a watery broth, which they called soup. This night was special because they had two small sausages to split between the five of them.

During dinner John thought Mike should be filled in on the dangers that awaited Christians in the city.

"Mike, you have to be careful when you go to church," he said as he concentrated on dipping up a small chunk of potato with his spoon. "The government doesn't understand us; maybe we scare them." He paused again, "If they fear us, they are not aware of it."

"Okay..." Mike had slipped past authorities before. "So would it be better if we all went separately, so we aren't so noticeable?"

"No, they know we all go to church. They know every move we make. That's not the problem so much — we just don't want to get caught saying or doing the wrong thing. They have sent spies to be in the church service."

"Why would anyone want to spy on us, especially if they already know we are going to church?"

"People spy to get party privileges," John continued. "If they can get information on us, they might get a promotion or a job they want."

"What kind of valuable information can they get at church?"

Ted interrupted, "They're just paranoid; they want to know who is against them, and who has influence."

This was a twist on church Mike had not considered. The government might perceive them as a threat. It almost seemed funny.

John persisted, "Mike, you really can't talk too much, especially to someone you don't know. Don't sing too loud, and just look straight ahead, and be sure not to look too happy. Your worship has to be in your heart, don't let it show on your face."

"Well, I don't get why they are afraid of us."

Maria stepped in. "They place us under suspicion because our church continues to grow. We don't try to make it grow, it just does. We have about a thousand people coming every Sunday. A group that large scares the government. The government says church is legal, but they only make it legal so they can watch us more easily. We have a power the government doesn't understand. We have a light for the darkness they have created. The government can't provide what the people crave deep down inside."

There was silence for a few seconds, then John continued. "Then if enough people find that Jesus is the answer, they will know that the government has lied to them about religion. A government that lies will, in time, lose the support of its citizens. That's why they fear us."

Ted broke in, "Anyway, I won't be able to go to church with you tomorrow. I have to work."

"You see, Ted has to work a lot on Sundays. He doesn't have to work on Monday or Tuesday, but he always has to work on Sundays," Maria mused.

"Yeah, they make most Christians work on Sundays. It keeps us away from church." Ilie added.

Early the next morning all readied themselves for church or work. Those who headed for church walked about a mile to a neighboring suburb on the outskirts of Arad. Meetings were held in a very large house. The inside walls had been taken out, and rooms were added on. The seats were filled, and people stood around the edges. Windows were left open so more could crowd around outside and listen. A high fence surrounded the back yard which was also filled with people.

Singing started the service, but it was done softly. There was a time of prayer, and everyone prayed in loud whispers, an almost eerie sound. Even though spies sat in the congregation, no one could ignore the overall feeling of solidarity, a pervading sense of refuge. Finally one or two of the pastors spoke. The meeting closed with one last song and a prayer.

Religion made the government paranoid. On Mondays, various pastors were called down to the police station and ordered to give an account of the previous Sunday's service. If the authorities did not like what they heard, the pastor could be jailed. Many pastors were beaten when authorities did not approve of services the day before. Some pastors suffered terribly, even to the point of death. At the same time other pastors compromised with the authorities. Still others seemed to have a gift of wisdom and supernatural protection when dealing with officials. Then there were those sad cases of pastors who cracked, and simply sold out to the government. Most Christians did not judge them, but left them for God to deal with. Many prayed that God would forgive them, and in time use them again.

Romanian Christians endured this unofficial standoff between the communist government and the body of Christ for over forty years. Christians went to church with harassment, but dared not speak of Christ publicly. It was strictly forbidden to mention one's beliefs in the work place. The government tried in a thousand little ways to keep believers from fellowshiping. It was always easier to break Christians if they were isolated. Keeping them out of church was an effective way to disconnect them.

Yet stories continually circulated of how God protected his own. It was impossible to verify anything officially, since the government refused to acknowledge a God. All newspapers printed the party's heavily censored version of the news. Official explanations of why the government did what it did were dubious at best. Yet in spite of these problems, trustworthy information was circulated in the body of believers. News of imprisonments, deaths, and miracles passed along the grapevine.

One such story was of a college professor who took a stand for Jesus. The police had questioned the professor many times and repeatedly asked him to sign a paper stating his denial of Christ. He stood firm. All interrogations were recorded. At one point the police edited the recordings, dubbed and spliced in such a way as to make the professor say outrageous things on the tape. Finally one day, as he was being grilled, his interrogator fell off his chair. Dead. The police department was so spooked by the death they decided to free the professor. His files were put on a shelf to gather dust. Eventually he was deported from the country.

The only protection Mike and his family had was their faith. Faith was their fortress. If one had enough faith, anything could happen. In theory one person could stand against the government, and win. From their perspective God was building faith in them, one lesson at a time. All these incidents were seen as part of the Almighty's blueprint to strengthen their faith.

Mike continued to gain spiritual and emotional strength from his family and church. In his mid-teens he experienced something many consider very curious. Mike believed the Bible clearly taught that God sends his Spirit to Christians as a comforter and an enabler. After Jesus came back from the dead, he visited many people and imparted encouragement. Then he took the eleven disciples, his closest friends, into the country, and gave some last instructions before he ascended into heaven.

One instruction was to wait for the Comforter to come. About seventy people waited upstairs in a large room in Jerusalem. They waited for days, not knowing what to expect. During the Jewish feast of Pentecost a sudden rushing wind filled the room. Small flames of fire danced above each person's head. All began to speak in foreign languages they had never learned. Virtually all Christians — Roman Catholic, Orthodox, and Protestant — accept this account as truth. The way they apply it to their lives in the twentieth century varies.

Mike believed any miracle recorded in the Bible could happen today. It was not something just for those people back then. He also believed when the Holy Spirit came to him, he would probably speak in an unknown language. This happened to other believers in the Bible, after the phenomena at Pentecost, when the Holy Spirit came to them.The rushing wind and flames of fire are not reported again, but there was always a report of speaking in an unknown tongue.

Due to the government's strangulation of Christian materials, false teachings began to crop up in some of the churches. One was the belief that if a person received this new closeness of the Holy Spirit and then fell away from the faith, there would be no hope for him. Damnation was certain, regardless of repentance later on. For this reason teenage youths were discouraged from seeking the Holy Spirit. Who was to know what a teenager might do in a phase of rebellion. Consequently Mike's mom tried to dampen his desire to receive the baptism of the Holy Spirit.

Mike was fearful. At the same time he felt drawn to ask God for this blessing. He attended special prayer meetings at the pastor's house. He felt very close to God, but although he fasted and prayed, nothing happened.

Then one evening Mike was at home alone, reading the Bible. Something came over him and filled the room with a powerful presence. His mouth was saying things he couldn't understand. A song was singing inside him, but he didn't know the words to the song.

Mike feared he would lose control, so he consciously stopped the utterance that came from his mouth. Still inside, the song continued to sing. In spite of his apprehension, this joyful presence filled every cell of his body.

He wanted to tell others in his church about this new experience. That night there was a prayer meeting at the pastor's house. Here Mike was enthusiastically encouraged to give full release to the new gift of the Holy Spirit. He let go of his hesitations and spoke in an unknown language. They sat Mike in a corner where he carried on for most of the evening, while others went on about their business.

Nearly two years later, during an evening prayer meeting, the Holy Spirit came over Mike and the man standing next to him. They began to sing a song they had never heard before, in a language they did not know. The harmony was perfect, even though Mike had never considered himself a good musician. The words coming out of both men's mouths were identical. A newcomer could have easily thought this was rehearsed, but Mike knew better. The Holy Spirit came over them without warning, and sang a song.

As time passed, life in Arad began to improve. Even school got better. While some students avoided Mike, others began to respect him. He climbed to the top of his class academically; his many hours of study now paid off. They also valued Mike as a team player in soccer competition. He loved this game, but noticed he lacked the energy to play well. No matter how rigorous his conditioning, he lacked stamina. Then he began to feel tired and sleepy all the time.

Mike was taken to the doctor — a truly rare experience — where they diagnosed hepatitis and put him in the hospital. While family and friends prayed, no miracle happened. For some reason God chose to use the long slow route of twentieth-century medicine to heal Mike.

Weeks later Mike regained his strength and he returned to school to be greeted by a small mountain of make-up work. His teachers were sympathetic and worked with him. However, he misjudged his Romanian teacher, who expected his work done immediately. Mike prioritized his assignments. It made sense to get his engineering and math classes caught up first, because he would use these classes most in his career. He would make up Romanian last, because he thought literature would be of little use.

A few days later, in his Romanian class, the teacher told Mike that he would be given an exam in twenty minutes. Horrified, panic tightened his stomach, knowing he had not the foggiest grasp of the test material. He had not cracked his Romanian literature and grammar books in weeks. Panic gave way to frustration. This wasn't fair; all the other teachers gave more time. If he had only known, he would have studied Romanian instead of math.

"Okay Mike, get a hold of yourself," he thought. "You don't have much time." Then he silently began to plead his case. "God, you know I have been trying hard. I haven't been wasting time. I have been doing my best. Please help me to know what to study."

Mike thought he could make it through most of the grammar, punctuation, and any writing problems the teacher might give. Literature was another story, so he pulled out his text filled with the famous writers of Romania and the communist era.

A thought ran through his mind. "Maybe I should read the communist writers, Marks or Engels. No, Lenin would be better." Somehow this didn't feel right.

Flipping through the pages he finally closed his textbook, holding it in his hands. "God, let me open to the information I am to study." He then let the book fall open and his heart sank.

There on the page in front of him was the biographical information for Mihail Eminescu, Romania's most famous poet. Mike thought, "This guy is too well liked in the West! He was too famous. The teacher will never ask a question about him. Maybe I had better open the book again."

"You prayed. This was your answer. Study this!" came a command from another corner of his brain.

So Mike read diligently. This exam would not be multiple choice or essay, but oral. The teacher would probe with newly made-up questions in any area he perceived Mike to be ignorant.

He was sure twenty minutes had not really passed when the instructor re-entered the room, and ordered him to put his book on the floor. As he closed his book Mike was assured, from down inside, that he had done his best under the circumstances. He felt bold as he stood up beside his desk, and waited briefly for the first question to come.

"All right, Mike, let's start. Who was the most famous nineteenth century poet this country produced?" The teacher started off easy.

"Eminescu."

The teacher seated himself behind his desk, and rested his chin in his hand. "What influences shaped Eminescu's perspective?"

"Well..., he studied at the universities in Vienna. That's where he got a German slant on things. Then he went on to study in Berlin. Uhmm..., there he was exposed to more German philosophy and other Western literature." So far so good. Mike confidently waited for the next question.

"Mike, tell me why Eminescu was so popular."

Mike paused. His memory still seeing what he had just read, he continued. "Some say he appealed to human nature's lonely side. His style could be very sad. Then to people in the West..." He paused, then continued, "...they like his mystical outlook. He worked his mysticism into all kinds of medieval legends."

"Are there any other reasons why he was so popular?" He had begun to probe.

"Everyone knows he used simple language," a tint of authority edged Mike's voice. "He was a simple master. They say his rhyme patterns were art. So people who really liked poetry liked his style, and other people just liked his stories." Mike was amazed, he had just read this!

The teacher raised his eyebrows, looked down, then looked up again. "Tell me how the factors of Eminescu's greatness lead to his downfall."

Again Mike could see the answer on the page. The only problem was, his reservoir of knowledge was rapidly draining. In his spirit he cried out to God, "Please stop this teacher!" On the outside Mike appeared confident. But inside, he knew that if the teacher sensed weakness he would move in for the kill, exposing Mike's ignorance.

Confidently Mike took a step forward from his desk. "We all know that dreary strands of melancholy are woven throughout his works." Wow! This sounded good. "People who are sad feel better when they read him. They can identify with a great poet. Eminescu could paint the pain of the human psyche. However, this pain led to his mental illness and his institutionalization."[1] Mike felt like he was reading a script, but nothing was in front of him.

The teacher had a pensive expression on his face as he turned his gaze down to his text. Flipping the page he began to speak, paused, then snapped the book shut.

"Mike, it is obvious you have mastered your material. You have a 'B.' An 'A' is for the teacher. Congratulations." A brief smile crossed his face as he rose to leave. "I'll see you tomorrow." Mike knew this guy never gave "A's." A "B" was the best anyone could expect. Mike walked home that afternoon and praised God for the "B." God had put him in a tight spot and pulled him out brilliantly. That night he hit the books early. To not study now would wrongly put God to the test.

High school passed quickly. He was in the top of the class. While classmates wanted nothing to do with Mike's Christianity, he had gained respect for his courage. Upon graduation Mike took his place in the ranks of mass transit engineers.

Eager to work hard and apply his newly acquired stockpile of knowledge, Mike quickly learned that qualifications meant little. His education was relevant and could be applied to his work; yet training and experience meant nothing when it came to advancement. Party connections meant everything.

*"You plotted evil against me,
but God turned it into good..."*
Joseph the Patriarch
Genesis 50:20 (TEV)

Chapter 6

Maria was the first to notice the fatigue in his face, and commented at dinner. "Mike, you look tired."

He looked blankly back at her, then over to his brother John. Everyone knew his rigorous schedule.

The transit system was run on a military paradigm. Supervisors and bosses were more like commanders. A boss never called an employee into the office to solve a problem, or simply to chat. A call to the office meant only one thing — trouble. Those higher up in the chain of command had little, if any, knowledge of how to run a transportation line. They were simply Party members feathering their nests. Communist Party membership meant job security, regardless of job performance. This led to apathy and dishonesty in the ranks. On-the-job drunkenness was common, but only non-party members received disciplinary action.

Mike had little choice of where he was to work, or the type of work he would perform. Those decisions come down the chain of command from high above. Nevertheless he was guaranteed a job that paid more than many. Mike was grateful. By American standards the pay was poor. He would not be able to move to his own apartment, nor could he buy a car. His paychecks offered little independence, but helped his family tremendously.

Mike did save a few lei hoping to buy a new bicycle. When he had accumulated one-month's salary he took it all to the store and purchased a new shiny Russian made bike. Never again would the purchase of an item excite him like this bike. For years he had wanted a bicycle, and now in his late teens he finally had one. On his bike he could go anywhere in Arad anytime he wanted, without paying bus fare.

Mike was well suited for his new job. The hours he spent studying blueprints and diagrams paid off as he applied his learning. The days were long, twelve to fifteen hours, plus he was on call for emergencies.

Almost immediately travel time began to wear on Mike. He rode his bike forty minutes across town to a train station. Once there he locked his bike in a rack and caught the next train to Timişoara. The trip was only thirty miles, but took over an hour-and-a-half. The train stopped at every village and hamlet along the way. Mike worked twelve to fifteen hours, then repeated the trip back. He had little time to sleep or do anything else.

"John and I were talking," Maria looked concerned. "It would be so much better if you could work here in Arad. You wouldn't exhaust yourself going back and forth to Timişoara."

Mike was too tired to be frustrated. "Yeah, that sounds nice, but how do I get a transfer? I agree I should be able to work here too, but you know how the game is played..."

"You know...," John narrowed his eyes in thought. "We have an in-law who knows a lady who works for one of the high-up bosses. He can put a word in for you, but it will cost you."

"How much does she want?" Mike had not the faintest idea where the cash would come from.

"She won't charge you anything, but the boss takes a 2,000 lei bribe."

"I don't know, it... it seems so corrupt, I don't like it."
Ted interrupted. "Mike! Mike, you're not taking a
bribe. You're giving a bribe." Ted raised his voice empha-
sizing the word *giving*. "And besides you wouldn't give
the bribe in the first place except that this is the only way
these guys do business. You're just trying to cope in a
corrupt system. Actually you are the victim of extortion."

Ted made it sound innocent. Mike hoped he was right.
"Okay, so if I decide to do this, where am I going to get
2,000 lei? That's two month's pay!"

"Ilie knows some people who can lend you the
money," John explained. "They can work out a payment
plan for you, just don't be late on your payments!"

In the end Mike decided to go with the plan and borrowed the money. They contacted the woman, and made
full payment. In a short while Mike received his transfer
to Arad. The system worked quite efficiently.

Mike enjoyed the breathing space in his new schedule. The saved travel time allowed him to become human
again. There was time to do something other than work
and sleep. He budgeted his salary to begin payments on
the loan. The cost had been worth it.

A few days later the woman who had acted as the
liaison called Mike's brother-in-law. She wanted to return
the money. "My boss understands that Mike is young and
doesn't have much money. He agrees Mike should work
in his hometown. He said he didn't need the money, so I
will be returning it to you."

The message and cash were passed on to Mike.

Later Mike had a chance to thank the woman. Still he
knew who had really worked behind the scenes. He knew
who had softened the boss's heart. To Mike this was a
miracle, not just a favor. Favors were not given to unknown non-party people.

Mike worked hard on his new job in Arad, and he found satisfaction in maintenance and repair of the railway. He showed up for work on time, didn't come to work drunk, and cheerfully did what he was told. Also, he did not complain when asked to work late or when called for an emergency. Most importantly he did his repairs right the first time, so they wouldn't have to be fixed by someone else. By applying these simple strategies, he gained the respect of his employer.

Things went well for about a year. Then Communist Party officials at the national level noticed something very alarming. In Mike's division of 200 workers, eighteen were Christians. This was totally unacceptable. The Party applied bureaucratic coercion to local bosses, who were told to get a denial of faith from all Christians.

Mike was one of the first to be called to his boss's office. His anxiety rose for the simple fact that he was called to the office. His superiors applied a strategy of separating Christians, each was called in individually. Mike entered the room to meet seven bosses and Party officials. He was politely asked to take a seat.

An older man leaned forward, with a sound of concern in his voice. "Mike, the officials have brought something very important to our attention. You have been attending church meetings. Now we know you are not a bad guy. We know that you work well. We also know that you are doing this innocently. You are doing this because you don't know any better. You are doing this because this is the way your parents raised you. No one as bright and intelligent as you could really believe this prattle."

The older man then leaned back in his chair. Mike returned the gaze with an expressionless face, as he tried to grasp this man's condescending words. He was amazed this man did not give him credit for thinking through his religious beliefs.

A second man began to speak, "Mr. Valentin is right. We think you are a Christian because those in your family are Christians. Maybe you are a Christian because your friends are Christians. But the government doesn't like Christians, and we cannot have Christians working here. Your being a Christian is the only thing we don't like about you. Everything else you do is fine. We have an order from the government for you to agree to stop going to meetings."

Mike felt no fear, he actually laughed. Not a nervous laugh, but a laugh at the absurdity of the situation. "What's the matter here? I have been working at this station for almost a year. No one has told me I have done bad work. Like you said, I have been working hard. I have been trying to please everybody."

Again the voices were warm and understanding. "Ya, ya we know that. And we don't want to hurt you. We just want to make sure you understand us."

The group of seven showed concern in their attempt to make Mike one of them. For if Mike could be convinced through warmth and logic to be what they wanted, it would be easier for all. Stricter discipline could be used later if this failed.

"Listen! You don't understand." Firm determination set in Mike's voice. "I am not a Christian because my parents are Christians. I am almost twenty years old. I know what's good. I know what's right and what's wrong. And I am a Christian because I am convinced it's the right thing to do."

"Hey, hey, don't say that." Fatherly concern edged a third man's voice. "Let's give you some time to think about this. We will give you two or three weeks to think this through. I think you will see the wisdom in doing what we say. We will have some papers for you to sign then."

From the far corner came another voice. A man leaned back in his chair with a pensive expression. "You know, I think this Mike is going to give you the same answer when he gets back in three weeks."

Mike lifted his gaze, his eyes squaring off with the man across the room. "You're right," was all he said, then smiled.

Mike left the conference knowing he had done the right thing. Still he wondered what would happen next. Would he lose his job, or be arrested later? He didn't know, but one thing he did know: he would take whatever stand was necessary. Jesus had done too much for him to back out now.

The next day Mike went to work and noticed a change. People avoided him. They did not want to be seen with him. He realized it was nothing personal; they responded out of fear. One's safety could be jeopardized if seen with a person on the Communist Party's black list.

During this time Mike felt a Presence very close. He knew the invisible closeness was Jesus looking over his shoulder. He knew Jesus would support him now. His Savior would not back out on him.

A couple mornings later Mike walked into work, and greeted a co-worker with a simple, "Hi, how are you?" The muscular man stepped from behind a podium, where he wrote in a ledger. With lightning speed he connected his right fist with Mike's jaw, followed instantly with a left blow to the side of the head. Stunned, Mike hit the floor where he was belted a third time. The room began to sway.

Instantly workers rushed in and restrained the man. Others helped Mike to his feet. He felt lightheaded and dizzy.

"Mike this is not possible!" someone was saying. "Call the police! That guy can go to jail!"

"No, I am not going to call the police."

"Mike, this is not right! If you don't call the police we are going to tell the boss when he gets back tomorrow!"

The next day Mike and his assailant were called into the boss's office. Mr. Lucia was a fair man who wanted the issue settled without police intervention.

"Why did you hit Mike yesterday?" Mr. Lucia asked the large man. "Assaulting fellow employees is not tolerated by the state."

"This Mike is a Christian. I don't like him. We don't need him around here! He thinks he has guts. He thinks he is not afraid of anyone..."

"How did you get that?" Mike's voice was tense and raised half an octave.

"Why did you talk that way to the bosses, when they called you in for being a Christian?"

"That's not your business. And you're not my boss." Mike was in no mood for this. "If they want to fire me, that's fine. I don't think you have to beat me up because I didn't say what you like. Besides, I didn't say anything to you or about you to anyone."

Mr. Lucia stepped in. "Look, you two had better drop this thing. Mike, you shouldn't go to the police. We will make sure this doesn't happen again."

"I am not going to the police." Mike's tone was as firm as before, but there was an air of reconciliation. "I don't hate this man. I have forgiven him already. I don't hold anything against him. As a Christian I can forgive him."

Suddenly Mike's assailant had nothing to say. He couldn't talk anymore. A look of shame crossed his face as he turned his eyes to the floor. He was not prepared for forgiveness.

"Now Mike, you really don't need to go to the police with this."

Mike reassured the boss.

Mr. Lucia appeared relieved. "Okay, if you're not going to call the police, then I guess you can go back to work."

As Mike headed for his work site, he reviewed the events. He was on a black-list. But still co-workers came to his defense. For this he was grateful. He didn't know what would transpire next, and he didn't know what pressure the other seventeen Christians endured. It was dangerous to talk to them, and he was not quite sure who all of them were.

A couple of weeks later he was called back to the office. As he entered the small room the door closed behind him; only three people met with him this time. They had some papers for him to sign.

"Mike, we just need your signature on some papers here." A Party member nonchalantly slid some papers across the desk. "We just need your name on the dotted line to protect your job."

"What am I signing?" Mike asked, knowing full well what they were up to.

"Oh, it's just a formality. It really doesn't mean a thing. It's just your signature. No one is going to check up on you," the Party boss reassured Mike as he handed him a pen.

"Check up on me?" Mike questioned.

"Right, no one is going to check to see if you are going to church. Just sign the papers and go on about your business."

"Look," Mike stood and faced the men. "If I sign a paper that says I am not going to church, you won't have to check on me. I won't be at church, because I keep my word. But I am not going to sign your paper. I am going to church. If that bothers you... I'm sorry." He left the papers unsigned.

A few days later there was a company meeting to which Mike was summoned. After various items of business had been discussed, the manager said, "As many of you know, Mike Olari is refusing to cooperate with the government. He still chooses to follow the silly superstitions of Christianity. These beliefs are like a cancer. They will eventually eat away at society itself. Religion, like opium, dulls one's awareness to society's issues. We here at the Transit Authority have tried to work with Mike, yet he remains insubordinate. We wish to warn you what association with this type of person can do. Mike needs to be avoided. Be careful not to talk to him. His ideas are dangerous." The manager paused, then as a mere formality he glanced at Mike and asked, "Do you have anything to say?" Without waiting for an answer, he immediately went on to other matters.

"Yes, I have something to say."

Ignoring Mike, the manager continued to speak. Other workers around Mike began to call out. "Mike has something to say! Mike has something to say!"

The manager was forced to yield the floor to Mike. "Say what you want to say."

Two hundred pairs of eyes turned to Mike as he stood up. He felt as if he were in a dream; part of him wondered whether he was sane. Then a tough courage sprouted deep inside and stabilized him.

"I am here today, and you want to judge me." As Mike listened to his own words, it seemed as if someone else was speaking through his mouth. "You want to make a big deal about my case, about my personal beliefs. No one cares how reliable I am, or how hard I work. Look at the number of employees here you can't count on. They steal many things from you. Is a thief ever treated like this? People come to work drunk. Does drunkenness ever get this treatment? How many members of the Communist Party just skip work when they feel like it? When you want me to work late, I do. If there is an emergency, I come in, even if it is the middle of the night. You can count..."

Mike's words laid bare the inequities of the system. In a rage the manager commanded Mike, "Leave now! Get out of this room!"

Mike had no choice. He left and went home. All kinds of thoughts flashed through his mind, among them, thoughts of death. It would not be the first time a Christian was killed in Romania, for uncompromised beliefs.

As a result of his stand, communist officials called Mike to meet at the government offices downtown. This was the third phase in the Party's plan to mold Mike to their will.

Mike was led into a moderately large room. He saw three long tables set out a few feet from the walls, forming a horseshoe. About twenty people sat behind the tables. Mike was given a chair in the center of the room, surrounded by people who had already judged him.

A man in a uniform began to address Mike. "Mr. Olari, it has been brought to our attention that you and one other woman in your sector are potential threats to the state. Sixteen of your comrades have seen the folly of their upbringing, and they have signed the papers." His gaze was steely, his expression was matter of fact.

News that sixteen had signed their faith away tore at Mike. It was not for him to judge them. He did not know their fears, but he grieved for them. This felt like a funeral. Meanwhile, some other official droned on about the follies of religion. When he finished speaking, all twenty began to ridicule Mike at the same time. There was no response Mike could give. All he could do was endure it. Finally the man in the uniform began to ask Mike questions again.

"Mike, do you find fulfillment in working for the people of Romania?"

"I like my job."

"Do you ever do work for your church?" The first officer continued.

"Yes."

"Do you come in to work for your boss, even if he calls late?"

"Yes."

"Just tell me which is better. Do you like to work for your church or for yourself? After all when you work here you get paid; the church will pay you nothing."

"You know what? When you work for the church, people do it because they want to. They're not just wasting time. Look at all the people here who waste time, and they waste time at the railway station, too!"

Mike's response was politically incorrect, for in a communist society the highest good a person can do is to work for the State.

Now ridicule turned to anger. "Get out of here! Leave!" The uniformed official pointed towards the door as he cursed, and shouted something obscene about Christians.

Again Mike could do nothing but leave and go home, and put the problem in God's hands. The next morning he went to work, and people avoided him as usual.

After two years of transit system service, an employee was expected to apply for advanced training. A candidate for higher education must first receive a recommendation from a Party boss above him. Mike applied, but received no recommendation. While his peers went on to further their careers, Mike was stuck at his entry-level position. He was the only person not approved for school.

During this time, God gave Mike favor in one boss's eyes. Mr Lucia had not said much when Mike was brought in before the other supervisors. He had been impressed with the way Mike had forgiven his assailant in his office. It was out of real concern that he approached Mike one day.

"Mike you need to be careful. These beliefs of yours are going to get you into trouble. I hate to see a promising young man like you be put behind the communist blackball."

"Thanks for your concern," Mike said quietly. "But Jesus is real, and He is my friend. I can not turn my back on Him."

"Well Mike, you have to do what you think is right. I wish you the best. Good luck!"The conversation was brief and both went on to their separate responsibilities.

Several weeks later a meeting was held for those in Mike's work sector. Mr Lucia had called the meeting, and he took care of odds and ends of business. Most there, including Mike, were bored. The last item of business concerned a new position soon to open. At this point Mike began to tune out. Mr. Lucia explained that this position would not be filled by appointment. The workers themselves would elect a new inspector. A man laughingly called out from the back, "I nominate Mike!" Snickers could be heard across the room.

Mike looked down at the floor.

"All right. Who thinks Mike would be good for the job?" Mr. Lucia called out.

Everyone in the room raised their hand in mocking gesture. More giggles could be heard as the bored workers amused themselves. Mike endured each agonizing second, and he knew the ridicule would continue over the next few days.

Mr. Lucia glanced quickly around the room. "You know, I think Mike would be best for this job. He is honest, and we know where he stands. We know he won't back down when he thinks he is right."

Mr. Lucia quickly shoved his papers into his briefcase and dismissed the meeting. "Mike, I want to see you in my office," he made brief eye contact with Mike. Then he ducked out a side exit.

Mike sat stunned. What had happened? Was this another attempt to mock him? Was this for real? Did he really have the new position? He got to his feet, and went down the hall to Mr. Lucia's office. There he learned that he would be second in authority to Mr. Lucia. All the other workers in his sector would report any technical problems to Mike. He would oversee all repairs. He was also put in a position to report any worker to those higher up.

There was one drawback. He would not get the pay raise that went along with the position. While Mr. Lucia thought he could slip the promotion past those in higher authority, a pay increase would be a red flag on Mike's file. He did not want to notify anyone that a Christian had begun to move up the ranks. Mike didn't worry about the pay increase, but praised God for the better position. He had almost lost his job, and now he was promoted.

Over the next few days he would overhear people talking. They couldn't believe Mike had authority over them. Even more baffling was the fact that they themselves had elected him to that position!

He found himself well suited for the work, even though he was only nineteen. Workers began to treat him with respect. In time they saw him as fair, and liked him. Some even admitted that God had given Mike the new position. How else could he have gotten the job? Curiously, the Party also let up on their harassment of Mike for the rest of his time in that sector.

*"We should never despair, our situation before
has been unpromising, and has changed
for the better, so I trust, it will again."*
General George Washington
July 15, 1777

CHAPTER 7

The crest Mike had ridden at work was about to crash into the stark realities of military service. Every Romanian male was called into active military service at the end of their teenage years. Just before his twentieth birthday Mike received his papers to report to boot camp.

This was not something he looked forward to, but it would only last sixteen months. During this time God would test and temper his faith. He had decided to make the best of it, and hoped to be trained in a career he could use later on in civilian life.

Day one of military life: all draftees stepped out of civilian clothes and mailed them home. A uniform would be their attire for the rest of their tenure. Heads were shorn bald, and bunks, in long rows of barracks, were assigned.

Winter approached, and cold dawn had not yet come on their first night in camp. Suddenly a lieutenant burst into the barracks spewing forth a tirade of obscenities. Draftees scrambled to attention at the foot of their bunks and squinted in the glare of lights just flicked on.

Of course draftees did not get out of bed quickly enough. They did not make their beds well enough. They did not run fast enough. They did not do anything right, no matter how hard they tried. Drill instructors screamed orders and insults, belittling men for the slightest infraction.

To give instruction in civil tones implied this was a civilian matter, so every order was screamed and yelled. In this way the army strove to break a person down. In return, the broken would be rebuilt into an effective Romanian fighting force.

In the brisk predawn air, draftees were put through their exercises. They consumed breakfast as the sun rose. The rest of the day was filled with every sort of military training, political indoctrination, and drill after drill. The next day they were tested on what they learned the day before. Officers wanted immediate input as to who promised to be the best soldiers.

Within a few days Mike and many others were taken to headquarters to be interviewed. Seated at a large table across from the colonel in charge of the entire base, Mike knew the screening process had started. From here medics, surgeons, technicians, members of the special forces, and so on would be selected for respective instruction. The colonel opened Mike's folder and scrutinized the papers.

From across the table Mike spied a notation scribbled on the inside leaf of the file folder. "Mike Olari is dangerous to society...." The colonel shuffled the papers back into the folder, and Mike could read no further. He was stunned. It never entered his mind that the incident at work would be in a permanent national file. The colonel asked a few questions, scribbled a couple notes, then dismissed Mike.

That afternoon, while draftees received instruction on how to handle their weapons, a disturbance erupted on the far end of the field. A draftee had been arrested and taken away in a paddy-wagon. Mike learned later the man was a Jehovah's Witness and had refused to pick up his gun. He was thrown in jail to reflect on his insubordination. This procedure became routine for Jehovah Witnesses, many of whom still refused to pick up their weapons upon release. Some went back to jail many times because they continued to leave their gun on the ground. Others were put into prison for years for this crime.

Mike was asked if he would also refuse to pick up his weapon. This was not a problem for him as there were no bullets in the guns anyway. He figured he would never have to kill another human being because criminals, gypsies, and Christians were not to be trusted in combat. Such undesirables were relegated to positions behind the lines where they could be chaperoned.

New draftees were divided into four platoons, each commanded by a lieutenant. The lieutenant in charge of basic training would go with his men to their next assignment. He would be their lieutenant for the full sixteen months of enlistment. Sergeants were selected from the draftees and put in charge when the lieutenant was not around.

It was the sergeants who, in the finest of military traditions, took it upon themselves to harass the new soldiers. Routinely, all draftees were awakened from their sleep to do calisthenics. They marched around the barracks in their underwear under a dark winter sky; then two hours later they would do it again. And of course they all had to do pushups at the sergeant's whim.

Towards the end of Mike's first week, the captain in charge of political indoctrination came onto the field. Mike's lieutenant went to meet him. After a salute the two conversed briefly.

When the lieutenant returned he called Mike's name. Mike stepped forward, and snapped to rigid attention. The lieutenant moved closer. Mike was frozen, his forward stare unbroken. The lieutenant moved still closer, his nose now inches from Mike's face. Mike's heart pounded, but not a muscle flinched.

The lieutenant screamed, "Soldier Olari! You have just volunteered to assist the captain!"

This was news to Mike. "Yes sir!" Mike bellowed back.

"Let's see if you can do better than the last syphilitic swine who slept on his posterior!" The lieutenant's voice actually went up a couple decibels. His tone was shrill and Mike felt the lieutenant's breath.

"Yes, sir! I'll do better, sir!" What else could Mike say?

"Screw up, Olari, and I will be all over your hopeless derriere! Make me look bad and I will harass you all the way to hell and back!" The Lieutenant's voice became more shrill. "Do you understand me?"

"Yes, sir! I won't let you down, sir!" Mike was able to match his lieutenant in volume.

"Then you may leave with the captain." The lieutenant's voice was suddenly civil. "You are dismissed."

Mike saluted and exited the field with the captain.

The tasks the captain had for Mike were easy, so easy that Mike wondered what kind of soldier could mess them up. The captain's office had to be cleaned in the morning and evening. A fire had to be started at daybreak in a small wood stove, and enough firewood for the day piled in the corner.

Mike performed his duties with meticulous effort. He already had a black mark in his file because he was a Christian. He had been slandered, but he did not want to leave room for a legitimate complaint. When he wasn't watched, he still did everything to perfection. He knew it would be noticed sooner or later.

There were advantages to these new responsibilities. While other soldiers grunted through predawn drills in the cold dark, Mike built a warm fire for his Captain. Afterwards, with time left over, he wrote to family or friends. He also prayed in his free time; this was important to him. Praying and listening to God in his heart were his only methods of spiritual connection now. He did not dare bring his Bible to boot camp. He only had one, and it would be foolish to risk confiscation here in the military.

The month of basic training passed quickly; however, military training seemed secondary to political indoctrination. It was as if the government was less concerned about invasion from a neighboring country than with not having its citizens tow the official Party line.

The captain had been impressed with Mike's attitude and work. One day he asked Mike, "Is there any position you would like to be recommended for?"

"What do you mean?"

"I think you are an honest, hardworking person, and you're smart enough to go somewhere in the army. I can recommend you for special training."

Mike pondered briefly, "Well..., I would like to work in the clinic. I would like to get some medical education."

"Okay, I will put in a recommendation for you." The captain smiled briefly and went back to the work at his desk.

"Thank you, sir!" Mike was truly excited about this opportunity. He had wanted into the medical field for a long time.

Days later the captain cornered Mike. Now he wore a stern expression.

"There is something you didn't tell me..." The Captain's cool perturbed gaze met Mike square in the eye. "You are a Christian."

"Yes, what's wrong with that?" Mike asked innocently.

"You know what's wrong with that," the captain quipped.

"Yeah, I know." Mike could feel disappointment build inside him.

The captain was disappointed in Mike, still he was a fair man. "Mike I am going to talk to you off the record, as a friend. I asked your lieutenant for a trustworthy reliable worker. You are that. Now I will not ask you if you have a Bible or Christian propaganda. I'll just warn you to send it home now. And I hope you will not give a second thought to spreading this religion of yours."

"No, I don't have a Bible, and I hadn't planned to preach to anybody. If people know I am a Christian, it's because I live differently."

"That's good." The captain never lost eye contact, but a hint of concern could be seen in his face. "You'd do better to give up this Christianity. I hope you understand why I can't recommend you for medical training."

From that time on the captain put more and more distance between the two of them. It was simply too risky for him to be identified with a Christian.

Profoundly disappointed, Mike never thought of denying his Christ. He reminded himself that his plans and dreams may not be the same as God's. He knew that his Father in heaven would work this out for good.

About this time, some faceless official decided Mike's military training would be terminated. There was only one thing people like Mike were good for, that was manual labor. A train was loaded with criminals, gypsies, and Christians. The criminals were young men who had a record as a juvenile delinquent; those guilty of serious felonies were already in prison. Gypsies were considered low class, because they spoke a different language, had a transient lifestyle, and held both theft and loyalty as a cultural values. Christians were in short supply on this train. Much later Mike learned that other Christians were there; but they found it difficult to live their faith under the circumstances.

The train took its human cargo 300 miles to a deep valley. Few direct rays of winter sun warmed this place. Rather, long cold shadows threw a chill over several barracks huddled against a now icy river. Here men gazed upward onto a steep mountainous slope. The remnants of an earlier rail line were clearly visible on the mountain's side. Trains did not travel here anymore. People rarely passed this way; forceful river currents had eroded the mountain's base. Slope and railway both lost their underpinnings. Year after year forgotten misfit soldiers built a new mountain foundation.

The Romanian army labored to build a rock wall rooted securely at the river's edge, which would hold the mountain's side in place. From this foundation, more gigantic man-made blocks of stone would undergird a new railway. Occasional supply trains brought tons of boulders and dumped them at the crest of the mountain's ridge. Soldiers swarmed over massive stones, and split them apart with sledge hammers slammed against great steel chisels.

The men loaded manageable chunks of rock into wheelbarrows, and carted them by hand down the mountain to the actual construction sight. Immense rectangular wire cubes had been formed. When empty, the wire cubes looked like giant chicken coops. Stones were singly situated inside these cable cages. As the cage filled, stones were cemented together. The entire structure was reinforced, a rugged bulwark that could endure the river's power.

Soldiers slaved on this project during every daylight hour. The cold winter brought snow, but snow did not stop construction. Mike swung his sledge hammer to a rhythm. Sweat dripped from his body as snowflakes fell. Coats and shirts were shed. Across the site faint trails of steam could be seen, illuminated in the cold horizontal morning light, as heat escaped from the soldier's half-naked bodies.

No one knew when this project started, or when it would end. This was a place to put human beings who did not fit into the system, and forget them. Days blurred into one continuous dreary episode, characterized by poor food, long hours, and interrupted sleep. Sergeants repeatedly woke up soldiers to run them through drills in the dark hours. At least the officers amused themselves in this cheerless place.

Most of the soldiers developed close bands of comradeship, then coagulated into tight cliques. Conversation was blue and sexual exploits were exaggerated. Off-color songs and jokes were the mainstay of humor. For soldiers with no God, no alcohol, and no women, they did their best. They saw Mike as different, and he was not welcome as a close friend. But this was nothing new to him. He had learned long ago that he was different. For him this difference made life worth living.

At some point in this endless series of days, Mike began to lose his appetite. When he ate, he often vomited it back up. With less food, he found he had less energy. Now each day drew into infinity. He wondered if he would get out of this valley alive.

Soldiers worked all along the mountain side. About midway down the descent was a small train station that had been converted into a cafeteria. All meals were taken here, well away from the barracks in the valley. During lunch the lieutenant appointed someone to guard the tools while the others left to eat.

One day Mike approached the lieutenant and asked him if he could skip lunch and watch the tools. Volunteers were unusual for this chore, so the lieutenant readily gave his consent. Mike's real desire was to be alone to plead with God.

When all had vacated the work site, Mike laid his distress before his God. "Father, you have been good to me in the past. You have always supplied my needs. You have always protected me. You have always listened to my problems. Now, Father, I feel death is present in this valley. I don't think I am going to make it out of here alive. My stomach is in pain, and I have no strength. I can't keep my food down, and most of the time I don't feel like eating."

As Mike continued to pray, he felt his anxiety lift. He thanked God for stepping in for him, and spent the rest of his lunch hour praising Him.

Although the lieutenant was a hard man on the outside, he inconspicuously showed sympathy for Mike. To him Mike showed promise and should be somewhere else. A week after Mike had prayed, the lieutenant assigned him to operate the large cement mixer. The job required little physical effort; all Mike needed to do was push buttons and pull levers. Mike began to feel better; and for awhile his appetite and strength returned. For weeks He felt his prayer had been answered.

Then one night, towards dawn, Mike was awakened with stomach cramps and nausea. He quickly slipped into his uniform and grabbed his coat. Snow squeaked underfoot as he headed for the outhouses. He felt lightheaded, and objects began to move. He could not stand, and felt himself hit the snow packed earth. Not unconscious, but unable to move, Mike lay in the snow.

A sergeant on duty noticed Mike had not returned, and went to locate him. He found him in the snow and lifted him to his feet. Then he put Mike's arm around his shoulder and supported him as they limped back to the barrack. There was no doctor in this isolated location, so Mike was sent to the nearest hospital.

Mike recovered quickly with proper treatment, and was returned to work. The doctors, however, located a cyst on Mike's spine, and ordered him back for minor surgery. Unexpectedly, the doctor wrote a pass for Mike which prohibited him from any work for an extended recuperation period, after which he could do no heavy manual labor.

Mike smiled inwardly at the roundabout manner in which God had answered his prayer. God had removed him from slave labor. In Romania, sick time did not exist. One was expected to show up for work no matter how they felt. The army was even worse. Now he had a doctor's pass, and no commanding officer could disregard a doctor's order.

Halfway through their military service Mike's platoon was transferred to another base, Prunişor. This base was closer to a town, but leave passes were rare. A new colonel and captain were in command. They had not read the soldiers' files and were unaware of Mike's legendary abilities to corrupt society. This was an opportune time for Mike's lieutenant to do a favor, so he recommended Mike for guard duty.

Mike's new responsibilities were simple. He was armed with a knife as no guard carried a gun. Patrolling the ground provided exercise and fresh air. He found it quite enjoyable, and later the captain promised to put him in charge of all the guards.

With increased responsibility, it was easier to get leave passes. Once he even visited his family in Arad. A few weeks later two brothers came for a weekend visit. They stayed in town, and Mike was able to get leave for Sunday.

Mike was on guard duty all Saturday night, but he still looked forward to his leave the next day. He and his brothers planned to attend church in town since he been unable to attend for months.

Mike's military peers could not understand this fascination with the fellowship of God's people. For Mike this was not a pious deed, but a time to warm himself in the love of God, a time to receive support and encouragement. As evening encroached, Mike returned to camp. He had not slept in over a day. While spiritually refreshed, his body cried out for sleep.

A major had been informed of Mike's exploits that day in town. He waited for Mike at the camp's gate.

"Private Olari," he said quietly as he stepped onto the roadway.

Mike jerked to attention and saluted.

"Where have you been all day?" A devious smile played with the corners of the Major's mouth.

"In town, sir! With a pass, sir!"

"Well, my sources tell me you were at church," the major said with mocking warmth.

"Yes, sir."

"You know, Mike, you Christians really don't need rest, you have God." He spoke with irritating calm. "I have a few things for you to do tonight. I have already made a list, and I want all the jobs done right the first time. We would hate to do them over again tomorrow night, wouldn't we?"

"They will be done right! Sir!"

Hours dragged as Mike pulled weeds, swept walks, and cleaned showers. All night the irony of the situation replayed in his mind. If he had spent the day abusing alcohol with his brothers, nothing would have happened. Destructive behavior went unpunished. The moral and spiritual values learned in church could only help build a strong society. Yet they punished this behavior. Mike wondered how long a society could last like this. Thirty-six hours without sleep focused the irony of the state's godless idiocy deep into his psyche.

Sometime after midnight the captain approached him. "Okay, Mike, you have done an acceptable job. However, when I consider that you are Christian, I am forced to the conclusion that you can't be trusted in charge of the guards. In fact, I don't think I can trust you being a guard at all. I'm going to reassign you to a work detail doing rail repairs."

Frustrated, Mike reminded himself that God was in control, that God's plan was to build a better Mike, a Christian who would yield to the impulse of the Holy Spirit. God's plan was not necessarily to place advancement on His children. Mike ran this concept through his mind, over and over, and began to feel at peace in his circumstances.

For the remainder of his army days he mended railway tracks. The work was not hard, but base brass again pegged Mike as a Christian, and would not allow him to transfer to another position. Mike did his time and got his honorable discharge. He was glad to be out of the army.

The army had taught him one thing: advancement was illusionary. In Romania one could always be knocked back a couple paces by the Communist Party. It could happen to anybody, especially to a Christian. It had happened in the army, and civilian life was patterned after the military. Mike did not know what life in Arad would be like when he returned.

"Next to God, we are indebted to women,
first for life, and then for making it worth having."
C. Nestell Bovee

Chapter 8

Arad was different now; although to the senses, things were much the same. The landscape of gray apartments, overgrown parks, and favorite places appeared unchanged. To be home with family and friends was a comfortable fit. At the same time though, everything had been altered while Mike was away. Many things had happened.

Changes had also fermented inside of him. He had become more determined to leave the country. He never knew when the wrath of the government would fall, for simply doing the right thing. Employment provided only illusory security. He wondered if he could support a family with his entry level position at the railroad. He always thought he would get married; now he began to think seriously about it.

Mike had followed a Romanian tradition. Marriage was not seriously considered until after military conscription was completed. Military service was a rite of passage for most. Now a man was viewed as responsible and mature; he could start a family. Mike's approach to dating was singular in purpose as he actively sought a wife.

Only a select few newly married couples could afford a place of their own. After a brief honeymoon the two would move in with mom and dad. It really did not matter if it was her parents or his. The primary consideration was: who has enough room for us?

Other changes happened too. At work many familiar faces were gone, and new ones appeared. Mike's position as supervisor was appropriated to someone else. He was demoted to his previous entry level responsibilities. When a serviceman returned, he was supposed to get a promotion and an pay increase. The reverse was true for Mike.

Mike did not give up easily. Again he applied to further his credentials as an engineer. He had done this before and had been turned down because he was a Christian. Once again he was rejected for the same reason.

Shortly after his discharge, a friend by the name of Ilie approached Mike. Ilie was older, and had worked with Mike before he left for the military. As a Party member he was privy to the formation of changes that would soon be passed down from above.

"You know, Mike, it might be better for you to find another job."

"What do you mean?" The same thought had entered Mike's mind, but he wanted to see what Ilie would say.

"I hear what Party officials are saying. They don't like you."

"Why?"

"Because you are a Christian! That's the only reason."

"But this work is what I trained for..."

"I know, I know, but they don't care. They just don't like people like you around here. And as far as training goes, they'll never let you take another class."

Mike knew Ilie was right; he kept his face expressionless. While Mike preferred to work with the railway, his attitude was cavalier. He wanted a good life but did not want to pay the communists' price. If the communists harassed him, he resolved to take it. Even if the communists killed him, he knew he would go to heaven.

"Mike, I'm talking to you as a friend, off the record. They are going to step up the pressure. They intend to make your life miserable."

"Well... thanks Ilie, thanks for filling me in." Mike said quietly. Frustration teased with him. He knew he needed to pray and seek God's wisdom. Would it be better to stay and buck the system? Or would it be better to leave?

It did not take long for Mike's plans to crystalize. While he was harassed at work, it was illegal for him to quit his job. His communist employers proclaimed the constitutional right of all citizens to hold employment. Workers were supposed to be so happy in their positions they would never want to quit, and it was illegal for them to do so. Mike saw how well the scheme worked. Workers were stuck in a profession until the government moved them. The majority were not happy with their positions, and pay was low. Consequently, workers would pretend to work, and the government would pretend to pay them.

Mike knew his brother could get him a job where he worked. It entailed the delivery of cakes and ice cream to different functions in Arad. To become a delivery man humbled Mike. His job with the railway transit system had given him a measure of prestige. A delivery man was considered very common. However, with tips, Mike could make more money if he delivered ice cream. This was an important consideration, especially as Mike hoped to find a wife soon. Financial security became a prominent consideration.

When he decided to make the job switch, he applied to the government for permission. This took time. In the interim, Mike focused his attention on other matters.

While employment was important, there was a issue of greater overriding concern. Mike felt it was time to get married. He had dated in his late teens. Now it was time to go on to something more intimate. He believed marriage to be of monumental importance, and thought it was critical to be with the woman God chose. Mike learned that a lot of time could be spent dating, without actually getting to know that person deep down inside. Only God really knew the girls Mike dated, and only God knew their hearts. It seemed logical to go to God for a romance that would last.

Mike remembered the Old Testament account where Abraham needed a wife for his son Isaac. He sent his most trusted servant back to Mesopotamia, their ancestral homeland, to find her. The servant wisely discerned that his task could only be done with the direction of God, so he asked God for a sign. When the servant arrived in his old village, he and his camels were in need of water. At the village outskirts, women drew water for daily use. He decided to ask them for a drink. He asked God to have the right woman also offer to water the camels, without being asked. The woman who showed this hospitality would be the one. A young woman named Rebecca had sympathy and gave him water to drink, then offered to water his thirsty camels. That evening the servant met her family, and she agreed to go back to Canaan to marry Isaac. An interesting thing happened; shortly after Rebecca arrived in Canaan, Isaac fell in love with her. This was not simply an arrangement they had to live with.[1]

Mike was versed in the stories of the Bible. Not only did he believe them to be historically accurate, he believed them to be lessons through the generations of time. To him there was a lesson in this love story between Isaac and Rebecca. Customs had changed, but the abiding truth of this account was that God must direct a man to his spouse.

With this central fact in mind, Mike entered into a time of prayer and fasting. Many Christians have difficulty remembering to pray about their concerns. Some will fast and pray for a day or two, then find the answers they need. This issue was of paramount importance to Mike. He felt it needed intense supplication so he set aside a week for that purpose.

Mike prayed for a woman he would love, and who would love him in return. He prayed for a woman who loved God and was committed to His service. He prayed for someone who would share common interests and would be a loving parent. He also prayed that God would bring her to him quickly. He had no idea where to begin his search. He waited for God to act.

The following week Mike chatted with his sister Maria. She spoke of a girl at work, and suggested he might like to meet her. At first Mike was not interested; he never liked blind dates. Maria persisted and began to list the girl's qualities. Then it dawned on him that she may be the answer to his prayers.

Originally Maria offered to introduce the two. Then Mike thought, "No, I'm brave enough to do this, I don't need my sister's help." The next afternoon Mike showed up at Ziridava Department Store, where Ana worked.

Mike glanced over the sales floor, but no one fit her description. Each department was relatively small. A man worked in appliances, an elderly woman worked in clothing, and no one was in bridal goods. There were few customers, and many shelves were bare.

A clerk stood behind a glass counter in hardware and caught Mike's his eye. With business-like demeanor Mike strode over and asked, "Is Ana Tipei working today?"

"Would you like to speak with her?"

"Yes, if she is not too busy."

"Just a minute, let me check. She might be in the back." The clerk quickly disappeared through two large doors.

A few minutes later Ana stepped through the same doors fully flushed. She was shy, and embarrassed easily, but she possessed a pleasant expression.

"Hi, I'm Mike." He extended his hand.

"Yes, I know, your sister told me about you." Ana smiled then glanced to the floor. "I can't talk long, I'll get in trouble."

"Are you busy after work? I would like to talk with you."

Ana thought for a moment, "Well... I was planning to walk to my sister's. You can come with me if you like."

"All right. When do you get out of work?"

"Four-thirty."

Their first date was set. In Romania it was common to walk across town. People thought nothing of a ninety minute walk to their destination.

Four-thirty finally arrived, and Mike was waiting for Ana. Together they set off across Arad in the mild April sun. They talked of many things: each other's families, work, hopes, dreams, and little bits of nothing. Ana was impressed with Mike. He seemed to be a nice guy and possessed a sense of humor. He was straightforward and said what he thought.

Mike was perhaps too straightforward, and took the direct approach. "Now that I am out of the army, I think it is time to get married."

Ana's stomach tightened.

"Of course, I think it is important to be friends first, so you get to know the person. You don't want to marry a stranger."

Ana did not want to hear this talk; she was too young to marry. She enjoyed her popularity with the boys at church. They teased each other, talked, and laughed; but she always kept a distance. She could welcome Mike into her circle of friends, but romance was out of the question. It was obvious she would have to set Mike straight on this marriage thing. It was fine if he wanted to get married, but not to her!

How to best deal with Mike's plans played in the back of Ana's mind while they visited her sister. Mike liked Ana's sister and her family. The visit was pleasant, but Mike knew he should not stay long. After a while he excused himself and said good-bye to Ana's relatives.

Ana walked with Mike out to the street.

"Well, Ana, I enjoyed our walk, and your sister seems to be a very nice person."

Ana smiled, "Yes, I enjoyed it too." She felt she should say something more.

But Mike quickly asked, "Would you like to go for another walk tomorrow?"

Another walk seemed innocent enough. Perhaps she could set Mike straight then, so she agreed to meet again at four-thirty the next day. Ana felt Mike would respect her desire to remain unmarried.

On their second walk through Arad, conversation flowed freely. Time passed quickly. Towards the end of their date, Ana paused on the sidewalk. She had to make things clear, she did not want any misunderstandings.

"Mike, I don't know what you have in mind; but I am only nineteen and I think I am too young to get married."

"I understand."

"I am very busy at church. They have a choir, and I sing in it. That takes a lot of my free time. I also work a lot of hours on my job, and I have many responsibilities at home. I know you guys like to get married when you get out of the army, but I am just not ready for that."

"That's okay, Ana. Right now I would just like to get to know you." Mike sounded reassuring. "Could I see you again?"

They met again the next day, and the next, and the next.... Soon Ana felt Mike should meet her parents, and they liked him. Later they teased Mike about quitting his job with the railroad to deliver ice cream. In reality they understood the impossibilities of the communist system.

Mike understood Ana's reservations. He, himself, did not know if this was the girl he had prayed for. Nevertheless, he enjoyed Ana's company.

Ana, too, had prayed for a mate, but she had not expected her prayer to be answered so soon. She wanted a man who was a strong Christian. A man who would take the initiative in spiritual matters. A man whom she would not have to drag to church, but would take her there. She prayed that God would let her know in her heart who this man was.

During the initial days of their friendship Ana stepped back and watched Mike. There were things about him she liked; he was able to fix anything, even her brother's motorcycle. She was fond of the nickname he gave her, "Ani." This was not an uncommon nickname, but Mike was the first to call her by it. She was impressed with his blend of seriousness, hard work, humor, and spiritual feeling. She found many things she could appreciate in him, but she did not want to be touched, not even a kiss goodnight.

For two weeks Mike and Ana spent a great deal of time together. When Mike stayed over in Timişoara for business, both missed each other, but neither had really fallen in love. Mike was focused on his prime objective of finding a wife. He understood a lot of time could be spent forming a friendship, but that girl may not be God's choice for him. They got along well and truly enjoyed each other's company. Even though the friendship was innocent in a physical sense, there was electricity between them that fueled a pervading peaceful feeling, especially when they were together.

Mike felt he must have some guidance from God if he were to continue his pursuit. He and Ana did not have to get married right away. He could wait, but he needed to know if this was the woman he should invest time in. If Ana was the wrong girl, he would resume his search and look elsewhere. Ana had made it clear she did not want to get married. Marriage was an impossibility. Mike realized it would take a miracle to get Ana to change her mind. God Himself would have to effect her thinking.

Therefore the test was this: if Ana agreed to get married this early in their relationship, in spite of her previous objections, he would take it as an indication that God wanted them to continue. If Ana had reservations or said, "no," it meant that Mike should search elsewhere. So Mike suggested that Ana and he not see each other for a few days and pray about which way the friendship should go. He did not tell her about the test.

Mike and Ana both saw God as a loving father. They believed He answered prayers, and gave the simple signs of guidance for which His children asked. They knew they had to be close to God for this to happen. Of equal importance, if God's plan dictated a change, then they would do it. They knew God did not rubber stamp human agendas, and only rarely answered flippant requests. God was not a horoscope to be consulted, nor was He an investment broker with great tips. He is God, and they were ready to follow His wisdom, regardless of their desire. They did not fear God's direction because they knew He loved them and wanted their best.

Many ask God for signs but God is not talking. The sign may occur but it is a chance occurrence, like the roll of the dice. However, in this case separate factors came into play. First, many days were spent in prayer and fasting. Then both Mike and Ana honestly wanted God's will above their own. With these criterion met, God will commonly answer - sometimes in mysterious ways.

For days they did not see each other, instead they prayed. Their vigil expired on Thursday night, when Mike showed up on Ana's doorstep. Ana had been to a week-night meeting at church, and the hour drew late. They stood in the dark out by the curb and chatted for half an hour. A street lamp glowed in the far distance.

Finally Mike asked, "Ana, what do you think about us?"

Ana stared at the shadowy pavement and spoke slowly. "I don't know, Mike. This is happening too fast. I think I need a little more time."

Mike felt his heart sink. It sounded like no. He was willing to accept this. He spoke softly, "Ana, that's okay. We can still be good friends. I am glad we spent this time together, but to me your answer means, 'no.'"

"But Mike, this is very important; we need to be very sure." Ana thought clearly, but not in the way Mike had hoped.

He was at a loss for words and thought he should leave. As he stepped away he heard himself say, "There was something I was going to tell you. But I think I had better go."

"Well, tell me," Ana coaxed. "You don't have to go this minute."

"No, I think I had better go." Mike felt foolish.

"No! Tell me what you were going to say!"

He shifted his weight and again moved away. "No, I need to go."

Ana clasped his arm, and pulled him back. "Michael Olari, I'm not letting go 'til you tell me."

Mike avoided her gaze as he organized his thoughts. He stared at the ground. His tone was tender, "Ani, your mom died when you were only three. You never knew her. I know your dad and stepmom are good people. But you are the only girl with all those brothers. You were the only one who helped your mom with the housework. Then you got a job and willingly helped the family with your paycheck. You only kept a few lei for yourself. You have worked hard to make everyone happy. Now, Ana, you need someone to make you happy. I think I can make you happy. I will take good care of you."

Tears filled Ana's eyes; she found it difficult to speak. "Mike, you don't know how good this sounds." She began cry softly. "I didn't tell you this, but before I met you, I started to pray for a godly man. I never thought God would answer my prayer this soon. I am just nineteen, this is a little nuts."

As Mike reached out to brush the tears from her cheek, something happened. Ana's mind changed in a instant, in her heart she knew it was right to marry this man. She consented. Within seconds reality changed. Now she looked at a whole new picture with different shades and color. This was the man!

There was much to do. Before a ring was purchased, or marriage license filed, Mike went to a flea market and bought 200 baby chicks. There would be a feast and celebration after the wedding. For this, they needed meat, but it was too expensive to buy at the store, so Mike decided to grow his own.

Backyards of suburban Romania are given over to agriculture. Most of the space was used for a vegetable garden, however, many families would also have a few chickens, a goat, pig, or a couple turkeys penned in the corner. As weeks passed Mike enlarged his chicken coop to accommodate the developing chicks. He fed them corn, so they would be plump and juicy for the wedding feast.

Typically a Romanian marriage occurs in two stages. First there is a function performed by the government; then a few weeks later there is a ceremony given by the family. For Christians this is performed by a pastor or priest.

On July 12, Mike, Ana, and some seventy friends and relatives crowded into a courthouse chamber where a public magistrate married Mike and Ana. For fifteen minutes he read a list of responsibilities the state required each to perform for the other.

Phase one of the wedding was quick; however, the entire clan lingered around the courthouse for another forty-five minutes while photos were taken. Then all walked to a nearby cafeteria for cake, ice cream, and Pepsi. The catering company Mike worked for helped provide refreshments. For most of the afternoon, the seventy friends and relatives chatted and celebrated. As evening drew on, about twenty family members from both sides went to Ana's parent's for dinner.

In the eyes of the local church, the state marriage was not valid. After the festivities were over Mike and Ana retired to their separate houses. A honeymoon would not happen until after the second wedding ceremony. Now their attention would be focused on the preparation for the next celebration.

At the second ceremony Mike gazed on his bride, now in her simple, long, white wedding dress. A delicate veil crowned with fine blossoms graced her head. She held a large bouquet of flowers. Mike would grow to love her innocent beauty, a beauty to which he was already profoundly attracted.

This time over 300 people came to the wedding, which was held in a new church built by the congregation.* The Christian ceremony was performed in the sanctuary. Afterwards everyone went down to the basement to celebrate with a splendid feast prepared by the families. They served all 200 chickens Mike had raised. The merriment, chatter, and laughter lasted late into the night.

After a honeymoon in the hills near Chisindia, Mike brought his bride home. The little Olari house in Arad had been disassembled and built into something bigger. Mike's parents and two brothers lived there when Ana became one of the family. There was enough space for

---

*This church was built without permission from the government. After repeated requests for building permits, and after repeated denials, the congregation built anyway. Once the church was up the government did nothing.

Mike and Ana to retreat into their own small bedroom, eight feet by eight feet.

Anna was accustomed to Spartan surroundings, yet this move was a major adjustment. She loved her family dearly, and she deeply missed them. Her musically talented family spent much time singing together over the years; occasionally they traveled to other towns and villages to sing as a family. One night, while in their little bedroom, Ana began to sob quietly.

When Mike came in he asked, "Ani, what's the matter? Why are you crying?"

"Mike, I miss my family."

"Ani, can I not replace your family?"

"We all used to sing. I miss the singing."

"Can't I sing for you?"

"Yes, but you cannot sing in so many voices."

Mike and Ana adjusted; in the early months of marriage, a deep love grew inside them. Within the year Ana was pregnant with their first child. Their commitment and sensitivity to each other grew.

Years later Mike and Ana would muse about their simple trust. In retrospect, their whirlwind romance had the earmarkings for disaster, yet their marriage worked. They both were committed to their decision, made in simple honest faith.

Years later, Mike looked back and listed the factors that made their marriage work. In his own words Mike states:

"You have to live your life clean, be faithful to God. You have to be a good Christian and trust God with all your heart. Then you must put God in everything you do. It doesn't mean you're not going to have ups and downs. It doesn't mean you won't get to the point where you will say, 'I don't know if it was God or not.' But when you started you knew it was God's will, even if later you say, 'Wow! Maybe I made a mistake.' But you go back and tell yourself, 'No I was praying for this, and this is what God gave me.'

"Usually you get married with a high level of love, and every year love goes lower and lower. But that didn't happen with us. We started with God, with little love, and after eighteen years we love each other more each year. Why? I don't look better to her; she is not more beautiful. We discovered things we didn't know about before in each other. We had our kids together.

"Another thing explains this: She was very clean before we got married, I was clean. I didn't know another girl, she didn't know another man. I was the best for her, she was the best for me.

"I don't know how many can buy this. But if you cannot buy this, you cannot have what I have. I think that's why we love each other more and more every year. We respect each other more and more every year. I gave myself to her 100 percent. When I said for bad or for good I meant it, and she meant it too.

"This is my experience. In our case I don't remember one full day to be mad at my wife. I am not talking about days, just one day. I make her mad, or she makes me mad, then a few hours later she comes to me and says, 'Honey, I'm sorry.' Or I say to her, 'I'm sorry.' Then we loved each other more. I have to admit that she was the one who came back more often, and said, 'I'm sorry, Mike.'

"I cannot say this is the example for everybody. I cannot say, 'do it my way,' or 'this is the best way.' This is my life."

Ani, Ani, Ani. The pleasant memories made her seem near. As he sat in a Yugoslavian jail, Mike he had no idea of the future blessing his wife would bring. He missed her terribly, but down inside felt assured that she would be all right. The file of memories his mind had just sorted through proved God's protection over him and his family.

An awareness built within him that he was protected, and that his Protector had nudged him out of Romania. Mike loved his people and wondered if he would return someday. He could not see the future, and the puzzle of the present was difficult to piece together. Still a sense of supernatural closeness ruled his emotions in this uncertain situation. In time he nodded off, and joined the other prisoners in slumber.

My Horizon the unforeseen,
And I am homesick,
Homesick for a land I have not seen.
Tristan Corbière

CHAPTER 9

Early sunlight woke the prisoners, settling on them with an awakening fear. All dreaded deportation to Romania. Anxiety tugged at Mike, but he reminded himself of how he had felt close to God the night before.

The apprehension felt by jailed refugees had a reasonable foundation. Who could forecast the political winds of this country? Through the Cold War years, Yugoslavia's dictator, Marshal Tito, held together the nation's rival states with an iron hand. He used a combination of force, fear, and compromise to keep centuries of conflict at bay. This Balkan region had seen rival kingdoms, clans, and religions slaughter each other for much of its written history. The monumental size of Tito's task became apparent at the close of the Cold War, when Bosnians and Serbs began killing each other once again.

Tito also found himself sandwiched between the two superpowers. To the west was the NATO alliance, and to the east was the old Soviet Bloc. Tito did his best to play both sides of the Iron Curtain. He claimed his country was communist, and for all practical purposes it was. However, when he pandered to the West, he received benefits. It was to his advantage, to remain in good standing with opposing international forces. Refugees were pawns in this international chess game. He could return them to show his communist commitment. Or refugees could be slipped to the West, many times secretly, as a gesture of goodwill.

It was in this helpless situation that Mike and his compatriots found themselves. Prisoners and guards filled in the details how the system worked. Here in jail, Mike learned that Romania would barter salt for refugees. Romania had large deposits of salt, and Yugoslavia had large quantities of refugees. Deals were often worked out. Policies constantly changed, but many times human beings were exchanged for salt.

Yugoslavia played its cards wisely. Refugees with any sort of criminal past were returned to Romania, along with anyone who seemed undesirable. Also, if a guard had a bad day, he could pull a refugee for return. Part of the rationale seemed to be: these people may be dangerous to society, so let Romania foot their prison bill. Still, if the quota was not filled, random names could be added to the Romanian return docket.

On the other hand, countries that granted asylum would receive the best refugees. While Yugoslavia's methods were dangerously flawed, they functioned as a valuable filter and strained out real problems. Of course western countries would never publicly endorse Yugoslavia's selection policies, but they were privately beholden to them.

Of those who were selected for freedom, some were put on busses and sent directly to Italy or Austria. These were the lucky ones; they would not be sent back to Romania. They were safe. Even if they were part of the criminal element, slipped through by mistake, they would be treated fairly. In the West they fell under the constitutional concepts of due process.

Other fugitives were selected for freedom, but not bussed out of Yugoslavia. Instead they were sent on to refugee camps within the country. From inside Yugoslavia they applied for asylum through an embassy belonging to the country of their desired residence.

After their capture, Mike and the others waited twelve days with no information, while the Yugoslavian government searched their backgrounds. In the meantime, cellmates consumed their time with the exchange of escape stories. Accounts were fantastic, filled with narrow misses, close encounters, and incredible feats. Mike began to wonder how much was true and how much was hyperbole. Then he reminded himself that his story was rather unbelievable also. Still he did not tell his story in this cell. The others boasted of their adventures and took little interest in other stories. He promised himself he would not allow his account to become a casualty of exaggeration.

In jail he got a fuller picture of the dangers he had just passed through and the possible dangers that lay ahead. He heard of a special cemetery on the Yugoslavian side of the Danube reserved for those who drowned as they attempted their swim to freedom. Some recovered bodies had bullet holes in them, others had severe head injuries. Romanian patrols often caught refugees, clubbed them to death, then dumped the battered bodies into the Danube.

Rumor had it that the Danube crossing was so dangerous that Yugoslavian officials felt pity for those who survived. For those who crossed the river, freedom was more certain, and their chance of return unlikely. Mike hoped the rumor was true.

In this group was a man who had escaped once and had been returned to Romania. This was his second try. He retold the stories of others who had been returned, some beaten senseless and released, some beaten and imprisoned for long periods of time. Halfway through their prison terms Nicolae Ceauşescu, the Romanian dictator, released many as a media goodwill gesture. However the next day they would be arrested again and sent back to prison. Most knew the game, so some broke parole and immediately fled the country before they could be rounded up again.

As Mike listened to his cellmates talk, he thought of Ana's brother. He had been caught in the act of escape and was attacked by a guard dog which had bitten him severely in the abdomen. After he was subdued, the guards continued to beat him. He was a bloody mess, but was still held in jail for a week. Fortunately he was able to prove police brutality, and the government granted him permission to leave the country. Ana remembered his departure, and how friends and relatives saw him off. Most had tears in their eyes; it was like a funeral to her. She felt sorry for him having to go to a country where he had no family. Now her husband had left for that same country, and she didn't know if he was dead or alive. All Mike could do was pray for her.

Another rumor began to circulate. Yugoslavia would not twice return a person to Romania. No one in the cell could think of any exceptions. Mike made a mental note of this rumor and checked it out later. It appeared to be true. Yugoslavia sympathized with those who fled a second time.

After twelve days of investigation, authorities could find no reason to send any of the refugees back. Mike and the others were crammed into transport vehicles and driven to Belgrade, the capital of Yugoslavia. Their trucks lumbered to a stop outside a small prison.

Herded indoors, they were separated from the criminals. Females were led off to some other place. Men entered a second story room, where twenty beds accommodated 150 inmates. Men slept two or three to a single bed, or on thin blankets between beds, under the windows, even under the beds. Mike considered himself lucky because he had a thin mat under a bed. It was impossible to sleep without touching another man. Masculine odor hung heavy in the air; few could shower in a day. It felt as if the room's oxygen had been sucked outward through the walls, and some other gas was left to sustain life.

Ten days later, Mike felt no regret when he was handed a bus token. He and some others boarded a city bus and traveled to a stop not far from the American Embassy. He had heard of the legendary freedoms and wealth enjoyed by Americans. Another reason Mike chose the United States was that his sister in Ohio could sponsor him.

Mike filled out forms. A staff member who spoke Romanian interviewed him. Then he filled out more forms. The Americans attempted to get a clear picture of what motivated Mike to flee Romania. Did he simply reach for a better material life, what many called the "American dream"? If the Americans thought he was after a higher standard of living, he would be turned down. However, if his goals were freedom to worship as he chose, freedom to speak what he saw as true, and freedom to hold his own political views, his chances were greatly improved. This is what America's founding fathers saw as the "American dream," and Mike pursued this dream. The fact he had family in the United States made his immigration almost certain. He planned a short wait while his paperwork made its journey through bureaucratic pathways.

❦

Once applications and interviews were completed, the Americans gave Mike more tokens and directions. In time he found himself on a bus that left the city and entered the scenic hill country that surrounds Belgrade. The driver pulled the bus to a stop at a sign that read "Cosuneag."

Mike and a few others disembarked, each clutching their earthly belongings. A long driveway stretched before them, which led through a well manicured lawn. At the lawn's distant side were tidy brick cottages scattered among mature trees.

Was this a refugee camp or a mountain resort? This certainly seemed like an amazing twist in fortune. They began their walk down the long drive, towards distant figures who milled about in the afternoon sun.

Upon closer observation the people looked like tourists, who motioned to the refugees. Their indication was to continue on down the drive. The refugees passed a few larger buildings. One appeared to be a cafeteria or dining hall. The drive then wound through a grove of trees. On the grove's far side were more cabins, only these were made of wood not brick.

Here the refugees were met by a camp official who spoke Romanian. All was well organized, and refugees were assigned to cabins. Families were given a lodge for themselves. Women and men without families were assigned to separate bungalows. Meals were eaten in a dining hall, and showers and toilets were behind another clump of trees.

The cabin walls were thin and drafty, but the air was fresh, and everything was clean. A few televisions had been installed at public locations. Refugees crowded around to watch the evening news. Programs were in an unknown tongue, but they put together bits and pieces of events. The food tasted good, but more importantly, there was plenty of it. Meals were prepared for the tourists, and extra was made for the refugees. Long lines formed at the few available showers. Everyone wanted to wash off their grime. Mike found it impossible to shower, as there was always someone ahead of him. So he rose early in the morning, around two, and scrubbed in solitude. Once clean, he returned to bed for a few more hours of sleep.

Mike heard many languages spoken, and quickly became aware of the international flavor of this camp. Refugees from Poland, Hungary, Bulgaria, Czechoslovakia, and even Afghanistan were sheltered here. He discovered that not everyone yearned for America. Most were on their way to Australia, and a few had Germany in their sights. Aid workers who ran the camp, came from the United States and Yugoslavia.

His heart lifted when he discovered telephones for refugee use. The fee was not expensive for the first two or three calls. He still had his Yugoslavian dinars buried deep in his front pocket, and he invested a few to make a brief call to his sister in Arad. Her family had just installed a phone. She was the first of the Olari clan to get one.

The phone rang several times. At last a woman answered, "Hello."

"Hello Maria, this is Mike." Conversation had to be brief, lines were probably tapped. "I'm fine, tell Ana I'll call tomorrow at five p.m."

"Five o'clock tomorrow?"

"Yes, I've gotta go."

"Goodbye Mike, we love you." She didn't want to keep him.

"Goodbye." The whole conversation lasted less than a minute.

Maria immediately got word to Ana that Mike was alive and well. Despite reports that her husband was dead, Ana had always believed he was alive. Nonetheless, her heart lifted as her intuitions were confirmed.

Shortly after five the next day Mike called a second time. This time Ana answered the phone.

"Hello," Ana's voice did not reveal her excitement.

"Ana! This is Mike, how are you?" Mike was especially concerned because Ana was due to deliver their second child shortly.

"Mike, I am fine. Cosmin is fine. I'm having no problems with my pregnancy. But how are you? Are you safe?"

"Ana, I am in good hands." That was all Mike could say. All the things that had happened in the last weeks would have to go unsaid. It was too risky, one day when they met again they could flesh out the real issues of their lives. "Honey, I have to go. Good-bye. I love you."

"Good-bye."

Their conversation was short. Briefly he had connected with his dear wife. But when the line went dead he was instantly removed to this faraway place.

The refugees agreed that life was better in the camp than in Romania. If life was this good here, what must it be like in Germany, Australia, or America? Security was minimal, and refugees freely moved about. They even walked to town during daylight hours. While they were essentially penniless, stores were open to them. Amazement was the only word that described what they saw: shelves filled with goods—soap, laundry detergent, toilet paper, and coffee. Mike had never seen so much coffee. He thought, it must be possible to drink a cup every day!

Yugoslavian law forbade refugee employment. However, locals came to the camp and hired day laborers. There was an occasional farmer who needed help with the last hay cutting, or the city dweller who couldn't find a local to work for the wages he wanted to pay. These jobs were always demanding, and the opportunities to work were scarce. Mike was glad whenever he could slip away and earn a little cash. However, he began to feel guilty. There were men in the camp who were absolutely penniless, who could not work when Mike did. Mike had a small roll of Yugoslavian dinars in his pocket. To him it seemed wrong to take work from another man who had nothing, so he passed the scarce opportunities along to others.

Mike was concerned about Ana. She was pregnant, could not work, and lived with his parents. Her funds were low, and she might not be able to get what she needed. He could not send his dinars back to her, since it was illegal for her to own foreign currency. Then an idea struck Mike. If he sent her chocolate bars, coffee, perhaps some soap, anything that was hard to get in Romania, Ana could barter them for what she needed.

It seemed wise to send his limited assets back to his wife. It cost him nothing to live in Cosuneag, and he hoped to leave camp for the U.S. within a few weeks. Mike made many trips into Belgrade and searched for bargains. When an item was purchased he went directly to the post office and mailed Ana a small parcel. About two months later Ana received it.

Mike had been in Cosuneag for about two weeks when another bus load of refugees rolled in. Among them was his brother, Ted. Ted was able to sell his house and car and, like Mike, he left his family behind, who then joined the others in the little Olari house. He too had crossed the Danube, and Mihai had been his guide.

Weeks turned into long months. Still life was good in the camp. Mike occupied his time with endless soccer games. There was still a little boy inside him, and he found great pleasure in his favorite sport. Others played chess, and Mike loved this game too. He could not count the hours locked in mental strategy and competition. He was especially challenged by one partner in particular, a doctor from Afghanistan.

Dr. Alisha could not speak Romanian, but he could speak English. This Afghan became Mike's English teacher. Mike found English an interesting language and learned

elemental conversation rapidly. In time, he learned Dr.
Alisah's story. His wife and nine children, all under the
age of twelve, lived in one of Cosnuneag's cottages. Originally they had ten children, but one was shot as they fled
Afghanistan on donkeys. Now Dr. Alisha was detained in
Yugoslavia while he made application for asylum in Germany. Some of his family were already German citizens,
so he was hopeful their sponsorship would be approved.

Dr. Alisha was a Muslim, and a man of high character.
As Mike increased his English vocabulary, the two discussed religion. Mike felt confined in his expression; his
phrases were broken and the topic was abstract. Dr. Alisha
believed in one God. He believed that Jesus was a great
prophet, but that Mohammed was greater. Yet the doctor
could not see how God would be concerned with his
insignificant life. God had too many other things to worry
about, like wars and international dealings. The average
person just had to do their best, and try hard to be as
good as possible.

With limited vocabulary, Mike searched for words to
explain how God loved us all. That God did care about all
the little people, not just the big issues, that we cannot
impress God, but we should just accept Christ's love. Mike
did not know if he made sense in his broken English, nor
did he not know if Dr. Alisha gave serious consideration
to what he said. Mike would be forever grateful for the
English lessons, the chess competition, and the good company. The only thing he could offer in return was witness
to the love of God. He prayed that a seed was planted and
would some day grow.

Resort refugee life eventually developed a down side.
Nights had became much longer. Leaves had fallen from
the trees, and the evening chill kept everyone awake. With
no heat in the cabins and few blankets, refugees did their
best to stay warm. They often slept in their clothes. Mike

slowly faced reality: he would not make it to the United States before the snow fell.

One chilly day an American aid worker made a casual comment to a co-worker, "I can't believe these people don't have coats. We're paying for them."

A refugee who could speak English overheard the comment and approached the worker, "What do you mean? We should have coats?"

"We pay for this camp. We give the Yugoslavs money for each one of you. You are supposed to get shelter, food, and clothing. It looks like you're getting everything but the clothing." The worker paused, then speculated, "Looks like someone's putting a little extra cash in their pocket."

Word spread quickly through the camp that each was supposed to get winter clothing, but something had gone wrong. One brave soul, a Romanian, decided to investigate. A few days later he was at the American Embassy in Belgrade. He explained the situation to an envoy, who quickly gave him cash to buy a coat. He was told not to make a fuss about this.

Other cold refugees knocked on the American Embassy door; they too received cash for coats. Mike chose a different tactic. He sent an air letter to his sister in Cleveland, and asked her for help. They lived at poverty level, but quickly sent cash for him to buy a light jacket.

Mike had not gone to the embassy for he smelled a coverup. Something was wrong here: the Yugoslavians had not met their responsibility and the Americans were awfully quick to hand out money. Two other unrelated incidents happened which heightened Mike's suspicion, and persuaded him to remain inconspicuous.

The first event occurred when Mike and his friends were in town. Some sort of political campaign was in progress. Posters of various candidates hung in public places. As they passed the picture of one candidate, Mike made an offhanded comment that he didn't like the man on the placard. Almost immediately two officials approached him on the street and told him to watch what he said about those in power.

A chill passed through Mike. He was familiar with this sort of surveillance in Romania, but hoped it was different in Yugoslavia. Despite the appearance of freedom, the secret police were constantly in operation.

The second occurrence happened to a nineteen-year-old boy by the name of Ghiță.* Ghiță was from a Christian family, but he had not personally bought into the faith. Like others, his escape from Romania was hazardous. At one point it was almost certain he would be caught. He began to pray for help.

"God, if you get me out of here safely I promise I will serve you." He was sincere.

Miraculously, Ghiță. made it across the border safely. For a couple weeks he appeared changed. He lived up to his bargain. Then he began to think, "I probably just got lucky. I don't think God had anything to do with this." He began to slip back into his old ways.

Things continued to go well for Ghiță. To migrate to Australia one did not have to have a sponsor. The Australian government gave approval for him to immigrate into their country, and provided him with an airline ticket. All appeared rosy, without God's help.

Ghiță's flight to Australia was scheduled to depart in one week. Everything was certain, so he decided to celebrate in Belgrade one night. In the course of the evening, he drank too much and his behavior was noticed. The following day the police showed up at the camp and arrested Ghiță. He was returned to Romania within forty-eight hours.

---

*Ghiță is the Romanian nickname for George.

In time, Ghiţă's fate become known to all. He was put in prison. Later he managed to get a letter to his relatives in camp. In it he said he learned that God is not someone you can fool. He knew God helped him, and then he turned against God. He was not sure he would flee again, but he said he would not turn from God again.

Mike quietly observed Ghiţă's experience and remembered his own brush with Yugoslavian officials. Their efficient law enforcement could strike without warning. Hence he decided to keep his name out of any possible controversy between Yugoslavia and America. He shivered in his light jacket and maintained a low profile.

Days grew colder. Both he and Ted knew something had gone wrong. They should have been in America by now. They had no idea why the Americans had not granted entry visas.

Frustration began to tear at Mike, then he received word that Ana had been given permission to leave the country. The Romanian government had granted her exit papers. This was extremely rare. Mike and Ana had repeatedly applied for these papers over the last two years. Others had applied for many more years, and never received permission to leave. Ana's intuition proved right, as she felt all along exit visas would be granted.

A few days after Mike's escape, Ana once again renewed her application to exit Romania. She stood in lines for days as she completed one bureaucratic requirement after another. Finally the government required one last thing; Ana must prove she owned nothing. Once she convinced the government she was penniless, they allowed her to travel to the capital. In Bucharest, Ana was examined by doctors and declared physically fit. That December, for some unexplained reason, a number of Romanians were granted passports. Ana was one of them. With passport in hand, she went to the nearby American Embassy and applied for a visa.

Still she could not leave for America. The U.S. would not let her in. Her husband was the only person who could sponsor her, but Mike was still in Yugoslavia and he could not return to Romania, because he feared arrest for illegal escape. Everyone now waited on the doorstep of freedom. Ana delivered their second child and named her Loredana. Mike was happy with the news, but was lonely in the distance. A sad sense of futility sprouted inside him.

A few days after Loredana's birth, the refugees were instructed not to leave the camp on the following day. No reason was given. Anxiety levels nudged upwards. That evening they all crowded around the televisions and watched the news, hoping to gain a clue for the sudden restrictions. Although the broadcast was in a foreign language, they were able to piece together the issue. Nicolae Ceauşescu, Romania's dictator, was slated to visit Yugoslavia.

Fear gripped the camp. Everyone felt the same apprehension. No one said a word for the next few minutes.

In a mournful tone of despair someone broke the silence. "They are going to send us back."

"That's why the extra military police have come," another added.

Faces were grim. All knew the perfect political gesture for Tito was to return a handful of refugees to Ceauşescu. This had happened before, accounts abounded.

The sun rose the next morning. The two national leaders signed papers, and had pictures taken. New agreements were reached. Bands played, medals and awards were given, but no refugees were taken from Cosuneag.

The next day Ceauşescu left, and the refugees were free to leave camp again.

This brief scare only heightened Mike's desire to leave. He wanted to be in a country from which he would not be returned—ever. Yet there was no word from the American Embassy. Months passed.

One winter day everyone was loaded onto buses and driven from Cosuneag. No one was sure of their destination. One hundred and fifty miles later the buses stopped at a new refugee camp called Banea Covilacea.

No one was really sure why they were moved. However, most speculated it could be traced back to the coat issue. Perhaps too many had asked the Americans for money. Had the Americans pressured the Yugoslavs? Now they were miles from an embassy. Now no one could hear their complaints.

Banea Covilacea looked like a refugee camp, with rows of barracks. The scenic beauty of Cosuneag was now a memory. The food was not as tasty, and there was less of it. The surrounding community was poorer, and no one came to the camp to hire day laborers. However, one thing made this place wonderful. The barracks were heated. Many refugees were warm for the first time that winter. There were hot showers with plenty of water!

Refugees also enjoyed more living space at this camp. When they asked for an extra room to have church, permission was granted. A pastor in camp from Timişoara gave communion and led services. All denominations worshiped together, Orthodox, Baptist, Catholic, and Pentecostal. The luxury of denominational division could not be afforded. The reality of the unity of Christ's church was evident in these sparse quarters. Things that Christians argue about seemed less important.

In spite of the good things that happened at Banea Covilacea, Mike became more discouraged. It seemed like he would never get out of camp. Five months had passed, and he had heard nothing from America. It was time to find a secluded spot and talk honestly with God.

"Father," Mike began, "am I ever going to be free? I have been in this camp for months. So far you have protected me like a shield. You have brought me safely out of a terrible country. I never could have done it on my own, and I thank you for your protection. Now, God, I am stuck. Nothing is happening. My wife has papers to leave, but I am stuck here, and she is stuck there. God, I miss my wife, and I have never seen my daughter. My son Cosmin is growing, and I can't talk to him. Father, I am sad and discouraged, please help me get to America."

Mike's sister in America was concerned. She had filled out papers of sponsorship months ago. Mike should have been in the U.S. by now. She checked again with the Department of Immigration, discovered the papers had been mislaid and were now lost. In no time she completed a second set of papers.

Weeks after the second set of papers were filled out, the base manager approached Mike with a smile. "Get your things together! You and your brother Ted are leaving for America tomorrow!"

Mike acted happy, but feared it was a trick. Again there was a problem, Nicolae Ceaușescu had scheduled another visit to Yugoslavia. More refugees could be turned over to Romania on this visit. The Yugoslavs could have lied about freedom, just to keep Mike and Ted from running.

Were Mike and Ted part of a peace offering to Ceaușescu? Was freedom really just a day away? Should they run? If they ran and were caught they would be returned to Romania for sure. Should they pack their bags and take tomorrow's bus to Belgrade? Should they trust the Yugoslavs?

Mike and Ted decided to take the bus to Belgrade. About a dozen refugees were on the bus with them. Once en route, an aide worker addressed them.

"You are not to leave this bus for any reason. We are going to sneak you out of the country. No Romanian officials will know you are leaving. Therefore, we need your strict cooperation."

This sounded good, but could it be believed?

The worker continued, "You will not disembark and go through the airport terminal. Stay on the bus and we will drive you directly onto the tarmac, next to the plane. You will get directly off the bus and board the plane."

Was this a setup? Were they told this just to quietly get them on a plane, only to have it fly to Romania?

As the bus entered the airport premises, Mike saw soldiers and military police stationed everywhere. Security was tight. It would be impossible to run now. The bus pulled into a secluded spot and parked. Everyone waited. Mike and Ted prayed silently. Hours dragged by.

Eventually a soldier walked out to the bus and talked to the driver. The driver started the engine and maneuvered the vehicle down a narrow alley between two large hangars then out on the tarmac. Fuel tankers and luggage carts went about their business. Their bus was only one of many vehicles on the tarmac.

They came to a stop in front of a large airliner with the letters D-E-L-T-A neatly painted on the side. Mike noticed this plane had no propellers, but was powered by jet engines. Could this be an American airline? Aircraft this large did not fly to Romania, but flew west.

None of the refugees were sure of their destination, but all saw the indications as hopeful, pointing towards freedom.

*The greatest good fortune
is the least to be trusted.*
Titus Livius, <u>Ab Urbe condita</u>. c.10 B.C.

CHAPTER 10

The plane looked new, the inside was clean and fresh. "This plane has to be going to America," Mike thought. "A plane this good would not fly to Romania."

Within minutes they were airborne. Belgrade stretched out below them. Everything went white as they passed through clouds. Minutes later they rose into the bright sunlight of the high atmosphere. Now Ted and Mike began to relax. Each sank deep into their comfortable seats. Freedom seeped into every muscle.

For so many years they had longed for this flight. Escape had been continually on their minds. Their previous attempts had only made them more determined. It now appeared that they had succeeded on Mike's fifth try.

Both Mike and Ted had failed to take note of the plane's flight direction. In a very short time the plane nosed downwards, back through the clouds. As they broke though the underside of white mist they saw a city stretched beneath them. A runway lay at its edge, and their plane made its approach.

Just enough time had passed to be comfortably back inside Romania! Had they been deceived? Still, Mike felt reasonably sure they would not be handed over. Ted sat in the aisle seat and glanced back over his shoulder to see tense expressions on the faces of the other refugees.

The seat belt light blinked on. The pilot said something in a foreign language. Mike thought he heard the word Zagreb. He and Ted listened to the conversation of passengers as they filed past to disembark. They strained for a hint in their talk. Again the word Zagreb was spoken, renewing their hope. Zagreb lay to the west of Belgrade. If this was Zagreb, the flight had taken them away from Romania. Perhaps this was just a stop before they went on to London, and then New York. Mike and Ted prayed silently.

More passengers boarded, and Mike noticed a few spoke English, another hopeful sign. English speakers would most likely travel west. But the most important clue was that all refugees were allowed to remain seated. None were escorted from the plane.

Soon the plane ascended a second time into the clouds. Once they crested in the bright sunlight, Mike made note of the sun's location. It was to their left. With winter sun on their left, they had to be heading west. The flight continued with its general west by northwest trajectory. Yes! They were, in fact, flying to freedom!

In a short time flight attendants began to serve passengers their meals. Mike and Ted had never seen anything like this before. Each meal was packed in plastic and Styrofoam. These substances were rarely used in Romania, and common people never saw them. Through a clear plastic container they inspected the main course and salad. A sealed white cup sat on the tray, along with a few other packets.

Mike and Ted stared at their meal in bewilderment. These strangers had unusual culinary habits. "How are we going to eat this without making a spectacle of ourselves?" Mike wondered.

Sitting near the window, he leaned over and whispered to Ted. "Look down the aisle and see how the other people are eating. Copy them, and I will copy you."

The plan worked quite well. The dinner was tasty, but the coffee needed sugar. Once the meal was finished they noticed three small packets on the tray. Mike picked up one packet and tried to read the writing. It meant nothing. He picked up another envelope, and he read "sugar." Carefully he tore it open, and sure enough there was sugar on the inside — about enough for his coffee. He would have to remember that for next time. The next packet contained powdered non-dairy creamer. This was something new to them. It must be for the coffee, but it might be good on the salad. They would have to pay close attention during the next meal to see how this was used. In the last packet they found a moist towelette. It was obvious what this was for. Mike and Ted were impressed, it seemed these people had thought of everything.

The flight across the Atlantic was long. The Romanians talked freely among themselves, confident no one could understand them. As they approached New York, a man in a business suit came down the aisle and spoke to Mike and Ted. His Romanian was perfect.

"Gentlemen, my name is Ken." He extended his hand.

Mike and Ted introduced themselves, and shook the man's hand.

"I need to know: are you going to Chicago after you land in New York?"

Mike explained, "No, we are going to Cleveland. My sister is sponsoring us, and that is where she lives."

"The reason why I came back here is to offer both of you a job. I have used Romanian immigrants before, and they work hard. If you are in Chicago and need work, call me. Here is my card." Ken bent down a little closer and lowered his voice. "I have been listening to the other refugees, and I was not impressed. You two don't use bad language, and you seem to be trustworthy."

Mike and Ted politely thanked the man for his generous offer. As Ken walked back to his seat, Mike and Ted looked at each other with satisfied expressions.

"Job. He offered us a job," Mike mused.

"There must be plenty of work." Ted stretched in his seat. "America must be a wonderland, with plenty of jobs, plenty of money, plenty of everything."

Both studied the English writing on the business cards before they tucked them away, deep in their pockets. Neither had a realistic concept of what lay ahead. In the early '80s unemployment gripped the northeast United States. Industry was moving south or out of the country. Factories that had operated for decades suddenly closed. Men and women lost jobs by the thousands. Politicians called it an economic recession. However, for those not blessed with unemployment insurance and not on welfare, this felt more like an economic depression. A migration from the industrial North was underway. Jobs were indeed very hard to find.

Economics was the last thing on these men's minds as they touched down in New York. With three hours before the next flight Mike explored the airport while Ted stayed with their baggage. Everything was so massive, a surrealistic dreamy mood settled over him. In front of an immense glass panel, he absorbed his first view of America. Below him on a well-lighted street, he watched cars move everywhere—beautiful cars, not like the little things that jounced along Romanian roads. There were so many cars, it seemed everyone must have one. He had seen a sea of lights from the plane. Now he gazed on distant skyscrapers, their lights stabbed deep into the night sky. He asked himself, "Is this the same planet I once lived on?"

In Cleveland Mike felt like an alien in a strange but beautiful land. Genuine compliments poured forth when he saw his brother-in-law's car. From his perspective the auto was exquisite, when in actual fact it had few miles left. His sister's house was a little mansion, although by North American standards it was very modest. How could Americans live like this? God must have really blessed them!

Mike's body slowly adjusted to the extended time change he had just experienced. Later he learned Americans called this "jet lag." He was up before everyone else the next morning. In no time he was out on the streets to explore the neighborhood, amazed by the way Americans lived. Mike wanted to see everything. He wanted to enjoy every little aspect of this new life. Everything was better in America. Even the snow looked whiter. His sister had such a variety of fruits, juices, and an unlimited supply of milk. Later that day he walked past a bank and observed people doing business at a drive-up window. This was incredible! How could the driver of the car be trusted not to just drive away with the money?

Quickly Mike and Ted learned that many things in America were not as magical as they first appeared. Nonetheless, they would always nurture a romance for their new country. There was much celebration those first few days. Two more had made it out! Slowly the Olari family was being reassembled on the far side of the Atlantic, in America.

After a few days Mike and Ted were informed of the serious job shortage. At the same time they were keenly aware of their sister's limited resources to help them. They needed to save money for their families' arrivals. The realities of a job search now emerged. Friends helped them look for work, but there were few leads. Both Mike and Ted spoke fragmented English, which potential employers found difficult to understand. Many would rather hire an American than a foreigner. Mike and Ted would work anywhere, doing anything, but jobs in Cleveland were not to be found.

After a couple weeks of fruitless endeavor, Mike's brother George arrived from Chicago, full of excitement and suggestions. Both George and Pete had escaped after Mike. They had slipped through Yugoslavia undetected, and stepped into the full protection of Italy. While Mike and Ted shivered in a refugee camp, George and Pete had been working in America.

In George's opinion there was more opportunity in Chicago. He offered Mike and Ted shelter in his basement apartment. He had plenty of room, now that Pete had moved to Phoenix. Briefly Mike toyed with the thought of Phoenix, but Chicago was closer, and George was persuasive.

So Mike and Ted decided to seek their fortunes with George in the Windy City. There they lived in a two-room apartment, buried in the basement of a large building. Pipes of all sizes zig-zagged across the ceiling. The dim light and the dampness did not bother them, for all they needed was protection from the elements. This was a base, a place to rest between the days of work they hoped to find.

Mike and Ted quickly unpacked their few earthly belongings in the bedroom. George was squeezed into the kitchen-living area. The next Sunday they went to a Romanian church of about 200. Everyone was very friendly and crowded around to congratulate them on their escape.

In a foreign sea of strange wonders, this small group of Romanians provided a island of familiarity. Bound together by their common faith, language, and past, they all faced the same challenges. They met others who had looked for work; some had looked for months. A feeling grew inside of Mike that Chicago could be a repeat of Cleveland.

On the way home Ted spoke. "Hey, Mike, remember that guy on the plane?" He dug deep into his pocket. "I almost forgot about this card." He pulled it out, and held it to the window for illumination from the passing street lights.

"Ya, I remember."

"It might be a good idea to call him."

"Do you think he was serious?" Mike raised his eyebrows. "But it wouldn't hurt to try."

The next day they called Ken who hired them both over the phone. They would start work in two days installing floor covering. The company worked in wood, mostly parquet. Ken promised them four dollars an hour.

Ken claimed this was a good deal because he took out no taxes. He said they would take home as much money as someone who made six or seven dollars an hour, someone who paid their taxes. Mike and Ted had no idea how the American tax system worked, and did not realize this deal could be suspect.

Quite simply they were thrilled to earn money, any meager income. Now they could help George with expenses. But most importantly they had money to pay the necessary application fees to bring their families to America.

The next Sunday Mike and Ted told the congregation they had found work during their first week in Chicago. Members were truly amazed, for many of them had searched for months.

Then a concept began to dawn upon Mike. This may have been God's timing. Had he been held in the refugee camp until just the right moment? Then at the exact time he caught a flight with the man who offered him a job. Mike considered this not to be luck or coincidence. This was a generous gift from God.

Mike now shifted his concerns to making ready a place for his family. He was not worried about their transportation. The cost of refugee flights was covered by an organization named after the Russian author Tolstoy. Later, when the refugees stabilized their income, they could pay back the loans interest free.

After sponsorship applications were filed, Mike bought an old Honda Civic. Now his family would have transportation. Next he began an apartment search. For weeks both Mike and Ted worked long hours. Both were able to accumulate a small savings. Then new job orders began to slow. Some days they would only work four hours. Some days they wouldn't work at all. Mike became concerned.

About this time he received good news. Ana and the children would arrive in two months. This was incredible! He had heard stories of families who had been separated for a year or even five years. But his family would be in the States just four months after he arrived!

Ana and the kids needed more space than existed in the tiny bachelor apartment. The basement was too dark and damp for children playing on the floor. How could Mike afford an apartment on his dwindling income?

George tried to help and told Mike of another job. This job would pay more. Mike was told he would clean an airport and do landscaping. He eagerly hired on. The job turned out to be heavy manual labor, mostly landscaping and laying sod. Mike was accustomed to hard work, and put in ten to twelve hour days. Mental calculations told him he would earn enough money for an apartment in a couple weeks.

However, Mike was profoundly stunned when he opened his first check. Only one hundred and fifty dollars was printed on the amount line, for more than sixty hours work! Perhaps the next check would be larger. But no, it was the same. Mike talked to his boss. He explained to Mike that taxes were high and he had to pay something called social security.

Mike worked for awhile longer. He was supposed to make seven dollars an hour. He didn't want to call his boss a liar, but he knew American taxes weren't as high as his boss claimed. He was being exploited. In reality Mike was making only two dollars an hour. Laying sod was dirty strenuous work. Every day he came home filthy and physically spent, too exhausted to look for another job.

Mike gave notice, then quit. Ana and the children would arrive shortly. Frantically he looked for another job. He called everyone he knew, and answered scores of ads. He desperately wanted his wife and children to have a place of their own.

Mike had handled his limited income wisely. His car was paid for, and he had saved $500. But this would not get him an apartment.

So Mike made a deal with a Romanian who owned an apartment complex. The man said Mike could live there for $350 a month, on a month-to-month agreement. The landlord even waved the security deposit, but insisted that Mike sign for food stamps. This was a humbling blow to Mike's self esteem.

His family had a place to stay for one month. But what would he put on the bare floors? What would his family sit on, or eat from? Mike borrowed $800 from a church member. At yard sales and the Salvation Army he purchased furniture, dishes, pots, and pans. Nothing went together - this was strictly functional decor, with a distinctly masculine nuance. Mike had everything ready, and ached to see Ana again. She would arrive at O'Hare International Airport on August 31.

Ana had taken a train from Arad to Bucharest, then had flown to New York. A large crowd of family and friends in Arad said goodbye for the last time. They stood on a simple cement platform outside the train station, alongside the tracks. She was close to her family; her eyes filled with tears. With the state of international relations, she honestly did not think she would ever see her family again. She could see nothing for her obstruction of tears. Someone, probably her father, helped her onto the train. Little Cosmin sat beside her, and took his mommy's hand, while Loredana slept in her arms. She continued to sob as the train pulled away from the station.

By a large window at O'Hare International Airport, Mike waited as he watched Ana's plane taxi in. Soon passengers filed into the reception area. Mike now fastened his eyes on the door. Then a short woman came into view. She carried a horizontal bundle of blankets, while a toddler clung to her coat. Ana was here! All reality now stood before him in the form of his family. Other problems faded away.

There was laughing, tears, hugs and kisses. Mike saw his six-month-old daughter for the first time. Cosmin had grown, and for the next few hours he wanted to be very near his father.

After loading luggage into their vintage Civic, they wound their way through Chicago and its traffic. Ana had never seen anything like it; so many cars, such tall buildings, and such endless sprawl. She was impressed with their little apartment, which contained more living space than she ever had in Romania. Obviously it needed a feminine touch, but she was amazed with what Mike had provided.

Most importantly, they were together. In Mike's mind they had not been married long, and over the months he missed his new wife immensely. He waited until the next day to tell Ana about having no job. He wanted to simply enjoy his family. When he did tell Ana, she appeared unconcerned. With all that God had brought them through, a job was a relatively simple matter.

Ana was astonished when she went into the stores. An endless variety of goods stocked every shelf. She was not bothered by her lack of money. The feel of plenty was new to her.America's poverty provided a much higher standard than middle class Romania.

Her mind went back to Romania's long lines. Some mornings she rose early to stand for hours in line for meat. Then the next day she stood in line for sugar. Another day she stood in line for toilet paper. On some special occasions, after she stood in line for hours, she was able to purchase a few ounces of coffee.Virtually every morning was eaten away by the line's long wait.Winter mornings were cold, many times made more miserable by freezing rain — still Romania stood in line. Many caught cold, and others came down with pneumonia as they waited in line during the dreary months. In these conditions simply standing in line — hour after hour — was a cause of death among the weak and elderly. Now Ana could buy everything in one store, on the same day, and make only one trip. The only line was at the cash register.

Mike continued his job search. He desperately wanted work, the thought of using food stamps embarrassed him. Not only did he feel cheap, he felt like he was taking advantage of American hospitality.When it was time to pay the cashier for groceries, Mike would walk away, head bowed with shame.Ana was left to pay the bill. She spoke no English. She fumbled through the food stamp coupon book in search of the right denomination as she attempted to communicate with the cashier.

The next Sunday, Mike and Ana prayed a long time for a job. Mike could beg from God, but to take government assistance was quite another matter. Early the next day a stranger called. This man explained he had heard about Mike through a friend and offered him a job over the phone as a painter's assistant. Mike and Ana could only praise God.

While Mike was very thankful for the new job, pay was meager. Six dollars an hour took care of basic bills, but Mike needed to pay off his loans. So he continued to look for other work.

In time he found a company of men who laid marble tile. Mike hired on as their tender. The crew could work most efficiently if those who laid tile did not have to run after their own materials. Mike insured each man a supply of tile and grout at arm's reach. This work was much harder but paid a little more than the last job. Mike observed those who fastened marble squares to waiting room walls, and thought, "I can do this."

The crew was remodeling a Holiday Inn. They installed new sinks and dressed the walls with marble. That afternoon the boss left the site for a couple hours. He gave instructions to keep the men busy, and then said, "Don't have Mike lay tile. He can clean up and assist."

Mike worked hard when the boss was gone and found he had a little extra time. He had carefully noted each step the laborers performed. Confident he could do a good job, he picked up a tape measure, level, and chalk line. With the level he checked the flushness of the wall. There was one small dip which he filled with "mud," then smoothed it out. He carefully marked a wall and drew squared lines where the tile should go. With a trowel he applied mastic glue to the underside of a marble square. Next he positioned the marble precisely on the line he had marked.

The boss arrived back early, and was surprised to see Mike installing marble. He went straight to Mike intending to reprimand him. But first he paused to examine Mike's work. It was good. "Mike, do you think you can do this?"

Mike's English was inadequate, all he could say was, "Yes, I think so."

"It looks good. I will start you tomorrow installing tile at eight dollars an hour."

This was awesome! Mike could pay off his loan and learn a new trade at the same time. Now things began to look up. As with many new immigrants, Mike's experience in the United States was an up and down affair. One week job security seemed certain, then a few days later he was looking for work. In America there was FREEDOM; in Romania there was JOB SECURITY. For Mike, to starve and have freedom was better than control by the government.

Mike became proficient in marble installation. His employer was honest, but rarely paid on time. The crew received their checks only when the tile contractor received payment. Consequently, weeks passed before Mike could pay his bills. The apartment manager told Mike he would need to go on welfare if rent was late again. The thought horrified Mike.

Mike found another job using his marble skills. Pay was better and on time. What Mike did not know was that his employer had hired him on the side. Only union members were contracted to work for the company. Mike was nonunion, but he worked hard and performed well. Even though Mike worked for less pay than union employees, he brought home more money than he had ever made. Mike thought he could get ahead. Once the company sent him to New Orleans for a special job. He worked feverishly at piece rate and earned over a thousand dollars that week.

Now Mike considered replacing his sputtering Civic. Pete, his brother in Phoenix, encouraged him to buy a car in the Southwest. He said the deals were better in Phoenix. Mike joined his brother in the desert, found a good car, and fell in love with the climate. The winter weather was mild, not like the biting cold wind of Chicago. Of course no one told him about the 115 degree days of summer.

He drove his new car back to Chicago only to discover he no longer had a job. New car, no job. The union discovered management's illegal hiring, and all non-members lost their positions. The whole union thing seemed strange to Mike who believed a skilled, honest, and reliable worker was all that mattered.

That night he took the bad news home to Ana. She was supportive and knew something would work out. Life was still better in Chicago than in Romania. But Mike wanted to get off the job merry-go-round. It was time to discuss their options.

"In one year I have had five jobs." Mike recounted each on his fingers.

"But Mike, we have all we need." Ana reminded him.

"You're right, and we have been able to help our family in Romania. Still it would be good to have a job that lasts. I would be happy to work for five dollars an hour if I would get paid on time and have steady work."

"What about Phoenix? Pete keeps asking us to come out."

"I don't know, it seems like God can give us something here. I really don't want to move across the country."

"Pete says the weather is really nice."

"He is right about that... Maybe we should pray about it."

For several days they took "The Phoenix Plan" to God in prayer, asking God for a sign. If he quickly found a job for five dollars an hour in Phoenix, he would move his family there. What Mike did not understand was Phoenix was a boom town, construction workers were in high demand, and his sign would be easily met.

Sunset Tile hired Mike to lay ceramic and marble tile in Phoenix. They paid well and soon he flew his family out.

In a little over a year Mike began his sixth job. Arizona was the third state in which he pursed the American dream. Americans were good people, but they had many strange and confusing ways of doing business. Life was good as Ana prepared to deliver their third child.

"Tell us, Epicurean, what things make us happy?
His answer is: Bodily Pleasure.
And you Stoic? Intellectual virtue.
And you Christian? The gift of God."
St. Augustine, <u>Sermones</u> 150, 3, 7

CHAPTER 11

America's money reads, "In God We Trust." In reality most Americans trust their money, and not their God. Mike's struggles in Romania taught him to depend on God, but in America his faith was also tested. No, he was never tempted to deny his God. Instead the subtle temptation was to put his faith in the American system, his own ability to work hard, and his employer to provide a secure income.

Mike liked his job with Sunset Tile; there was plenty of work. His English continued to improve, but at times he struggled with the language. Ana delivered their third baby, whom they named Linda. With three children, they talked about buying a house, but Mike's past experience taught him to be wary. What if the job didn't last, like the previous five?

The vice president of the company, Mac, noticed the quality of Mike's work. A friendship developed between the two. One day after Mike loaded his truck with marble tiles and bags of grout, he cornered his boss. "Mac, I need to know how much longer I can work for you?"

Mac looked a little surprised.

"I want to buy a house, but I don't want to be without work and out on the street."

"Good grief, Mike!" Mac laughed. "You won't be without work. Both you and your brother are good workers. As long as we have a company, you can work for us. Trust me." Mac's tone reassured Mike. "The way the construction business is going, we will be in business for a long time."

With Max's guarantee Mike and Ana bought a house in Sunnyslope, a low income area in north Phoenix. Many immigrants, most from Central America, lived there. The house was small, but it was theirs.

Not long after they had moved into their house, a Romanian brother in Christ came to them. He needed $150. With this additional cash he could make a late house payment; otherwise, foreclosure would start the next day.

Mike's mind made quick calculations, "I need to make my truck payment, that's $150. Ana needs to send seventy-five dollars to family in Arad. As it is, we only have the truck payment, and I don't get paid for two weeks. God, what should I do?"

This was tough, but almost immediately Mike knew what should to be done. The brother needed cash immediately, and Mike's bills were not due for a few days. He felt God would provide in the days that followed, so he happily parted with the money.

Ana supported Mike when he gave the cash away. Satisfaction was theirs, confident they had done the right thing. Still Ana wanted to help her family, and Mike had to make the truck payment. They could only do this with God's help, so they prayed — quite sincerely.

A couple days later when Mike came home from work Ana meet him at the door. She had a curious expression on her face, a mixture of puzzlement, fear, and excitement.

"Mike, did you hide some money in the dish towels?"

"What do you mean?" He hardly took this silly question seriously. Hot and thirsty from a day of labor in the desert heat, he kissed Ana, and headed for the refrigerator. "You know I gave away our last dollar the other night," he called back as he pulled out a pitcher of cold lemonade.

"Mike!" Ana raised her voice. "I took a dish towel out of the cupboard and there was money folded up inside!" She now had Mike's fill attention.

"How much?"

"I counted $175." She gestured. "It's on the table."

Mike glanced to his right, and saw neat pile of dollar bills. He counted it, $175. Questions sprang up. Where did it come from? Who else had been in the house? They asked the children if they had seen anyone. They had not. Both Ana and Mike counted the money several times that night, each time it was $175.

The next morning Mike went to work. Ana put the cash on a high counter, away from the children, afraid to touch it. This money was like a stranger, unintroduced, and unaccounted for. She avoided it, yet as the day went on curiosity got the better of her and she counted again.

When Mike came home she was so excited she could hardly speak. "Mike, there is more money!" Immediately she grabbed his arm, pulled him to the kitchen. "You count it! There is fifty dollars more!"

Sure enough, the total now was $225 — enough for the truck payment, and cash to help Ana's family in Romania! They stared at each other in amazement and disbelief.

Where did this provision come from? Ultimately, they knew it was from God. They had prayed for that exact amount, enough for the truck and for their Romanian relatives. They had told no one of their need. No one was seen in the house. They never solved the mystery of who actually put the cash in their kitchen.

On this occasion God provided for Mike and his family in an amazing and unusual way. All other bills were paid the old-fashioned way, with wages from hard work. Mike was promised job security and he felt comfortable that his income would cover his family's needs. He laid tile at many sites and quickly learned the layout of the sprawling cities that make up Metropolitan Phoenix. On a clear day the city was beautiful, surrounded by scenic desert mountains. His company negotiated a contract to lay Mexican tile in a resort in the North Mountains. The Pointe Resort at Tapatio Cliffs was under construction on a mountain slope. Mike and Ted were to lay most of the tile. Mike could almost see his savings account grow from the extra hours of labor.

Truckloads of tile were unloaded at each mountain villa, restaurant, and recreation area. Laborers were assigned to tend to Mike and Ted's needs for adhesives, grout, and sealants. They checked instructions and blueprints to be sure the correct shade and size of tile was installed in each area.

About halfway through their job the builder came out to inspect and went into a rage.

"What are you using to cement this tile in with?" he demanded.

"Thinset. See the bags." Mike said innocently.

"Right! Is it waterproof?" he demanded. He said something else but Mike and Ted could not understand him because he spoke so quickly.

"This isn't waterproof, but it will hold. It is what they send out." Mike tried to explain in broken English.

The builder continued, "We specifically told you guys to use a waterproof adhesive."

"We just use what they give us." Mike wanted to say more but his English was poor. Mike and Ted looked at each other, not knowing what to say or do. "Why you not talk to our boss, he tell you — dees what they send out!"

A mistake was made at Sunset Tile. The wrong product had been sent to the site. All the tile that was installed would have to be removed and new tile laid. This would cost thousands. Mike and Ted were fired. It did not seem fair to them, they had simply done what they were told. It appeared the general manager blamed them to save his own job. Neither had an idea of how to protest this. Their English was poor, and they tried to explain as best they could.

Mike's friend Mac told them their jobs were gone. Mac knew this was wrong but felt nothing could be done. He also knew that Mike depended on this job to make house payments. Discouragement weighed heavy on Mike as he returned home. He was glad to be in America, but he desperately wanted a job that lasted. In the past, when he prayed, God provided him with a job. But this time his job search stretched for three months and produced nothing. It was as if doors were deliberately slammed in his face. Finally Mike had to borrow from friends and relatives to make payments.

When he prayed, Mike realized he had made one critical mistake. His mistake had nothing to do with job performance. Rather it had to do with trust. He had believed Max when he said, "Trust me, there will be work." He had trusted Sunset Tile to supply his needs. He now got a very clear picture that he served a jealous God. God would not allow Mike to trust anyone but Him. He began to believe his unemployment was disciplinary action from the Most High.

Mike's only option was to place his full trust back in God. He prayed for work, searched the want ads, and contacted every contractor he knew. With borrowed money he bought a couple of cars, fixed them up and tried to sell them. The car venture fizzled, and the job search was unfruitful. Mike refused to collect unemployment, food stamps, or welfare. His experience with government assistance in Chicago left him humiliated, and he refused to repeat it.

At the end of three months he sat down with Ana. They collected all their money, including loose change, and counted. There was enough to buy a bag of potatoes and a jug of milk.

Mike then prayed, "God, I am not going to borrow any more money. I won't beg from others any more. I am going to spend the rest of my money on milk and potatoes. I would rather starve than borrow anymore. So I ask you to provide me with a job."

An impression went though Mike's mind. "Apply at Letco."

In his mind he responded, "But I have already applied there. I have been there so many times they know me by name."

The impression came back, "That's okay. Now is the time to apply again."

Mike followed the prompting. He had a good idea where it came from. He set off for the store to spend his last change on milk and potatoes. But on the way he stopped at Letco Construction.

As soon as he stepped inside the door, Mike heard his name called from across a large room. "Mike!" It was Tom, the man in charge of hiring. "Do you want a job?"

"What do you mean, 'Do you want a job?' I have been coming in for months looking for job." Mike grinned.

"When can you start?"

"Now..., well I have to go home and change."

"Great!" Tom gave Mike a firm slap on the back as they walked back to the personnel office.

Mike paused briefly, then asked, "Do you have enough work for my brother too?"

"When can he start?"

"Today."

"Sure! We have lots of work. Give him a call."

God came through again. Of course it was in the eleventh hour, but that was typical for God. Mike praised God all the way home. His elation was evident when he walked through the door.

"Honey, I'm home!" he called out. "Who's the man with milk? Who's the man with potatoes? And who's the man with a job?"

When Ana ran into the room, Mike grabbed her and swung her around. The kids rushed in, jumping up and down in the contagious excitement. They all danced around and praised God. Then Mike hurried off to phone his brother. He slipped into his work clothes, and raced off to his new job.

Letco was a good company. Mike and Ted were treated fairly and honestly. However, like most companies in the Southwest, Letco did not provide dependent health coverage. Employees could buy it for $200 a month.

This seemed like a lot of money to Mike and Ana. Two hundred dollars could do a lot in Romania. They knew so many people who needed help, and recent reports from Romania indicated things had gotten worse.

Mike and Ana talked it over. God had blessed them. They were much better off than those trapped in their homeland. Instead of health insurance, they would send an extra $200 a month back to Romania. In Romania they had trusted God to keep them healthy; they would do the same in America.

Mike and Ana could not send money directly to Romania because it was illegal for Romanians to own U.S. currency. Checks could not be sent because it was virtually impossible to cash a check there. If a person attempted to cash a check, he almost certainly invited Securitate or secret police scrutiny. To be associated with an American, especially a Romanian-American, meant being put on a Securitate black list. So Mike and Ana held their contributions in a stateside account. Then when someone returned to Romania for a visit, they gave him cash to deliver. The courier always traveled with a U.S. passport and was consequently allowed to hold American currency. Once inside the country, dollars were exchanged for Romanian lei, either at the government bank or on the black market. Then they distributed the money.

Mike and Ana made their pact to help Romanians still under communism's yoke. The next Sunday night, Mike went to church to hear an evangelist. Afterwards he visited friends for dessert and coffee. About four hours into the evening his son Cosmin called.

"Daddy, Mommy is sick. She won't talk to us, and we are hungry."

Mike talked to him for a few minutes. He found it difficult to get a clear picture from his five-year-old son. Apparently Ana laid down shortly after Mike had left. She had not gotten up to feed the children, and dinner was four hours overdue. This was not like Ana.

In a few minutes Mike arrived home, and went directly back to their bedroom. The children asked questions, "What's wrong with Mommy? Why won't she talk to us? Why is she saying those funny things?"

Mike calmed them, "We are all going to pray for Mommy. We are going to ask God to make her better."

Ana lay in sweat, her sheets were soaked. She heard their voices, but responded with nonsense. Her skin was cold and clammy. In a short time her fever began to rise. Apparently it had been rising and falling for the last couple of hours.

Mike could not take her to emergency without insurance. That cash was marked for Romania. He had trusted God to keep them well, and now they were in a major crisis. Mike knew God had not let them down. Rather he saw this as test to see if he would really trust God.

Mike and the two older children knelt beside the bed and began to pray. Linda, the youngest, toddled around and whimpered occasionally. As true Pentecostals, they all prayed at the same time, and with great volume. The children simply wanted their mom to get well. When it comes to prayer, it is not the words that matter so much as the faith of the person praying. Mike did not feel he had a lot of faith, but the children were strong on faith.

The phone rang. No one answered it — their prayer could not be interrupted. Then it rang again, again they left it unanswered as they prayed on.

The children prayed for a long time, but finally left the room and wondered about the house. Mike continued at his wife's side. Most of the time he prayed in the language given him when he received the Holy Spirit. He also prayed very specifically for Ana in Romanian, his first language. Ana's fever began to fall once again, but this time color returned to her skin. The fever did not rise as before. After twenty minutes of prayer, she asked quietly, "Where are the children?"

"They're in the other room," Mike answered and continued to pray.

A few minutes later Ana spoke again, "Have the children eaten supper yet?"

"No, we have been praying for you." Mike said, then continued to pray.

Ana's condition continued to improve minute by minute. She became fully coherent and soon sat up in bed. Her strength began to flow back into her body. "I think I had better feed the kids," she said as she moved to the edge of the bed and dangled her feet over the side.

"Okay, you go and take care of them. I feel I must stay here and pray some more. I am really getting through now."

As Ana went down the hall, she began to sing an old Romanian praise song. The children were happy to see their mom feeling better, and chattered in excitement as she fixed dinner.

Mike stayed in the bedroom and prayed, praising Jesus for the miracle that had just occurred. Then a beautifully strange thing began to happen, something never before experienced by Mike. In his mind he saw a vision, an incredibly lucid mental picture. Jesus stood before him with an open notebook in one hand and a pencil in the other ready to take notes. "Mike," he said, "ask me what you want, and I will give it to you."

"Jesus, I want a church. A Romanian church in Phoenix. There are quite a few Romanians now in Phoenix and we need a place where we can worship and praise you in our own language. You know we have met in classrooms on Sunday afternoons, but we need a place of our own."

Jesus assured Mike that within a short time they would have a church of their own. Later he wondered why he had not asked Jesus for more. After all, He did have his notebook open, ready to take notes.

The next night Mike went to a small prayer meeting at the house of a friend. None of the people there had been with Mike the night before, and Mike had not told them about what had happened. He was still trying to sort it out in his mind.

During the prayer meeting a woman began to speak as if the Holy Spirit spoke directly through her. She addressed Mike in the first person. "Mike, I came to you last night, and I healed your wife. You asked for a church, and that is going to happen. Believe in Me, and you will see it happen."

A couple weeks later Mike and Ana's commitment to send insurance dollars to Romania was challenged again.

Mike had worked a long day. That night he slept the sleep of the weary.

Ana woke him. "There is something wrong with Cosmin, come and see."

Groggy, with sleep still in his eyes, Mike stumbled into Cosmin's room. Cosmin burned with fever and gasped for breath, unable to speak.

Mike began to pray, "God we don't need this!" He was tired and in no mood to mess around. "We have been faithful in our giving to those in need. We really don't have the money to take our son to the doctor. I am so tired; I can't be in the emergency room for hours. We know you can heal my son quickly; so, Jesus, please just heal him now." Mike felt a surge of anger inside him. He was not angry at God, but with the enemy who tempted him.

Almost immediately Cosmin's breathing returned to normal; then his fever broke. He drank a glass of water, rolled over, and went to sleep. Mike and Ana went back to bed, and all woke the next morning refreshed.

Mike learned an important lesson while they lived in Sunnyslope. For him, trust in God must be total. Blessing can be God-given, but God's blessings cannot be trusted in place of God Himself.

In the years that followed, Mike was amazed at how quickly God improved their lives. He worked piece rate, long, hard hours, and it paid off. He saw it this way: God had given him a strong body, so why not use this gift of strength God had given?

As Mike assimilated more English and learned the ropes of the construction industry, he decided to apply for a contractor's license. He passed the test, and started his own business. God blessed, and the business grew. He opened his own showroom, and named his company, Active Tile and Marble. Then he opened a second showroom in nearby Sun City. Before long he had twenty-five men working for him.

Sunset Tile, the company that fired Mike and Ted, went out of business. But Mac, the vice president, remained Mike's friend and later came to work for Mike's company.

Mike eventually bought a bigger house because his family continued to grow. In time, he and Ana would have seven children, four girls and three boys, following the Romanian tradition of large families.

Six months after Mike received the vision, Romanian believers purchased land for a church north of Phoenix. A year later they worshiped in a nearly completed building.

THE OLARI FAMILY
Back Row: Loredana, Mike, Ana, Cosmin
Middle: Linda, Emanuel, Melissa
Front: Angela, Andrew

"Where there is no vision, the people perish..."
Proverbs 29:18

CHAPTER 12

1986 was a good year for the Olari family. God blessed Mike and Ana's hard work which brought them the prosperity of the American dream. But one night Mike was awakened by a different dream. In his sleep a scene had played before him like a video — so real he felt he was there — so lucid he would never forget it.

On a lawn he saw people eating — little children, teens, adults, and old people. The people were distinctly Romanian. A hungry person would take his plate to a large machine and press a few buttons. The machine constantly dispensed food to all who came to it.

Suddenly, for some reason, the machine stopped working. A line formed. Somebody banged and kicked the machine, but nothing came out. People on the lawn began to starve, and babies cried.

Mike turned and looked. Famished faces, close to death, were before him. All was peaceful, but abject destitution lay before him.

Mike called out, "God, what can I do to help these people?"

A man came down and floated vertically in the air. Mike suspected this stranger was an angel. The man had a key in his hand, and the key held Mike's attention.

"Take this key and open the machine from the back," the man commanded.

As soon as Mike grasped the key, the man disappeared. Immediately, Mike ran to the machine and opened it. The inside was filled with food, and the starved gathered around, as Mike gave them food. Everyone was excited and happy.

In an instant, the scene was gone. Mike awoke in the darkness of his bedroom. Ana slept quietly by his side, but they were not alone in the silence. The air was thick with a separate atmosphere. Mike recognized the Presence.

Mike sat up and spoke into the Energy. "God, how can I help these people? I don't have the money or resources. I am just one man. How can I make this happen?"

There was only silence in response. Silence, and the faces of hungry people, now burned into Mike's mind. Mike flipped on the light and woke Anna. This could not wait till morning.

Ana's first muddled inclination was to complain, but she checked herself. Even though she was groggy, it was obvious something had happened to Mike. If this was from God, she knew she had better listen. With conscious effort she held her eyes open and listened to Mike recount the dream.

"Look, Mike, I believe you. I believe you saw this in your dream. But how can this happen? It is impossible. It is difficult to send money back to family. How can you help more poor people? And besides, you're not an American citizen. If you go back, you will be arrested."

What Ana said was true, but still Mike persisted. "But this is what I saw. I think God wants me to help."

"Maybe this is to happen years from now. Maybe God wants you to get ready for something in the future." This sounded plausible.

They talked about it, then prayed. They decided to tell no one of the dream, not even Mike's brother Ted.

Their plan was to set the dream aside, but it indelibly stuck in Mike's mind. In his thoughts he repeatedly asked God, "Do You think this is going to happen?"

Almost two years later, Mike and Ted drove to California to explore the possibilities of real estate speculation. All day they visited different properties, but found nothing worth their investment effort.

That evening they went to a prayer meeting held at the house of a friend. Many people were there, including a woman who had the reputation of being a prophet. At the end of the meeting she pulled Mike aside.

"Mike, I am not sure what this means." She paused briefly. "I don't even know you." Still she was focused and sure of what she said. "While I prayed I saw a vision in my mind. I saw you standing on a large platform and a crowd was before you, perhaps a couple thousand. The people were hungry, and you held a large loaf of bread in your hands. Then God said to you, 'Give the people bread!' And you said, 'But I have only one bread.' And God replied, 'No problem, just give it.' Then you began to break off large chunks, and give it to the people. You were excited and said, 'Oh my goodness, this bread will never finish!' That's all I saw, and like I say, I don't know what this means."

But Mike knew what the vision meant. This woman had just validated his dream of two years earlier, the content closely paralleled. Yet questions remained. How was this to happen? Where would he get food for these people? Mike was able to provide comfortably for his family. Yet he had few resources to take on a job of this size. Was he supposed to literally provide food for people? Or did the food in the dream and vision symbolize spiritual nourishment? After all Jesus said, "I am the bread of life." Was he to share the gospel with his countrymen? But how could he share the gospel with the communist restrictions? Or did the calling have both a spiritual and literal application? After all, Jesus met both the physical and spiritual needs of the people around him.

Unsure of the next step, Mike felt the time for action drew close. The next year, he received his American citizenship, and immediately applied for a passport. Now he could visit Romania as an American. It would be very hard for the authorities to arrest him. He decided it was time to act.

Towards the end of August, Mike purchased a round trip ticket to West Germany. In the first week of September he returned to Europe with a large sum of money withdrawn from his personal accounts. From a friend in Germany he borrowed a late model German manufactured Ford Sierra. Then Mike went shopping and bought goods that were difficult or impossible to obtain in Romania. He stuffed everything into the station wagon. Somewhere in the cargo was a very valuable package of Romanian Bibles.

Mike drove from Germany through the scenic Austrian countryside and into Hungary quite uneventfully. The Hungarian border patrol cared little about what Mike had in his car. The next border was Romania, where more restrictions applied. The guard refused to let Mike cross. He claimed Mike had too much merchandise in his car. He knew that Mike was either going to give it away or sell it. His cargo was obviously not for personal use.

Denied access to Romania, Mike was forced to turn back down the road into Hungary. After a few miles, just past a small village, he spotted a parking lot by an unidentified building. For a few hours he slept in his borrowed vehicle, awoke and waited for the sun to rise. He hoped a different set of guards would be on duty, and they would be more liberal.

In dawn's twilight, he ate yogurt and bread purchased from an Hungarian grocer the day before. Once filled, he turned the key in the ignition, flicked on his high beams, and pulled out onto the lonely pavement. About two kilometers from the checkpoint he pulled over again and shut the engine off.

He prayed. "Father, I believe you have told me to return to Romania and help my people. I don't really know how I am supposed to do this. Right now I am doing what I can, but they won't let me in. Father, I really don't want this trip to be wasted, so help me get in. If you have to make the border patrol blind, then make them blind. If you have to open a gate for me, then open the gate. I can't do this on my own, I am totally helpless. You are my only hope."

Mike felt his concern lift. In less than two minutes he was at the checkpoint. Two or three cars pulled to a stop behind him.

The guard was friendly and greeted him with a smile. "Hey, how are you doing? Have you been traveling long?"

Mike broke into a broad smile. "It's been a good trip, just spent the night in Hungary." He handed the guard his American passport.

The guard's face hinted surprise as he took an American passport from one who spoke perfect Romanian. "Tell me, is America like they say it is?"

"Well... you have to work hard, but you can do well."

"This is a very nice car!" The guard paced down a couple strides and admired the grillwork and headlights. "How long did you have to work to get this car?" he called back to Mike.

"Listen, I tell you most families in America have cars this nice — some are a lot better!"

The guard shook his head in disbelief. "How long did it take you to become an American?"

"Almost seven years."

"Hmmm." For a brief moment there was a distant look in the guard's eyes, then his smile returned, and he slapped the car's roof two times. "You can go my friend, have a good trip!" He called down the road to a second guard who operated a barricade. "Let this one through, they are starting to pile up." As an afterthought, the guard quickly stamped a visa inside Mike's passport and handed it back.

Mike lightly touched the gas, and maneuvered out of the checkpoint. The road stretched before him unobstructed by any more military police. He thanked God with genuine gratitude.

Once inside Romania, Arad drew Mike like a magnate. His foot mashed accelerator to the floor. This is a land where speed limits vary from car to car. Autos with larger engines were allowed to travel faster. One's objective was to cover as much road as possible before being slowed by a horse drawn wagon. Mike wrung the most from his vehicle's performance. Suddenly he popped over a hill, only to be met by an unmarked curve. Immediately he crossed the pavement, violently jounced into the countryside, and narrowly missed two trees.

As he pushed his visceral organs down from his throat, he maneuvered back onto the narrow highway. A fleeting thought crossed his brain, "What if I had hit that curve last night in the dark?" He knew he would not have driven slower just because it was dark. He easily could have hit those trees. An eerie gratitude smoldered for being turned back at the border. Of course, this incident would never change Mike Olari's driving habits. Once on the road the accelerator was again pushed to the floor, and he arrived in Arad within the hour.

Every friend, relative, and distant acquaintance knew Mike was on his way. The hour he arrived, word went out, and visitors began to stream in. Late into the night stories were exchanged, and news of the last seven years was brought up to date. Then Mike began to distribute Bibles, clothes, shoes, razors, chocolate, gum, and cash.

Mike was dismayed when he saw how economic conditions had worsened while he was gone. Inflation had eaten away the people's power to provide. While most Romanians owned their houses, they found it difficult to put food on the table. Local pastors told Mike of families who ate one meal a day.

Churches in Arad and Timişoara invited Mike to speak. The churches had grown in spite of increased government harassment, frustrating the secret police. The government claimed to allow religious freedom — actually they tolerated a religious veneer. When a church began to step out from under government control, Big Brother increased intimidation. The more abuse the Securitate applied, the more determined Christians became.

When Mike spoke, he was asked not to mention anything about America. When he visited a church, he did not give goods or money. Any assistance was done quietly through the pastors, who had a more intimate knowledge of individual needs. He spoke only of the love of God, the good news of Jesus the Messiah, and the power of the Holy Spirit.

Mike felt uncomfortable when he spoke in large urban churches. He knew Securitate agents were in the audience, and his presence could put Christian brothers and sisters under increased scrutiny. Mike thought it more prudent to visit rural gatherings of believers. The Securitate saw these people as country bumpkins and were less likely to descend upon them.

Mike's pastor back in Phoenix was a man named Cornel Avram. He was from a small village in the eastern part of Romania where poverty was more profound, and Mike was asked to deliver assistance. The trip to Lemniu took one day, and Cornel's family warmly welcomed Mike. He was not a stranger for long and was asked to speak in the little church.

That night Mike pulled his car into an inconspicuous place behind the church, a result of his inbred habit of maintaining a low profile. Word traveled among the people, and the church was packed with standing room only. Windows were swung outward, and people crowded around the open portals. Despite the serious faces, it was evident that God had moved in this village. The excitement of His presence was just under the skin of conditioned solitude.

After the meeting, some locals from a nearby village approached Mike and asked him to come to their church too — that very night!

Mike objected, "But I can't, I am tired, and I've got to drive back to Arad before morning."

But they persisted, "If you can't come to our church, then meet us in a house closer by."

In the end Mike consented, and met for a second time that evening. Over thirty teens crowded into the house, excited to hear what Mike had to say. The hosts were poor, and could only offer a cup of warm goat's milk to each of their guests. That is all they had, and no one expected more for everyone was poor.

But there was an invisible guest among them, who filled all with a separate refreshment: the Holy Spirit, who made Himself evident. The teens were bound together in Christian love, and hung onto every word Mike spoke. Two hours instantly passed. Shortly after midnight, Mike left the simple farmhouse with a new energy in his veins. He could not sleep now if he had wanted to. He made it back to Arad just as the workers of Romania readied themselves for their day's labor. Mike had people to see, so rest was out of the question.

That night he visited his brother-in-law Peter. When it was time to leave, Peter walked Mike to the car. Mike unlocked the door and started to get in, when Peter, on an impulse, invited him back for a cup of coffee. Mike took him up on his offer.

Without a thought he went inside leaving his car door unlocked — a habit he picked up in America. He was tired and never thought about his billfold and 2,000 American dollars tucked under the driver's seat.

When Mike returned, he saw the car door open and the dome light on. A few items were scattered on the street. A mental picture of $2,000 stuffed in his billfold leapt into his mind. Panic gripped his abdomen. In an instant he was on his knees beside the open door. He groped under the seat and found nothing.

Mike was angry — angry with the thief who stole his money, and angry with himself for not locking the door. The police were called.

While they waited for the police, Peter tried to console Mike. "Look, Mike, up until now you have had a good trip, and you have done a lot of good. You have helped a lot of people, and you have spoken in churches. You can't let the money ruin your trip." He put his arm around Mike's shoulder.

Mike pulled back. "No! I worked hard for that money! And there are people who need that money to simply live."

"But Mike, you will never see those dollars again." Peter's sympathy did not obscure his perception of reality.

"No! I'm not going to be happy till I get the money back!"

"Come on, Mike, you know how things are in this country! Thieves steal all day long, and it's never seen again. Besides, the guy who did it probably doesn't have enough to eat himself."

These words had little effect on Mike, "Look, Peter, $2,000 will buy a lot of food, far more than one family can eat. This guy will waste it, and I know families that need help. You know what is going to happen?"

"Tell me."

"God is going to put fear in that guy's heart. He is going to be afraid of being caught with American dollars, and he is going to return it."

Peter raised both arms in the air. "Just like that, he is just going to walk up and give you your money back?" Peter could not believe his brother-in-law.

"No, he is going to throw it up in the grass, or on the steps, or something."

"Okay Mike, I hope you are right." Peter realized the futility of further discussion.

The police arrived and began to record the details of the robbery. At that time, a little boy ran up with Mike's billfold. Everything was there but the $2,000.

The next afternoon Mike was visiting friends on the other side of town when he received a call from Peter. He did not say what the problem was, but just told Mike to come home quickly. Mike drove directly across town to find a very excited brother-in-law.

"We were afraid to touch it! We called the police because it is American money." He led Mike around to the back yard.

The police were already there. An officer handed Mike $1,500. He thanked the officer, and quickly counted the cash — $500 missing. "Well, this is a good start, but I won't be happy till I get the rest."

Blank shock spread across Peter's face, "Come on, Mike! This is a miracle. Be satisfied. I mean, I thought this would never happen. Last night I thought you were nuts for thinking anything would be returned. Just be happy with what you have."

"No, Peter, all of that money is for God's work, and God will get it back for us." Mike was surprised at his own resolve, but he firmly believed in his mission.

The following day the police called again, this time to report the thief had been caught. An additional $400 was recovered and returned to Mike.

An electric excitement crackled in the home where Mike stayed. No one had ever heard of anything like this before.

Mike confided in his brother-in-law. "This is good, but I am not all together happy about it. There is another hundred dollars out there, and someone needs it more than the thief who stole it. I think we will get it back."

Peter stared back at Mike in disbelief. "Mike, be happy! God has answered your prayers. Let the hundred dollars go!"

On Sunday Mike got a call from the Securitate. They said they had recovered the last $100, but Mike needed to claim it at headquarters.

Mike knew the Securitate's treachery and was suspicious. This could be a trap. They were not like regular police and swore allegiance only to Ceauşescu. A person's most basic rights meant nothing. Mike was not sure his American citizenship meant much at their headquarters.

Peter agreed to go with Mike to at least witness an arrest should one take place. Hopefully he would have time to report it to the American Embassy. But this time concern was unwarranted. The Secret Police simply returned the money; they claimed it turned up later.

On the way home Peter shook his head in disbelief and said repeatedly, "This is truly a unique case."

Mike's three weeks passed quickly, and it was time to return to America. He gave away the last of his goods and said his good-bye's. By every measure he called the trip a success, yet as he boarded the plane he felt overwhelmed. He looked out his window and silently spoke with God. "How can I really help? What I have done is like a drop in the bucket. I have used all my funds. The Romanian government may not give me a visa next time. Father, my hands are tied. What else can I do?"

Mike felt the only thing he could do was to put his vision on the shelf, and wait. He, along with the entire Western World, was unaware of how rapidly the Iron Curtain would unravel. All the might and rhetoric of this godless system rested on a foundation of sand. In a matter of weeks, one communist government after another would shift from its false foundation and fall.

Like a row of dominoes, totalitarian regimes of Eastern Europe fell to the concepts of western democracy. In December of 1989, the people of Romania took their stand. Once again the citizens of the free world stood by in jaw-dropped astonishment as the news reported the fall of another lifelong enemy.

Through December, exiled Romanians in America called each other cross country in an effort to get the latest information. Timişoara was in chaos and rumors of killings abounded. News networks showed gunfire in government complexes. Romanians in the United States were anxious. For days they did not go to work, as they stayed home and watched CNN. Between broadcasts Mike and many others prayed that communism would be ripped out of their country forever. They prayed for the safety of family and friends.

Reports came of army mutinies — of soldiers who refused to carry out heartless, inhuman orders. These soldiers refused to slaughter their own countrymen. Then came confusion over the apparent disappearance of a dictator.

REVOLUTION!

PART 2

*"There were so many years I did not come to
church for fear of the government.
Now there is shooting in the streets,
but I come because I trust God."*
Victoria Ioniţa, Bucharest, December 1989[1]

CHAPTER 13

Riveted to network news and international radio,
Romanians in North America were spellbound by reports
they heard. In their most irresponsible fantasies, none
dared dream of anything so phenomenal. However, much
rumor and speculation clouded the real picture. Fantastic
stories abounded. All happened so fast. As with any social
upheaval, reports varied; yet, core facts remained in common. In time a full and reliable picture came into focus.

Revolutions do not just happen. The road to revolution is paved by earlier grievances. The events that shaped
this revolt crystallized into two realms — the physical-
political world and the spiritual dimension.

The physical-political world of Eastern Europe was
closely watched by pundits. Yet these experts were
amazed when Ceauşescu fell. World leaders and analysts,
stunned by Ceauşescu's excesses, realized they had blindly
endorsed a killer. To the free world, Ceauşescu portrayed
himself as a forward-thinking maverick, a socialist who
could be trusted.[2] Had this been a media coup? Were the
intelligence services of England and the U.S. not reliable?
Probably this was the cold glint of *Realpolitik*, an example
of the West siding with anyone who nettled the Soviet
Union.

It was Ceauşescu who, over the years, openly criticized the policies of the Soviet Union. He had his picture
taken with three American presidents. In 1968, just after
the Prague Spring, he criticized the USSR for their invasion of Czechoslovakia.[3] When the Soviet Bloc boycotted
the 1984 Olympic Games, Romania participated in the
Los Angeles events.[4] This led many Americans to see
Ceauşescu as an enlightened socialist. The United States
gave Romania "most favored nation" trading status.[5]
Queen Elizabeth knighted Ceauşescu only months before
his fall. Norway gave both Nicolae and Elena Ceauşescu
their most prestigious decoration, the Cross of St. Olaf.[6]

But it was the Romanian people who lived in the reality of Ceauşescu's oppression, for theirs was a land where
Securitate registered all typewriters.[7] Big Brother's ten-
tacles reached inside every person's skull. With all his
power and control, Ceauşescu continued to ratchet down
the pressure, turn after turn. His desire was an ethnically
pure state. German and Hungarian communities were
forced to give up their cultural identities. Peasant villages
were bulldozed, and their inhabitants forced to live in
agricultural centers or in cities. Jews were sold exit visas
to Israel.[8]

Ceauşescu decreed that Romania's foreign debt be
paid off, even if the people were pushed to starvation's
brink. He cut back government-supplied electricity, forc-
ing citizens to use low-watt bulbs. During the winter, Romanians shivered in their houses and gray cement apartments. The government sold unused electricity to neighboring countries. Food was sold on the international market to pay the national debt, while countrymen went hungry.[9]

Against this backdrop Ceauşescu began to build his
own palace with thousands of rooms and a facade of
marble.[10] The edifice was three times larger than

Versailles; in fact it was larger than the Pentagon. 50,000 people were displaced; their apartments and houses razed, to provide land for its construction. The main reception hall was the size of a football field, 240 feet long and 90 feet wide. Over the grand staircase hung a five-ton chandelier, consuming enough electricity to supply two Romanian villages (two villages forced to use low watt bulbs). Hand-carved marble columns supported the ceiling. On a weekly basis, Ceauşescu inspected the palace construction site, then routinely changed the blueprints. Many times completed rooms or whole sections of palace were torn apart and rebuilt at Ceauşescu's whim.[11]

Ceauşescu's palace is larger than the Pentagon. Romanians are quick to point out, that like an iceberg, two thirds of the structure is below the surface. In time or war Ceauşescu wanted to be able to sustain direct arial attack, and still live in luxury.

Elena Ceauşescu was revered in the state-controlled press as a great scientific mind; the recipient of numerous bogus awards. She was the "author" of many works written by ghostwriters. In actual fact, she had not attended college, and in earlier days she repeated the fifth grade.[12]

The state media created an aura of royalty for the
Ceaușescus. Towards the end of his reign, Nicolae
Ceaușescu harangued Romanians for two hours a night
on TV. In those last months, with much pomp and cir-
cumstance, they performed coronations on television with
regal pageantry. Ceaușescu received the crown of Michael
the Brave and the scepter of Mircea the Old, serenaded
by peasants in the background. Dressed in ethnic garb, all
waved flags, clutched bunches of grapes, or held sheaves
of wheat. This costumed choir sang state-composed folk
songs, which praised the holy name of Ceaușescu.[13] In
his megalomania, he ascribed to himself almost divine
power.

Ceaușescu securely held power with the protection
of his own private battalion of secret police called the
Securitate. They swore allegiance only to Ceaușescu, and
by conservative estimates were 180,000 strong. This elite
fighter-police army was more feared than the East German Stazi.[14] Many soldiers in this fanatical force were re-
cruits from orphanages. Their indoctrination imprinted
Elena and Nicolae Ceaușescu as parent figures.[15] These
orphans were very effective. They cleverly gained Western secrets and sold them to the KGB. It is widely held
that the Securitate worked intimately with Libya, the Pal-
estine Liberation Organization, and Iran.[16] During the revolution, Romanians were so angry with Arab Securitate that
innocent Arab students fled into hiding.[17]

In Bucharest a network of secret tunnels fanned out
from the Central Palace, and led to a variety of destinations concealed with hidden entrances. Securitate moved
about the city as no one else could. At will they appeared
and disappeared through these secret entrances and tunnels. Some believed the designers of these passages had
been killed, so as not to divulge their location.[18] In the
tunnels, and underground complexes they stored weap-

ons and supplies. If necessary, Elena and Nicolae Ceauşescu could hole up for weeks while Securitate defended them on the surface.

In the early days of 1989, Ceauşescu appeared strong and secure. The army and Securitate stood firmly behind him. He held the press was under his fist. He and his family enjoyed absolute power. Then the Ceauşescu regime was jarred by the first tremor of discontent.

In early March, six top party officials with impressive records broke ranks. They delivered a public letter of scathing criticism, opening with this statement; "....we have decided to speak up. We are perfectly aware that by doing so we are risking our liberty and even our lives..." At first nothing happened. A few days later the letter was extensively published outside Romania. At that time all six officials were arrested, and sent into internal exile. Under house arrest their only contact was with the police and their guards.[19]

Challenges to authority had recently erupted in other totalitarian countries, but Ceauşescu did not appear alarmed when it happened to him. Instead, he focused on the positive. On April 12, he announced that the Romanian foreign debt had been paid in full.[20] This major feat made Ceauşescu feel resolute, secure, and confident enough to deride Gorbachev for diluting communism in the USSR.[21] On July 7-8 the Warsaw Pact countries met in Bucharest and unanimously endorsed ideological diversity. However, "unprecedented disunity" was the reality.[22]

In the fall of 1989, the communist bloc began to quake and splinter. When Eric Honecker of East Germany fell on October 10, a shock wave was felt throughout the entire communist world. Still Romania stood firm and unruffled. Next door to the south Todor Zhivkov of Bulgaria had given lip service to Gorbachev's reforms. He was toppled in a coup on November 10, with the nod of the Kremlin.[23] Nonetheless, two weeks later, on November 24, Ceauşescu was reelected as party chief without one dissenting vote. Most foreign analysts confidently affirmed that Ceauşescu would survive reform.[24] Communism was crumbling in all Eastern Bloc countries but one. Poland, East Germany, Czechoslovakia, Hungry, and Bulgaria were each in some stage of massive reform. Only Romania stood alone, unchanged and unchallenged.

Superimposed over this arena of political intrigue hung a sphere of spiritual power. The physical is inseparably linked with the spiritual. While political pundits analyzed the physical realm, the spiritual world went unobserved. This realm rarely yields to scientific tests and measures, and is, therefore, overlooked. For the most part the spiritual world must be revealed.

If this revolution was more than physical cause and effect, then what elements in the spiritual realm impacted events and caused revolution? Many times God moves like the wind, unpredictable by human criterion. When Ceauşescu was found wanting in the court of the Almighty, nothing could save him. His security forces were not strong enough to stand against the angels of heaven. As a consequence of elevating himself in false pride, he was left without an ally in the visible world, without aid in the invisible realm of the spirit. In the end, fear drove his feet.

We cannot adequately analyze the realm of the spirit. We can, however, gain hazy insight into its function through precedents and instruction from the past. God told Moses at the burning bush that He had heard the groanings of His people in Egypt. God for certain heard the groanings of His people behind the Iron Curtain. In His time, He delivered His people. Also a close look at the underground church in Romania showed a shift in the way believers related to each other. Consider the following teaching:

Two thousand years ago, shortly before His execution, in an upstairs room, Christ prayed with His disciples. He prayed for His church, that they would be one, just as He and His Father were one. This unity would cause the world to believe.[25] The implication is that a godly supernatural power will be released into the world when believers are unified. This healing power draws people to their God.

For various reasons, and many times for reform-minded causes, the church has splintered over the past millennium. Sometimes the grounds for separation were justified. Many times there was simply a divisive spirit among God's people that worked counter to the kingdom of God. It is natural for believers to see things differently and associate with those of like mind. Yet the suspicion of believers towards fellow brethren of slightly different persuasion has been carried too far, weakening the cause of Christ.

The suffering church in Romania was not immune to such distrust. To illustrate, consider three denominations: the Orthodox, the Baptists, and the Pentecostals. The Orthodox Christians considered the Pentecostals a little strange with their speaking in tongues and high energy worship. And those Baptists were a little stuffy. Besides they lacked the traditions of the Orthodox Church. On the other hand, the Baptists could sometimes agree with the Orthodox, that the Pentecostals were a bit unstable. However, the Orthodox could not be trusted because they had sold out to the government: the Communists now, the Nazis before. Besides, no one taught the Bible like a good Baptist. Now the Pentecostals agreed that the Orthodox were sold out to the government. Yet the Baptists did not have the power of the Holy Spirit. And so it went, each denomination became an entity unto itself.

This was not a new problem. First-century Corinthian believers followed different teachers: Paul, Apollos, Peter, and so on. St. Paul had to ask, "Is Christ divided into groups? Did I, Paul, die on the cross?" Obviously not, Paul says we are all servants. "I planted the seed, but Apollos watered, and God made the plant grow." We are all workers in God's field, and God gives the harvest. [26]

The Orthodox have a fine historic heritage and over the centuries have brought many to faith in Christ. The Baptists have taught many deep truths of the Scripture and have grounded believers firmly. In this century Pentecostals have been moved powerfully by the Spirit of God. While some may castigate many Orthodox for selling out to the government, all must remember they too can sin. Forgiveness is the cornerstone of the Christian faith. It should also be noted that within the Orthodox Church there was a renewal movement of one and a half million. These believers drew Securitate harassment, and were forced to meet secretly in small groups. [27]

Twenty centuries after St. Paul wrote, we still work in God's field, and it is still God who gives the harvest. Christians everywhere can learn from their sister denominations, who worship Christ the Messiah. Naturally we hold pet doctrines and passionately debate them. But, in the end, we must lay aside our differences and work together. In doing so we develop a spirit of unity. There is no organizational ecumenical membership. We simply love our brothers and sisters of slightly different faith. We work with them, we pray for them, and we look out for their best interests. The Father, Son, and Holy Spirit are flawlessly united, not by organization, but by perfect love and common purpose. Yet each member of the godhead maintains His individual personality. So the churches in

Christendom have their personalities, but beneath it all we rest on one firm foundation — Jesus Christ our Lord. We get a picture of the way the Trinity works when Christ prayed on the Mount of Olives, shortly before His death. Jesus, in anguish, sweated great drops of blood. He prayed that God, His Father, would work something else out, "to take this cup from Him." Jesus did not want to die, yet He submitted to His Father in love.[28] Jesus had power, He could have called armies of angels to rescue Him. Instead He laid aside his power and submitted to His Father in love. Notice how Jesus laid aside the power He could rightfully claim. Much of the division in Christendom is little more than a grab for power. We disguise our thirst for power with all manner of pious impediments, yet power is our game, not submission in love.

<hr/>

The umbrella of Christendom gives shelter to many, however, it is not universal. The way a person enters the kingdom of God is amazingly simple. First, one has to realize that he is far from perfect in thought and deed. Because of our imperfections we are separated from a perfect God. Yet this perfect God sent His Son as a human, to show us how to live. Ungrateful, imperfect people killed God's Son. But God has power over death, and His Son, Jesus, returned to life in three days. If one acknowledges his shortcomings and humbly asks Jesus to forgive him, believes Jesus to be God's Son, and that God raised Him from the dead, he will be adopted into God's heavenly family. This is something done by faith, the fruit of which is love for God, self, and fellowman. This is the Good News of Christianity in its simplest form. All are welcome, all who believe are brothers and sisters in God's family. They have no business castigating those who might see various points of theology differently.[29]

Nothing brings humans together like a common enemy. For the Christians of Romania, the common enemy was dictator Ceauşescu, with his increasingly insane policies. As the end drew near, persecution of Christians increased. Churches were locked, then later bulldozed. Yet when Christians stood in front of their churches, linked arm in arm in prayer, the bulldozers were held at bay, at least for a while.

In villages around Timişoara, the government targeted churches for destruction. At times believers slept in the churches so when they heard the rumble of a bulldozer the alarm went out. Quickly believers of every denominational stripe crowded around the church to pray and sing until the bulldozers backed off.

Nearby in the village of Bіştrita, a church neared completion. It wasn't so much a new church, as it was a remodeled and expanded church. The government would not give permission to build, so the Christians expanded anyway. Repeatedly, government bulldozers arrived. And repeatedly, all Christians rallied around until the bulldozer retreated. After several attempts in the fall of '89, the government successfully razed the church. (Later, after the revolution, the new government rebuilt it.)

While other nations of Eastern Europe teetered and fell, a curious thing happened in and around the Timişoara area. Spontaneously, small groups of Christians secretly met for prayer. These were not organized cells of a revolutionary front. Rather these were prayer cells that cut across denominational lines. Here simple believers, who had lived their lives under oppression, begged the King of Kings for deliverance.

One small group called themselves the "Bapticostals." Their membership consisted of two Pentecostals and three Baptists. In the months before the revolution, a very important concept dawned upon them. God was not building a kingdom of Baptists, or Catholics, or Pentecostals. God would build His kingdom and the kingdom of His Christ. In prayer groups across the city others reached the same conclusion.

From Timişoara and across the nation, Romania's Christian minority prayed. Romanian broadcasts from Radio Free Europe encouraged people to pray. Exiled minister Joseph Ton called for a day of prayer and fasting on his radio program.

Christians felt that God would step in and deliver Romania. A Pentecostal parishioner near Timişoara claimed to have received revelation that Ceauşescu would be dead by December 25. The man did not know what to do with the information, for such talk would lead to imprisonment or execution.[30] A similar revelation happened near Bucharest. In a worship service a man in the audience became distinctly aware that Ceauşescu would be executed soon. Afterwards he spoke to the pastor in the front of the church. The pastor immediately warned him not to let anyone hear him, because they all could be in trouble.[31]

It was in this air of solidarity that a minister in Timişoara had become very popular. His name was Father Laszlo Tokes, pastor of a small Hungarian Reformed Church. The revolution started in Timişoara with Christians. The Marxists did not need to fear the opiate of religion. Rather, it was the breath of the Holy Spirit that would melt this regime. The people would feel a boldness come over them, and fear would vanish. This breath would in turn unite the Serbs, Germans, Romanians, and Hungarians of this land. With incredible courage they stood unarmed, but united, against an army with tanks, guns, and bullets.

Father Tokes, an ethnic Hungarian, came to symbolize the revolutionary spirit. The downtrodden Hungarian population was concentrated in the Timişoara region. When Tokes spoke about God's love and against the abuses of Ceauşescu, he touched a common place in all hearts, not just the Hungarian.

The previous August, Tokes had been interviewed on Hungarian television. On air he criticized Ceauşescu's urbanization policy which destroyed 8,000 villages and relocated peasants to concrete apartment buildings. When Tokes returned to Romania, he was denied a ration book.

Parishioners tried to care for him now that he could not provide his family with meat, bread, or fuel. The kindness of these people was rewarded with police harassment. The Securitate limited visitation at the Tokes household, even of relatives. His phone was disconnected. Occasionally his phone was reconnected to receive threats from the Securitate. He was then billed for the abusive calls.

Tokes sent his four-year-old son to live with relatives, well away from the tension. Yet his pregnant wife stayed by his side. In November he was stabbed and beaten by four masked men who broke into his home. Fortunately, two friends who had been allowed to visit helped drive the attackers off.

Manse windows were broken on an almost daily basis. When vandalism spread to the church, members of the congregation slept in the sanctuary. But these were just part of Tokes' problems. Church hierarchy desired that he be moved to southern Romania, to a less controversial environment. The bishop petitioned the government and obtained a court order to transfer Tokes.

On December 15, 1989, Father Tokes spoke in his small church. He was known for his position on human rights and spoke against the excesses of dictator Ceauşescu. He had spoken out before, but always with carefully selected words. Criticism was calculated, many times subtle, because informers were always in the audience. Because of government pressure and the bishop's position, Tokes's expulsion was certain. This was to be his last sermon in the old Romania.

A court order was issued to have the pastor moved to southern Romania,[32] but his little flock saw things differently. This time the church building was not slated for destruction, but it was the pastor himself who was to be silenced. Word was put out to brothers and sisters in other churches across the city.

Reverend Tokes went home that Friday night to contemplate the ramifications of his transfer. Soon some 300 people had gathered in his yard and encircled his house.[33] He recognized members of his congregation, but there were other faces too. Timişoara is a city of one million people, and Christians from all over the city made their way to the Tokes residence.[34] Some held hands, others locked arms, and they began to sing and pray.

As the police took up opposing positions one man called out, "Down with Ceauşescu!" The unspeakable was verbalized. Stony silence followed—on both sides.[35] Without warning, a boldness fell on protesters. Thick courage permeated the air. An invisible Presence evaporated fear of what the consequences might be. Demonstrators began to chant: "We are not leaving! Ceauşescu, run away from us! God is with us!"

The police were alarmed. The Securitate had a peacetime policy: break up groups of five or more, even if people just chatted on the street. Truly threatened by a protest of several hundred, the police advanced with truncheons and nightsticks. Shop windows were broken so that the protesters could get their hands on anything to throw at the police. They unloaded cans and bottles from sparsely stocked shelves, then hurled these objects at police. Fire trucks were soon on the scene, and dispersed the crowd with high pressure water.[36]

This uprising became known as the "Tokes moment". It was the spark that ignited the dry tender of revolution — a revolution not organized by one person or group of people, but a spontaneous event that took the country.[37] Fire trucks successfully disbursed the crowd, but some fires cannot be extinguished by water. Many protesters went to the university to recruit students. Others spread the news across Timişoara. All night smaller protests erupted in other locations. Armored vehicles patrolled the streets, and the army was activated.

When the sun came up, all was calm. A few people cleaned debris from the street. Store managers replaced the broken glass in their shop windows. Eerily, these people acted as if nothing had happened. That afternoon the mayor of Timişoara addressed the people. He took a stance of calm and reassurance, but the people were left with the impression there was little he could do.[38]

<hr>

Sunday, December 17, was an unseasonably warm, spring-like day. Protesters swarmed Father Tokes' house until there was no more room. Securitate and army troops took positions around the city. Protesters filled downtown squares and plazas, breaking down doors to the Communist Party headquarters and throwing pictures of Ceauşescu out the windows.

Meanwhile in Bucharest, the Executive Political Committee ordered the use of live ammunition. The current constrained policies were denounced. Word came from the highest levels to let blood.[39]

Military restraint brought hope to the demonstrators. Across the city soldiers were encouraged to break ranks and join the cause of freedom. The protesters' mood was festive, sharing food and singing long-banned songs with gusto. Children sat on fathers' shoulders. Such expression of liberty was unknown to this generation.[40]

Many in the city did not realize the gravity of the gathering crisis, and went about their Sunday activities. By word of mouth they learned that tanks were near the plaza area. Choppers filled the sky, but radio and TV continued regular programing and mentioned nothing.[41]

Then, in early evening, as if on cue, an armored car and a newsstand exploded. Small fires ignited along side streets, and breaking of glass was heard everywhere. People began to shout, "We are nonviolent!" Within a half hour soldiers were ordered to fire. Those who refused were pulled from their ranks and executed immediately.

As the army first opened fire, some called out, "Blanks!" Many soldiers had fired over the heads of the protesters. But it was obvious the bullets were real. People fell. Unarmed men, women, and children received direct rifle fire. Parents held their children up and screamed, "Brothers, don't shoot our children!" The protesters carried away the wounded, but the dead were left where they fell.[42] Securitate now opened fire from machine gun nests located in commanding positions. A whole row of children were mowed down.[43] Human blood bathed sections of pavement. Panicked citizens tripped over the dead and dying as they tried to flee. With iron resolve others held their ground and sang, "Arise, Romanians!"

Along side streets, the wounded were shot in the head by the Securitate. Wounded were even shot in ambulances. Reporters from Yugoslavia, Hungary, and the Soviet Union put the death toll at between five and ten thousand.* No Western reporters were on the scene.[44]

---

*It was to Soviet advantage to villanize Ceauşescu and report a high body count. If Russian troops were sent in, their need would already be established. Tudor Peţan, a Romanian media specialist, who participated in the Timişoara uprising, suspects the death toll did not pass 1,000. (Interview, August 6, 1996, Timişoara.)

That night garbage trucks loaded with corpses drove to an undisclosed location. Some say they took the bodies to a mass grave, others say to Bucharest to be cremated. Later four mass graves were exhumed, and relatives dug through stiff rotting bodies in search for loved ones.[45] Before sunrise a powerful thunderstorm, unusual for the season, cleansed the streets of blood.[46]

News of the events spread like wildfire across the country, in spite of official silence in the media. Romanians turned to Radio Free Europe and other foreign broadcasts.[47] Some in Bucharest got news about Timişoara from gypsies who provided a fairly reliable grapevine of information.

The following day in Timişoara sporadic gunfire was heard. Securitate and army forces could have massacred half of Timişoara's population. Instead they chose a macabre form of terror to control the masses. Snipers fired from hidden positions. No one was safe. Both the person who looked out of his window and the protester on the street could fall victim to the sniper's bullet. Some twenty children hoped to find sanctuary in the Metropolitan Cathedral, but were slain as they ran up the steps. At the same time other children were on the streets. A young girl saw the Securitate butcher victims they had hanged earlier. They watched in stunned silence.

"Why do you stand there?" asked a secret police.

"I want to see what you do," was her reply.

"If you stay, you will follow."

The girl ran in terror.[48]

A surreal insanity settled upon the city. Streets that had always been safe, were now treacherous. Not everyone grasped the magnitude of danger; no local warnings or news reports were broadcast. In some locations children played on the streets as usual. An estimated eighty percent of protesters were youth in the first days of revolt.

People mill about on the steps of the Metropolitan Cathedral, the same place were children were once mowed
down with Secuitate gunfire, as they sought sactuary.

Something from deep down inside, something suppressed for decades, erupted to the call of freedom. Did these people have a chance? They had been led to believe that this regime was invincible, but now cracks appeared in this communist bulwark. Timişoara's revolt happened in spurts, surges, or waves. People vented their rage by protest then returned home, only to be back on the streets in a few hours.[49]

Soldiers were everywhere. Initially the water purification plant was guarded like a fortress. Communist officials feared a terrorist poisoning of the water supply.[50] In time important locals began to speak from the balcony of the Opera House, urging their countrymen to take courage.[51] Soon Romanian flags were flown with a large round hole cut in the center. The hammer and cycle had been clipped away.[52] In the crowded central plaza, protesters raised their fists and chanted, "God exists."[53]

International condemnation of government action was swift. Censure was led by former Warsaw Pact countries. Solidarity workers drove convoys of medical supplies provided by the Polish people. Border guards flagged the trucks past. Traveling under the cover of darkness, drivers received hostile fire from the Securitate. Not all the trucks made it through.[54]

On December 19, soldiers in Timişoara could no longer deal with their consciences. The people they killed were their countrymen, the very ones they were sworn to protect. Then the army mutinied and sided with the demonstrators. Now the Securitate received gunfire.[55]

On December 20, government negotiators were sent to Timişoara to buy time. Back-up Securitate units followed shortly, and once again demonstrators were fired upon. But now army units returned fire. Flames consumed the interiors of stone-walled government complexes. Judeţul

Timiş, the county surrounding Timişoara, was on the verge of civil war and placed under martial law. No one knew where Father Tokes was. He had been arrested and taken away.

Judeţul Timiş was under siege. A news blackout was imposed, and phone lines to the outside were cut. Terror escalated. Evidence of tortured civilians surfaced later. Naked bodies of the executed were found, some with their ankles tied together with barbed wire. A three-year-old boy lay dead, partially covered in freshly fallen snow. Nearby a mother lay disemboweled, her seven-month fetus on her ashen breast.[56] An old man lay with his hands cut off, his body disfigured by boiling water and acid. A number of bodies had stomachs crudely sewn together, after they had been sliced open.[57]

To the north in Arad, people listened to their radios. The BBC, Voice of America, and Radio Free Europe had been their "Daily Bread" through the dark decades of the Cold War. When the free world informed Arad of Timişoara's events, Arad's populace flowed into the streets. They swarmed around city hall and felt no fear. Faces that had known only oppression now bore big smiles as they sang songs with delight. Reflexively, the military moved in to keep control — to the left Securitate and to the right the regular army. Authorities on bull horns and loudspeakers told the people to disperse. But the people stood with united resolve, believing it was better to die than to live under Ceauşescu.[58]

Again the church was instrumental. The people knelt before the soldiers and said the Lord's Prayer. Signs read, "God is with us!" There was gunfire and people died, but the carnage of Timişoara was not repeated. Rallies were held; speakers encouraged the people to pray and stand their ground, stressing to them what freedom could mean and what justice could do. They were also told how to find God. Most of the speakers were pastors from the various churches.

One of the many spontaneous leaders who sprung up was a young local actor in Arad named Valentin Voicilă. Like the others, he spoke fearlessly for the cause of freedom and human rights. Later he would be elected governor of Judeţul Arad. Then he would be converted to the cause of Christ and become a minister of the gospel.

To the secular Romanian, this display of Christian leadership was a curious turn of events, as Romanians had been led to believe Christians were weak. They only went to church because they needed the superstition of religion to help them cope. Christianity was nothing more than an opiate. But now these weak Christians fostered courage, and spoke of a God who cared for all the people.

Across the country, the scenario of spontaneous protest was repeated in many cities and towns. Reports from the city of Sibiu said troops had fired at everything that moved. In Iaşi protesters burned Ceauşescu's writings.[59] Confrontations erupted in Cluj, Braşov, Ploieşti, and Constanţa. But the main revolutionary play would be in two acts: Act I in Timişoara and Act II in Bucharest. In Timişoara many felt there was no turning back after the first massacre. Even though they were under siege, the soldiers stationed in Timişoara were with them. More importantly the boldness had not left, but spread instead.

"Today if death did not exist,
it would be necessary to invent it."
Jean Baptiste Milhaud,
when voting for the death of Louis XVI
January 19, 1793

CHAPTER 14

At the time of the Timişoara massacre, Ceauşescu returned from a visit with Iran's Ayatollah Khomeini. Angry that such mild action had been taken in his absence, he advised, "You do not silence your enemies by talking like a priest. You burn them." Apparently he was unaware of Timişoara's present carnage.[1]

Ceauşescu did not seem to believe international press reports about the slaughter in his country. Apparently he assumed his soldiers had used blanks. Now he ordered them to use real bullets, but to shoot the people in the legs after warning shots. He criticized Defense Minister Milea and Securitate Chief Vlad for not having this matter under control. They alone protested the use of live ammunition that Ceauşescu now ordered. Ironically, these were the commanders who would have given the nod for slaughter in the first place. Elena Ceauşescus called the generals cowards. Nicolae threatened the firing squad for such ineptitude. Discussion was adjourned with unanimous agreement in the twenty-five member Central Committee. All endorsed Ceauşescu's policy. "Burn them." There was not one dissenting vote.

Defence Minister Milea retreated to his office with an officer's pistol. There he put a bullet through his heart.

Milea's bodyguard said he was instructed to tell Milea's widow, "The Minister of Defence could not obey such criminal orders." Or was he murdered? After the revolution, evidence surfaced that Ceauşescu gave the order for Milea's assassination.[2]

Romanian state radio belatedly reported Timişoara's troubles, calling it a simple uprising of disgruntled Hungarians, protesting for Transylvania to rejoin Hungary. These individuals were labeled as bandits, Hungarian spies, and traitors. Radio commentators went on to quote Ceauşescu as saying, ".... their demands will be granted when poplars have pears." The next day hundreds of paper cut-out pears adorned the poplars of Bucharest.[3]

A natural question arises here. Did Ceauşescu and his entourage actually grasp reality from their lavish and sheltered world? This was a man who liked to be called "The Danube of Thought" and "The Genius of the Carpathians."[4] A person filled with such vanity is many times open to obvious mistakes and flattery's manipulation. Some believe conspirators began to feed Ceauşescu bad advice. Perhaps now was the time to topple him in the mist of civil unrest. Regardless of the origin of the plan, Ceauşescu called for a mass rally on December 21. This was a fatal mistake.

The rally was scheduled for early morning. Faithful Party cadres were to be shepherded in from factories and offices around the vicinity. On cue, they were to cheer and applaud. They had dutifully done this before as their deified leader harangued them for hours on end. This media event was intended to convince the world that Romanians still basked under the rule of Ceauşescu's benevolent utopia.

Loyal workers assembled in Republic Square, which spread before the Central Committee building. Some were given signs and placards, but most just stood and waited.

Ceauşescu was to appear from above on a balcony and address them. However, there was a change in plans, and Ceauşescu would not address them after all. All were thanked and sent home.

Later there was a second change in plans, Ceauşescu decided to speak after all. Now the Party faithful were dispersed and could not be located. A second group of workers were brought in, a large crowd was needed for the eyes of TV cameras. Some of these folks were actually hostile to the party, therefore they would be an unreliable cheering section.

As Ceauşescu expected, supporters dutifully assembled, but there were others there too. Three cordons of police held back youths and students from the nearby university.[5] Party bosses had gone from shop to shop, office to office to round up supporters. Others were caught up in the excitement and impulsively decided to show up on their own accord. This was the best show in town, and no one wanted to miss it. Spontaneously formed groups coalesced and approached Republic Square. Young children helped swell the mass to a sea of humanity.

Ceauşescu began to speak. He blamed the uprising in Timişoara on "CIA spies, fascists, hooligans, and Hungarians."[6] Everyone knew better. The crowd was silent, except for students on the sideline who booed from behind cordons of police. Without warning a strange sound crackled over Ceauşescu's words.[7] At the same time an electric defiance surged through the crowd. Ceauşescu was interrupted in mid-sentence. In moral outrage they began to cry, "Give us back our dead! Give us back our dead! Death! Death! Death! Down with Ceauşescu!" Others chanted, "Rat! Rat! Rat!" or "Go to hell!"

With arms outstretched, Ceauşescu froze, words would not come. Before him churned a cauldron of anger and righteous outrage. He staggered back, but with a sharp jab Elena pushed him once again onto the balcony. Still no words came.[8] The sound system was switched to recorded applause and patriotic music. Cameras rolled, the nation had seen their deified dictator falter.The world also saw.

The workers who were ordered to attend tried to escape from the plaza. Police strained to hold back students who surged forward. Others, who had come on their own, pressed towards the Central Committee building.Apparently Elena and Nicolae exited through a secret passage. Some say they stayed in the building.

In the meantime army and Securitate reinforcements encircled the entire area. Securitate readied themselves in underground tunnels for a deadly strike. Protesters retreated and poured into Magheru Bulevard. Soldiers, tanks, and choppers herded protesters into two nearby plazas: Piaţa Universităţii and Piaţa Romană. A tank rolled over two civilians. Those who rushed to their aid were shot down by automatic rifle fire. The American Embassy reported thirteen dead.[9] By mid-afternoon special riot police, armed with nightsticks and shields, marched down a wide avenue called Calea Victoriei and took up positions. Plain-clothes policemen began arrests.

By five p.m. the crowd had not disbursed. Warning shots were fired, but no one was in the mood to leave.[10] Then the Securitate and army opened fire. To some it sounded like artillery and machine gun fire. A number of buildings went up in flames, including the university library where many priceless documents burned.[11]

Journalists, staying at the Intercontinental Hotel, witnessed demonstrators as they were blasted by near freezing water from firehoses.[12] This failed to deter marchers. Instead they built barricades, only to have tanks roll over them in short order. Securitate fired on protesters from hidden positions with rifles equipped with night vision scopes and silencers. People simply dropped with a single bullet to the head. By dawn the demonstrators had been cleared. Bodies of the dead were removed, and blood washed from the street.[13] Around trees stood puddles of water stained red with blood.[14]

December 22 — the sun rose on another day in Ceaușescu's compassionate kingdom of communist brotherhood. During the night a new newspaper was birthed, entitled: *People's Spark.* The headline read; "CITIZENS, MEMBERS OF PATRIOTIC GUARDS! ANYONE WHO CAN USE A WEAPON, TO ARMS! DEFEAT THE ENEMIES AND TRAITORS OF THE COUNTRY, KILLERS AND VANDALS."[15] At seven a.m. demonstrators began to reassemble. By eleven a.m. huge crowds faced off against rows of soldiers and tanks backed by Securitate.[16]

By this morning, word of General Milea's suicide had been leaked. Rumor was he had taken his life rather than order his troops to fire on the people. Soldiers, who hated their grizzly duty, were even more reluctant to fire on civilians. Now they knew their general would have opposed such an order.[17] Demonstrators chanted, "The army is with us!" Then the people swarmed the troops, and offered them cigarettes and flowers.[18] Tank crews could not resist the charms of fraternizing citizens who stuffed Christmas trees down tank barrels.[19] Faced with such Yuletide goodwill, the Securitate withdrew, to regroup at the Central Committee building.[20] Other army regiments soon followed the lead of troops in Timișoara and Bucharest. The entire Romanian army joined with the people!

Soldiers had been in an exceedingly difficult position. A good number were draftees, and never wanted to be in the army, furthermore, the majority detested the job with which they were faced. Two accounts illustrate this dilemma. A CNN reporter filed this report: "I saw soldiers facing a woman. A (Securitate agent) ordered them to shoot the woman. The soldiers refused. They threw down their guns.... The (Securitate agent) shot the soldiers."[21] The other account is of a company commander who was directed by a Securitate officer to order his company to fire on demonstrators. The commander refused. The Securitate officer warned the commander that he would be shot if he did not issue the order. The commander pulled his pistol from his holster, and pointed it towards demonstrators. He ordered his soldiers to aim their rifles. Just before the order to fire was given, the commander pivoted, discharged one round, and punched a tidy hole in the Securitate officer's forehead. The soldiers were ordered to lower their weapons and not to fire on civilians.[22]

Few in the army were sorry they joined the people. Yet the Securitate could easily fight on; their only allegiance was to Ceauşescu. Protesters now moved to the Central Committee building where Ceauşescu had faltered the day before. They believed he was still inside, or had returned through a secret passage.

Belatedly, Bucharest radio officially announced the suicide of General Milea. They labeled him a traitor, then announced a state of emergency. This would be the last major announcement on Communist radio in Romania. More people poured into the streets to join the others at the Central Committee building.

Ceauşescu still believed in his ability to sway the masses. Around noon he stepped onto the balcony once again.* Immediately people booed and threw objects.

---

*Many reliable sources only mention one balcony appearance by Ceausescu. However, the flow of events seems to suuport other sources, who mention two balcony appearances.

Ceauşescu dodged one of many projectiles, and was forced back into the building by the pelting mob. In a state of near panic, Nicolae, Elena, and top brass took the elevator to the roof, where a helicopter waited.

Angry citizens forced their way through the doors, while guards stood by, unresisting.[23] Pandemonium ruled in the Central Committee building. Ceauşescu's writings were heaved over the balcony. Romanians below heaped his bound speeches into piles and kindled a fire. Ceauşescu was a long-winded speaker, so fuel was not in short supply.

For hours in the plaza unrestrained joy and celebration reigned. Dictatorial rule was all most Romanians could remember dating back to the days of Hitler's expansion. Now the millstone was lifted. For some it was giddy elation, but for others tears streamed down faces that had known only oppression. Citizens kissed the soldiers and danced around blazing bonfires, fed with copies of Ceauşescu's printed propaganda.

In spite of the chaos within the Central Committee building, groups organized giving birth to the National Salvation Front, (F.S.N.). Perhaps the groundwork for this organization had been quietly been laid days before, drawing a wide spectrum of dissidents and dissatisfied communists. They would be the caretakers of reform until elections could be held.

The F.S.N. was taken to the television station via armored vehicle. Two poets, Mircea Dinescu and Ana Blandiana, were recognized in the crowd. They arrived at the station on the shoulders of the people. The self-appointed revolutionary leaders and common people addressed the nation over the air. In short order tanks encircled the station to provide protection.[24] The revolution would be run from Studio Four.[25]

At one point Securitate entered the station through the air vents. Six people were wounded in the fighting that broke out inside the building, but the revolutionaries held their ground. Not once did they go off the air.[26] On December 23 at two a..m. all hell broke loose. The thirteen story building shook as Securitate gunfire slammed into it. Soldiers inside returned a withering barrage. Most of these soldiers had only fired their guns a few times during basic training; now they fought for their lives and the liberty of their countrymen.

All night Romanians were fed information from their TV sets. At one point their screens flicked during the assault. But Free Romanian Television stayed on the air, and broadcast a desperate appeal for help. Within minutes people left their homes and made their way to the TV station. Brazen courage gripped them as they formed a human shield around the station, 3,000 strong. When gunfire reached the lower levels of the building, they scattered, only to reassemble again and again.

Unarmed civilians located machine gun nests and attacked. Many were mowed down. The brave were students and fathers with families that depended on them. The Securitate withdrew, and Free Romanian Television continued to broadcast.[27] Gunfire would be directed at the station over the next two days, but freedom fighters always remained in control. The new government was conceived on air, live, with occasional incoming fire.[28]

A familiar face appeared on television — former foreign minister, Corneliu Mănescu. Mănescu was one of the six put under house arrest the previous March for signing the open letter of criticism. Now he pleaded with Securitate who fought on. "Don't blindly obey orders. You love us. We love you." To the common Romanian he appealed: "Slave workers of Romania, cease your work, support us, and come here!"

Mănescu was 73 and thought to be too old to head the National Salvation Front so Ion Iliescu, 59, was chosen for the job. In the 1950s Iliescu had attended university with Gorbachev in Moscow. Ceauşescu had accused Iliescu of "Bourgeois liberalism," and had him purged in 1971. He was demoted from Central Committee secretary and forced into a variety of low level jobs. When Gorbachev visited Romania in 1987, Iliescu was sent into the Carpathian Mountains. Ceauşescu feared the two men would collaborate.[29]

The National Salvation Front was presented to the Romanian populace via television as a caretaker government, made up of a broad spectrum of Ceauşescu critics. There were Communists on one side, all the way to Reverend Tokes on the other. They promised free elections and reforms. Freedom of religion and freedom of the press were officially granted on air. The F.S.N. hoped Romania would evolve into a democratic socialist republic along the lines of Sweden.

Amazingly General Vlad, highest commander of the Securitate, was in the station while crucial decisions were made. He claimed to have defected to freedom's cause. He claimed elements of the Securitate had gone renegade and were not under his control. According to Vlad, it was these "loose cannons" who were responsible for continued attacks. However, these loose cannons always knew what was about to happen next, thus the cause of freedom was placed in jeopardy several times. Then someone noticed General Vlad using the phone a lot. He was finally arrested, and the Securitate immediately became disorganized. The cause of freedom began to right itself.

Still the Securitate were a force to be reckoned with. Terrorists popped out of subway entrances connected with secret tunnels, and killed whomever was in sight. These same tunnels led to fake gravestones from which agents stepped and sprayed mourners with bullets. A wounded Securitate terrorist was brought into a hospital. In a preprogrammed insane state of hysteria, he screamed, "I'm dying for Ceauşescu! I will kill you!" The doctor administered phenobarbital and diazepam. Still he screamed, "I will kill you! I will kill your children!" Blood tests showed he had been injected with a powerful amphetamine.

With the army firmly behind the F.S.N., citizens now reported Securitate activity. Then the army swiftly moved in and took out the resistance. Suddenly, without notice, the Securitate withdrew, and nobody knew where they were. The revolution was further aided when Ceauşescu's son Nicu was paraded as a bruised captive on national television.[30]

During these days of chaos, Gorbachev got a message through to the leaders in Studio Four, offering the assistance of the Soviet army.[31] While Gorbachev was a reform orientated person, Romanians, remembering what happened when Soviet troops were sent into the Baltic Republics, Hungary, and Czechoslovakia, declined the offer of Soviet assistance.

It remained a mystery, as to what had happened to Ceauşescu and his entourage. One account said Ceauşescu's overcrowded helicopter just barely lifted off, as protesters ran across the roof of the Central Committee building.[32] They flew thirty-four kilometers north to Snagov, an eleventh-century monastery, later fortified by Dracula, and fortified again by Ceauşescu.[33] Now it was used as his summer place. Two ministers of state disembarked before the rest headed off to an airbase near Piteşti.[34] Allegedly a jet waited to take them to China. In flight, the helicopter pilot switched to a coded frequency and received word they would be shot down if they did not surrender.

Bucharest and Pitești are connected by a superhighway called the Auto Banda. A section of the highway was built to double as a military airstrip in case of emergency. The largest military aircraft could land for emergency fuel and repair.[35] The helicopter pilot claimed to have engine trouble and set down on that section of highway-runway. The passengers were unaware of the threat to shoot them from the sky. All four passengers got out to discuss their options. It was the pilot's turn to contribute to the revolution. He simply lifted off leaving the Ceaușescus stranded. Their discussion turned into an argument, as three workers from a chicken farm approached. When they recognized the Ceaușescus, Elena shouted to them, "Get back to work!"

The Ceaușescus hid in the bushes while their Securitate body guards began hitchhiking. When a driver pulled over, they commandeered the car.[36] Accounts vary as to what happened next. But eventually the Ceaușescus were arrested and stowed inside a tank. For the next few days they were driven around the countryside. The army successfully kept their location a secret, so that Securitate could not rescue them. Since there were numerous tanks on the roads, it would be almost impossible to locate this one key tank.[37] Nicolae was supposed to have an electronic homing device in his wristwatch. However, its signal could not be transmitted through the tank's thick steel casing.[38]

The National Salvation Front has been criticized for not having a public trial for the Ceaușescus. A public trial would have been nice, thorough investigation and cross examination may have revealed much. However the F.S.N. was pressured by real danger; if Ceaușescu were rescued by the Securitate, civil war could erupt. The Securitate could fight on against the army. If, however, the Ceaușescus were dead or proven insane, there would be no reason for the Securitate to fight on. The sole purpose of the Securitate was to protect Ceauşescu.

The tank bearing the Ceauşescus came to a stop at Boteni Military Base,[39] where a trial by military tribunal was scheduled. Nicolae and Elena were escorted indoors and their blood pressure was taken. They would be tried in a small room. On one side the defendants sat behind a simple table. From the opposite side of the room they faced a judge, prosecuting attorney, and two defense attorneys. A couple of solders stood guard with automatic rifles. Along one side of the court sat a half dozen other individuals.

Five charges were brought against the Ceauşescus: genocide, abuse of military power, destruction of public buildings and private fortunes, economic sabotage, and theft of currency and conspiracy to leave the country.

From the onset Nicolae stated that he did not recognize the court. According to the constitution he was to be tried by the Marea Adunare Naţională (M.A.N.) or the Great National Assembly. The M.A.N. was made up of representatives from all cities and provinces of the nation.

The judge informed Nicolae and Elena that the Marea Adunare Naţională had been dissolved. The Constitution was no longer in effect. The rules had been changed. He told them to stand to address the court. Neither stood through the whole trial. Nicolae then restated, "I do not recognize this court." Then he added, "If I do talk to you, it is because I am speaking to you as simple peasants."

At this time two defense attorneys solicited the bench for permission to counsel their clients. With permission granted, they approached both Ceauşescus and spoke loudly, perhaps to be picked up on the video camera. They advised both Nicolae and Elena to plead insanity. With an insanity plea the Ceauşescus could possibly save their lives.

When the defense lawyers first gave counsel, both Nicolae and Elena appeared to pay attention. But the insanity plea was too much. Anger was plainly visible in the accused. From then on they had nothing to do with the defense attorneys' counsel.

As the defense lawyers backed off to the opposite side of the room, the judge read the charges again. Then he accused the Ceauşescus of trying to build their own private kingdom. Next he informed them that the court was assembled to judge the former rulers of Romania, and everything they had done.

Ceauşescu interrupted, "Nothing you are doing here is real; everything is a masquerade."

The judge shot back, "You have performed the masquerade for twenty-five years! Now it is time for you to pay for what you have done!"

Elena tried to help, but Nicolae persisted. "I don't talk anymore, I don't respond. It doesn't matter what you ask me. I will not sign any papers you produce." Then he gave a gesture with his hand, meaning it's over — end of discussion.

The prosecution ignored Ceauşescu's antics and pressed the charge of genocide, the slaughter of over 60,000 people. Then the prosecutor asked, "Did you ever think about the future, that all this would end? That you would have to pay for what you have done?"

Ceauşescu struggled to hold his peace then blurted, "I will not answer to this court! I will only answer to the Marea Adunare Naţională. I will answer all questions before them. You have taken over the power, this is a coup! You are abusing your power!"

"If we abuse power, why are the people fighting in the streets? Why have you hired mercenaries to kill your own countrymen?"

Nicolae took the defensive. "I didn't order the killing of people. Everything you say is lies and not based on truth! And I don't want to talk about it anymore! You are just trying to confuse me."

The accusations continued. "You have destroyed the property and economy of this country. You have a secret army that is still resisting the people. What can you tell us about this?"

Ceauşescu didn't answer.

"The foreign mercenaries you hired are killing people in the streets! Now! As we speak! And your citizens cannot fight back, they have no weapons." Ceauşescu was chided for not answering, followed by more bickering about the court's right to try him. His anger remained visibly obvious.

"Tell the court why the people are fighting in the streets."

"They are fighting for me, for the existence of the communist state." It was evident Ceauşescu had not heard any news locked away in the tank.

"Do you know you are not the President of Romania? Do you know you don't hold any of your other positions? Do you know, you are not the Commander and Chief of the Armed Forces?"

"I am President of Romania! I am Commander of the Armed Forces! I have to tell you again, I treat you like simple peasants. You are not my judges. I am the Supreme Commandant of the Army! I am the President of Romania!"

"Do you know that people would walk miles to Bucharest to buy a little piece of bread? Do you know how hard it was for your people to feed their bellies?"

Ceauşescu laughed. "I don't want to answer this. I took care of the people well. For the first time they had enough wheat and flour. I am speaking to you like simple peasants. I was so good to these people. I brought electricity to the small villages. I built hospitals, I built apartments, and schools. Never before have the small villages of Romania had such success. How can you accuse me of destroying this country?"

"We hear stories of the fine imported food you dined on. Wasn't the bread of your countrymen good enough?"

Elena came unhinged, "How can you say this! How can you talk to us like this"

"You have $400,000,000 dollars stored away in secret foreign accounts."

Elena, still angry, "Give us proof! Let's see your proof!"

Nicolae interrupted. "Everything you say is false! It is all lies! You all will pay for what you have done to us. This is simply a coup! You perjure me, and I will sue you for these insults! I will only answer to the people."

The judge then reread each of the five charges. Each charge was followed by a simple statement: refusal to answer. When presented with the charges, Ceauşescu refused to sign.

Still there were more questions, including an inquiry into the suicide of General Milea to which Ceauşescu responded, "I heard after his suicide that he was a traitor, that he didn't carry out my orders."

"What kind of orders did you give him? To kill people in Timişoara? And he didn't want to execute these orders? Now if you are not responsible for this, if you have mental problems we can talk differently."

The defense tried once more to make them understand that they were in danger. They urged the Ceauşescus to answer the charges, or to plead insanity. Both rejected the defense team, and claimed the defense was in league with the prosecution.

The prosecution chided Elena, "We knew your birthday, but we never knew what year you were born in."

She snapped back with a cold, "So what?"

Both defense lawyers then took the stand to explain why they couldn't really defend the Ceauşescus well. They asked the court to consider that the Ceauşescus were totally uncooperative. While the defense tried to excuse themselves, they actually incriminated the Ceauşescus. But they did ask the judge to carefully consider his actions, not to take revenge, and to act only within the confines of the law.

The judge then wrote the sentence: Death.[40]

Unknown to the Ceauşescus, 300 soldiers had volunteered for a three-man firing squad.[41] A lottery was held to select executioners. It was an honor to be chosen for the task.[42] A sense of urgency reigned. Their former leaders must be dispatched as quickly as possible, before the Securitate could rescue them. The Securitate chain of command must be decapitated. Hopefully, civil war would be avoided.

Nicolae and Elena were escorted outside, to stand against a stucco wall. Both received some thirty bullets each before the order to fire was even given. Elena fell to the left, coat and scarf thrown up around her head, and a long trail of blood flowed forward. Nicolae crumpled backwards, both lower legs folded under his thighs. No blood could be seen, his eyes remained blankly open.

Nervously orders were called. Soldiers were to take their positions, and guard against Securitate attack. But the attack never came.[43] To the physical eye, two well-guarded bodies lay at the base of a bullet-flecked wall. The corpses grew cold. But to the spiritual eye, that wall was a gate to eternity.

"The antichrist is dead on Christmas Day!" was the announcement from Romanian radio. [44]

To Heal a Wounded Land

Part 3

CHAPTER 15

The bullet-riddled bodies of Nicolae and Elena
Ceaușescu were shown over and over again on Free Romanian TV, the video camera lingering on each face with
its vacant stare. There was no doubt that both were dead
along with their regime and any potential dynasty. The
replayed image confirmed the Securitate's worst fear. With
Ceaușescu gone there was no cause. How could they fight
on? What was there to fight for? The new provisional government made an offer of leniency to any Securitate who
turned themselves in. Those who would not surrender
faced death sentences. News reports now referred to the
Securitate as "terrorists." Bulletins were broadcast, and
some terrorists surrendered. A few fought on and sealed
their fanatical fate, but most evaporated into the milieu.

In the revolution's final hours, citizens broke into a
Ceaușescu mansion in north Bucharest. They were
stunned by his wealth and military preparedness. Beneath
the mansion, in a maze of tunnels, they found a command
center equipped with the latest in electronic technology.
Deep in an underground bunker they discovered a set of
switches, each connected to a charge of explosives located in strategic locations throughout the capital city.
Ceaușescu had the ability to virtually destroy Bucharest
in an attempt to save himself.

As a few well-organized Ceauşescu terrorists fought on in an attempt to destabilize the National Salvation Front, the F.S.N. stocked store shelves. Huge stashes of food were found in warehouses — food produced by Romanians but slated for sale on foreign markets. Other goods, which Ceauşescu routinely imported for his elite, now appeared in stores. Electricity that once flowed out of the country was diverted to consumers in Romania. Factories that operated at a loss were shut down. Gas and oil were diverted to heat cold apartments. Heating fuel came just in time; the warm December days of revolution now gave way to bitter cold. With these quick emergency measures, the F.S.N. gained majority support.[2]

As the F.S.N. freed the flow of information, the world became aware of new destabilizing problems. Family ideals were strong, but under tremendous stress. For social and religious reasons families have traditionally been large—six to ten children were the norm for many.

Under communism, family planning policies had fluctuated wildly. Incomes withered with the advent of Marxism, and parents found it virtually impossible to provide. In 1957, the government issued a decree: abortions could be had for about two American dollars. By 1965, there were four abortions for every live birth. Population declined. A panicked dictatorship issued State Decree No. 770 in October 1966. Suddenly abortions were illegal along with contraception. Tax breaks were given to those who increased their families. Penalties were assigned to those who did not produce. Ceauşescu called on the nation to increase its population to thirty million by the year 2000, a net increase of seven million souls. In 1967, the first year of the new policy, Romania's mothers responded with stamina. The birth rate soared 300 percent.[3]

Women received gynecological examinations at work. Once a pregnant woman was tagged, "Demographic Command Bodies" were called in to monitor the woman. Mis-carriages were investigated by the Securitate.[4]

Families were poor and could not support their increases. Black market birth control was expensive. Poor prenatal care and nutrition endangered many women. Infants and unborn children were at horrible risk. Infant mortality was eight times higher than that of Western Europe.* One baby in ten was born under 1500 grams (1 lb, 5 oz). These tiny humans were considered living miscarriages, and were refused medical care. Larger, healthier babies, that could not be afforded, ended up in orphanages. To further exacerbate the problem, Ceaușescu banned all books on human sexuality and reproduction. These were now deemed state secrets, to be used as medical texts.[5]

After the revolution, the world was shocked as reporters exposed conditions in Romania's orphanages. Babies were left in their cribs all day; many were underdeveloped. Older children slept two or three to a bed. But most shocking was the incidence of AIDS. One third of children tested positive for HIV. It appears the babies received unscreened blood from used needles. Babies were injected with blood in an attempt to fortify their immune systems. This practice was forsaken by most doctors generations ago; yet, it was widely practiced in Romania's orphanages through 1989.[6]

Confusion followed the regime's collapse; there were questions about the new government. Questions loomed in people's minds. Where were the dead? How had many perished in the revolution? Could the new regime, which included old communists, be trusted? How much personal

---

*Western Europe has less than ten infant deaths per 1,000 births. Romania had eighty-three infant deaths per 1,000 births.

freedom would come from this? Some answers came slowly, some never emerged. International attention was diverted elsewhere, and Romania wrestled with her problems unnoticed.

No one knows how many were killed in December of 1989. At first casualties were listed at 64,000, then reduced, reduced again, and yet again. The final death toll was set at 750, with just over one hundred killed in Timişoara. Many did not feel comfortable with the new government's figures. A haunting sense continued to grow. Maybe they would never know how many Romanians had lost their lives.

As the list of atrocities is reviewed, one has to wonder: can anything good come of a communist regime? The F.S.N. had old communists in its ranks. Could the National Salvation Front be trusted? The students of Bucharest did not think so. Evidence surfaced that the Communist Party itself had planned a *coup d'etat*, for some future point. They just had not expected events to fall into place so quickly.

It was said the hastily constructed F.S.N. took power after a spontaneous revolution was in progress. They claimed to be a caretaker government, and would step down when elections were held. Later F.S.N. members decided to run for office, winning the presidency and a majority of seats in the National Assembly and Senate. Suspicious students and intellectuals took to the streets again. This time they were cleared away by coal miners who supported the government.[7] The general Romanian population was in the mood to give the F.S.N. a chance, most perceiving it as the guardians of freedom who made an honest effort to improve their lives.

The fall of Ceauşescu was the last domino to crash in Eastern Europe. The West breathed a collective sigh of relief. The world had just taken a step back from the brink.

Constitutional reforms became the law of the land in Romania, so the West turned their attention elsewhere. In a very short time forty percent of all Romanians would not have enough to eat.

The dark days of communism bred desperate conditions. While events are laden with hope and promise, the return to dictatorship is a distinct possibility — unless economic conditions improve. The former Soviet Bloc countries lost a war, the Cold War. While bombs did not fall, their economies showed an effect similar to a country defeated in actual war.

It would be a mistake to blame the West for Eastern Europe's poverty. Their poverty is directly linked to forty-five years of godless communism. Under Ceauşescu it was illegal not to work unless enrolled in school so everybody worked for the sake of being occupied. Factories had been ordered to simply employ people as a way to provide paychecks. Many factories were unprofitable because their goods were not marketable. These plants closed after the revolution. Thousands of people now had no income.

From this century's history we can draw a compelling parallel. Allied forces won WW I but were in no mood to help conquered countries. President Wilson of the United States was the only Allied leader who did not desire revenge.

In defeated Germany, people suffered in poverty until a strong dictator offered a way out. His name was Adolf Hitler. We do not need to review the misery he brought the world. What we need to note is: the German people would have never supported Hitler if they had not been so desperate.

After WW II, U.S. Secretary of State, George Marshall did not want a repeat of mistakes made after the First World War. He came up with a plan to rebuild all countries devastated by war. The Marshall Plan rebuilt countries that had been our former enemies. Now, years later, at the close of the twentieth century, former Axis countries— Germany, Italy, Austria, and Japan — are all American allies. There is no chance they will go to war with the U.S. in the foreseeable future. We helped our old enemies; now they contribute to our security.

An eerie repetition of events has occurred. NATO's most feared enemy for over forty years finally fell. The economies of most Soviet Bloc countries are devastated. The mood of many in the West is: why should we help them? They got what they deserved as the natural outcome of communism. Their suffering reinforces our belief that we were right. Their misery fuels a smug attitude of relief. They are so crippled, how could they threaten our security? Finally many ask: Why send aid over there when we have problems of our own? Very similar attitudes existed prior to World War II, and look what happened when we isolated ourselves.

We fail to realize two things. First, the majority of these people were not our enemies. They were powerless victims, captured under the iron hand of a godless system. They wanted freedom, and many tried to escape. Second, if desperation continues, a leader not unlike Hitler could easily gain support. Fortunately, the current move is toward more democracy in Romania. However democratic gains can be lost if conditions do not improve.

Mark Twain supposedly said, "History does not repeat itself, it rhymes." Western governments have faltered, and continue to let slip an opportunity to make our world secure. Through neglect, they imitate the mistakes that followed WW I, and God only knows how the rhyming score will end.

While worldly governments falter with neglect, all is not lost. There is another government that is not of this world. It is the government of God and of His Christ, and God calls his believers to help those in need. Regardless of denomination, Christians are called to bind up the wounds of the fallen. We can help in a thousand little ways. Not only can we feed the hungry, we can feed the soul, something no earthly government can do.

This may sound like simple naivete. Many will smile in condescending disbelief. But we serve the Lord of the Harvest when we give our five loaves and two fishes, and watch God work. Sure it would be nice if NATO or the U.N. came up with a new Marshall Plan. But the nations of this world can only do so much; sometimes they do a lot. In time they will pass, and be no more. It would be nice if our God did not call on us to relieve suffering. But our God does call us. What is done humbly in the name of Jesus will not pass, but will last forever.

Some would like to help, but are overwhelmed by the need. It seems our singular efforts are like a lonely drop of rain evaporating over the great Sahara. The comfortable defense is to isolate ourselves, surrounded by material blessings. There we feed our delusion which says: "God blessed me, so he must expect me to enjoy it." This is not truth. When God blesses us, he expects us to use that blessing to bless others.

Citizens of God's kingdom need to remember who we are. We are commanded to pray, to go directly to the "President." The "Commander-in-Chief" will give us our orders. Yes, he has something for us to do. When we yield to Him in the stillness of our soul, He will direct us in a hundred different ways. We must set aside our goals, ambitions, and sense of security. We must ask God to fill us with his love and show us where and how to share it. Our efforts may be small, but if ordered of God, that is all that is needed. Only what is ordered of God will last forever.

Mike Olari held these ideals as truth. As history played itself out in Romania, he felt a continual urge gnawing in the pit of his stomach. He had received his "orders," but still he did not know exactly how to carry them out. He harbored no illusions. The occasion was monumental compared to his few resources. To make Mike feel even more helpless, his tile business took a down turn when a contractor went bankrupt and his company lost money, draining his personal funds. He questioned God, not from doubt, but from a desire to do the right thing.

Daily, the "vision" replayed itself in Mike's mind. He had no idea what to do next. In late winter of 1990, Mike unloaded his frustration on a friend. Paul listened closely as they walked down a Phoenix street. He could offer no answers or solutions, but Paul perceived that Mike spoke from a real burden given by God. This was something much bigger than the two of them. Paul Larue suggested they pray, immediately, at the side of the street, not for pious show but from honest concern. The two prayed at the same time.

A couple hours later Mike was stuck in traffic and his cell phone rang. It was Paul, and he was unusually cheerful.

"Mike, it hit me about an hour after we prayed. I think you need to talk to my father-in-law."

Mike wasn't sure what to think, "Yeah...okay.... who is he?"

"This guy has traveled a lot, done writing, and has tons of connections. I went ahead and called him. Are you free this afternoon?"

"I can be." Mike was cautiously optimistic and rescheduled his afternoon.

At two p.m. he knocked on Verne Nesbitt's door. When Verne answered, an uncanny awareness passed over them both. It was as if they had known each other for years, and yet they faced each other for the first time. Verne was a cordial man who listened with great interest. Mike recounted the events unfolding in Romania, and shared his concern and inability to help. At this time, he was not as worried about the material needs of the people as much as the needs of the heart and spirit. In Mike's mind, the immediate challenge lay in the lack of scripture.

Bibles had been destroyed while the Communists ruled. Now it was time to put Bibles back into the people's hands. Urgency ruled after the revolution, for no one knew how long the borders would remain open. Was this another Prague Spring? In 1968 Czechoslovakia had thrown off the yoke of communism, only to have Russia force it back in with tanks and soldiers. Would a similar thing happen now in Romania? Just in case, loads of Bibles must be delivered as soon as possible.

A few days after their meeting, Verne called Mike. He had secured funding for a trip to Romania. His church had bought Mike a plane ticket, and a church member put up enough cash to buy 500 Bibles.

Quickly Mike booked a flight to Germany. Once there, he rented a car and trailer, filled both with Bibles and goods, and set out for Romania. As he drove across Hungary he was reminded of the past fall's trip. He remembered the guard who refused him entry. Now he mused at carrying such a large load of Bibles with no attempt to hide them. Last fall such blatant activity would have been lunacy. This spring Mike honestly expected to deliver his goods.

There was a short line at the border checkpoint. The officer took a quick look at Mike's passport and waived him through. As the checkpoint disappeared in the rearview mirror, Mike was overwhelmed by the gravity of the scene just played out. For longer than Mike could remember, his cargo was forbidden. Now he transported it freely! Now he could express beliefs for which he and others like him had suffered. Sheer joy came over him, tears rolled down his cheeks as he drove on to Arad.

The National Salvation Front has been criticized, sometimes fairly. However the F.S.N. took bold action when it came to basic human rights. The gift of religious freedom was a courageous step. Now people could worship, read their Bibles, and speak candidly of their faith, free from fear. If the nation could take the next step and truly learn to seek their Creator, then they would be truly blessed.

Arad was a changed city. Freedom had breathed an invisible difference. Mike unloaded his Bibles, which were rapidly distributed. Securitate informers were absent from the churches. No one would be turned over to the government.

He saw something else beautiful. Christians from Europe and America sent Bibles to Romania, as well as to other former Communist Bloc countries. With this development, Mike began to reconsider his objectives. Anybody could ship Bibles, even those who did not know the language of the people. Mike had two advantages: fluency in Romanian, and an American passport. In the early 1990s Romanians admired America and anything American. People came to hear Mike, simply because he was American. It was obvious his talents would be better used in evangelization and teaching the word of God.

Mike mulled this plan over in his mind on the way to his brother's house in Arad. This particular evening the house was unusually crowded, and English was the *lingua franca* among the new faces. One visitor was from Phoenix and pastored a large church — The Valley Cathedral. Don Price was profoundly interested in the way God moved in Romania, and took notice of Mike's efforts. He invited Mike to present his ministry to the mission board when he returned to Phoenix. Later, believers at The Valley Cathedral funded Mike's next trips to Romania.

Still Mike had a wife and seven children to support. At home, business problems grew in his absence. When back in Phoenix he resolved company issues, then prepared to return to Romania. Ana held things together amazingly well. She was skilled at being both mother and father to the children when Mike was away. The children understood, from the oldest to the youngest, that Daddy wanted to be with them. But they also understood Daddy was needed back in Romania. Mike felt it would be a mistake to take his family back with him before the government became more stable.

In 1991 and 1992 Mike made several trips to Romania to preach and was amazed at how the people soaked in the gospel message. After forty-five years of communist rule, many had little concept of what it meant to be a Christian. Most had a vague nebulous concept of God; they just thought He must be out there somewhere. Suppression had bred much ignorance. Still many were nagged by a desire to know more about their historical faith. All Christian denominations experienced a surge in growth after the revolution.

Mike spoke in churches and home gatherings. His words were like the first rain after a desert summer. The Spirit of God connected with the longings in their souls. Not all believed, but many did.

Shortly after the revolution Mike visited his childhood village of Chisindia. People were excited and rented the "Casa de Cultură," the village assembly hall. Everyone attended en masse to hear him speak. They received this Romanian-now-turned-American with enthusiasm.

Mike felt he should do something for the small Pentecostal congregation there. They had always met at his grandparents' home, and it was time to build a church. Property was available near the center of town. Mike bought it for (U.S.) $500, and quickly notarized the deed.

A curious event followed. Denominational friction was not dead. There was an Orthodox church down the road. Many people did not trust the Orthodox Church because it had been recognized by the very government that had tried to stamp out religion. The local priest went to the woman who sold Mike the property and asked her to buy it back.

The priest was worried about the rapid growth of Pentecostals. He had read a book about them and told the woman what happened in America. He spoke of a healing crusade where people lined up in wheelchairs desiring to be healed. Then someone rushed into the building, and yelled, "There is a bomb! A bomb's been planted in the building!" Everyone ran from the building including the "crippled" in the wheelchairs.

The priest had a legitimate concern. There have been more than a few accounts of false healers, some documented by the FBI. Those who claim the gifts of the Holy Spirit need to be less gullible, especially when it comes to traveling salvation shows. There are fakes in the fold who, like hungry wolves, feed on innocent lambs. Such nonsense causes many, who would like to believe, to turn away.

Lenuţa, the woman who sold Mike the land, now had second thoughts. She believed her priest and asked Mike to return to return the money.

Mike's response was businesslike. "Lady, did I not pay you for this land?"

"Yes."

"Did I not pay you well?"

"Yes."

With the deed firmly gripped in his hand, he said, "This land is ours. We are building a church. Sorry."

A few days later Mike was back in the states. He needed about 7,000 American dollars for this project. Romanians in the U.S. gave, but the largest single donor was The Valley Cathedral, and today there is a sister church, called The Valley Cathedral in Chisindia, Romania.

A year later, as the church neared completion, Lenuţa became ill. The doctor numbered her days at less than a year. As she looked at death, she asked Mike to pray for her. She had seen God work in the small group that built the new church. Still these people were not Orthodox, so she was uncertain. She decided to seek a second opinion from another priest, her son-in-law. (Unlike Catholic priests, Orthodox priests may marry.)

The Valley Cathedral of Chisindia

The young priest said, "Sure! Why not have Mike pray for you?"

The next time Mike was in Chisindia he prayed for Lenuţa. Her faith was strong, and she trusted Jesus completely. The presence of the Holy Spirit was sensed in the room. Mike felt something good would happen.

A few months later, Mike was at home in Phoenix. One night he dreamed in lucid detail of Lenuţa. She was clothed in white, and walked down the center street of Chisindia. Other villagers followed at a short distance. Lenuţa was an attractive woman, beautiful in her youth. Mike dreamt of the young, beautiful woman he remembered from his childhood. He awoke and pondered. In the morning he told Ana, "Either Lenuţa has been healed tonight, or she has gone to be with the Lord."

Later that week Mike chatted with his brother on the phone. John had called Chisindia a few days before. Lenuţa had just passed away. She parted about the time of Mike's dream.

Mike continued his journeys to Romania. While he was well received by churches in Arad and Timişoara, he felt drawn to forgotten rural areas. Sometimes he spoke in small churches, but many times he met in crowded homes. He grew accustomed to a receptive audience. Always there were some who opened themselves to Christ. A unique satisfaction that accompanies this sort of work filled Mike.

One night was different. In a small village, he spoke to a home group. His presentation went well, and as usual he sensed the closeness of the Holy Spirit. When he closed the meeting, no one responded. This was a first. Mike felt he had failed, and he was embarrassed.

A year later Mike passed through the same village and spoke to the pastor's wife. She had good things to say about that night.

Mike was puzzled. "Actually I am kind of ashamed of that meeting because nothing happened."

"But two women came to know Christ. They just didn't tell you."

Mike felt he should open himself for instruction.

The woman continued. "Those women went home. One talked to her husband and father-in-law. They became Christians too. So the three of them decided to open their house for a church in Săliște. Before this they didn't have a church there."

Mike was humbled and said nothing.

"I don't think these women knew what they were getting into," the pastor's wife snickered. "They just came to see what an American looked like."

This relatively minor event rolled around inside Mike's head, teaching him that it was not his responsibility to gain converts. His job was to present the gospel of Jesus Christ. The Holy Spirit would perform the harvest. For Mike to assume a responsibility reserved for God was a sin. Furthermore, the Holy Spirit deserved credit for the new converts — not Mike.

After four or five trips to Romania Mike's cousin, Gheorghe Rașca, came to him with a business proposal. The village of Chisindia needed a mill. Villagers grew wheat, but had to travel many miles to grind it into flour. A mill would provide employment and a valuable service. Profits could be used to fund traveling pastors, or pay for their education.

The plan sounded good. Mike presented it to the board of The Valley Cathedral in Phoenix. After a period of prayer and consideration, they agreed to buy equipment: grinding stones, electric motor, sifters, storage containers, and so on. Mike had the responsibility of building a structure to house the equipment.

The plan was simple. The villagers in Chisindia erected the structure. Mike supplied materials funded by Romanians in the U.S. The project should have taken a year to complete, but there were delays. Fittings for the machinery were not compatible. Costly new adapters were ordered from outside the country. After an investment of more time and money, they were ready to go into production.

Now all that was needed was a five-ton truck to transport grain to the mill and to carry flour to market. Mike had a plan. His Volkswagen Fox could be sold for a large profit. If he added a couple thousand dollars, he could buy a truck. Maybe. Mike contacted a Christian brother in Germany. With luck, he might find a eight-year-old truck for about (U.S.) $7,000.

It did not take long for Mike to find a buyer for the Fox. That same day, just before the actual transaction transpired, the Fox was hit broadside in the driver's door. Mike was uninjured, and walked away from the crash. Perhaps he should have rejoiced because he was safe. Instead he was angry —his plan was crushed in the intersection. It was doubtful the Fox could be repaired.

Marathon runners, when well into the race, become extremely fatigued. Every muscle aches as the body screams to shut down. They call this "The Wall." Once The Wall is passed, the rest of the race is not so bad. Mike's spirit felt like the marathon runner's. Discouragement penetrated the essence of his emotion, then solidified. Disillusionment hit hard and caused him to doubt. He canceled his afternoon appointments and went to the small room where he stayed. There he prayed in frustration.

"God, I am not asking for favors. I am not asking for cash. All I ask is that you protect me while I earn a little money. A little money to help these people. You gave me this vision, at least I thought you did, but now I'm not sure. I don't want to be here if this is not your will. God, I have traveled back and forth across the world. I miss my family. God I tried to help out, but everything takes so much energy! It takes so much time. I destroyed my business in America because I am gone. God if you don't show me by tomorrow morning that I should be here, I will go back to the United States and forget about Romania."

Mike was serious. The thought of American life pleased him. He relaxed, and the fantasy of uninterrupted months with family and friends allured him. Deep down inside a faint whisper could be heard, "Maybe you should help these people here." The whisper was not loud, so Mike chose to bask in the dream of America. He slept well that night.

In the fresh morning light, Mike walked to his Uncle Pavel's office. There he planned to finalize his departure. He had not received a sign or indication that he should stay in Romania. He was ready to check out. With a smile on his face, he strode through the office door around nine a.m. Immediately his uncle handed him a fax from Germany.

It read: "I don't know who needs the truck, but who ever they are, they must be in the will of God. A stranger called yesterday, asking if I wanted to buy an almost new, five ton truck for DM 3,000 (US $2,000). Let me know by 3 p.m. if you will take delivery."

This was an incredible deal! A newer truck for thousands less. Mike sat down. This was the answer he asked for. He felt humbled and ashamed. He knew he was in God's will. He was stunned, as if hit by God.

The flatbed truck was purchased and delivered to Chisindia. The truck delivered wheat to the mill and the mill began production of fine whole wheat flour.

There was still one problem, Mike had not done his marketing research. The village people did not like whole wheat flour. Everyone assumed they would get white flour and were disappointed when they saw the actual product. Mike assumed they wanted whole wheat flour because it was the healthy choice. He had eaten it as a child, and he knew villagers had used it for years. The point had never been discussed.

Mike tried to explain, "Look, this flour is better; it has more protein; it has more vitamins; it has more fiber!"

To the villagers this meant nothing. What was fiber anyway? They wanted white flour.

Mike tried again, "In America, people who want to be healthy buy whole wheat bread."

The villagers held a different perspective. With freedom, they should be able to buy white flour. Ceauşescu had given them whole wheat, and told them it was better. They wanted white flour, the kind they had seen advertised in Western magazines. Now, Mike wanted to pass this whole wheat stuff off on them too, the same as Ceausescu. What good was the revolution if you could not eat white flour? One should have the freedom to eat what they wished!

A shriveled old lady stole off to her home and returned with a loaf of bread. She broke it open, and held it out to Mike. "This is what we want! See how white it is? We want our bread to be white!"

The village unanimously endorsed the woman.

Frustration rose in Mike. This project had looked like such a good idea. It had such potential. How could he have overlooked such a simple issue as white flour? The entire project stood in jeopardy. In time the villagers agreed to try the whole wheat flour out of respect for Mike. But they did not like it. Bags of flour soon stood in storage. No one would buy it.

Mike could not let the project go to waste. His mind worked other angles. As it turned out the mill could also make very good corn flour. There was some demand for this product, so the mill project wasn't a total loss. Some were employed, but production was not at the levels originally hoped for. Corn flour production continued for four years. In the summer of '96, a new mill was purchased and the building expanded. Finally white flour could be produced.

Mike learned from the mill that anything he did would be difficult. Nothing would be done on time. New problems would appear from nowhere. There would be failures before there was success. The frustrations Mike felt were a microcosm of the nation as a whole. Romania's economy had been jolted backward before it was ready to move forward.

In the Summer of '96 the mill was expanded. Horse-drawn wagons are still very common. In this case, the cargo is large blocks of gypsum to be used as giant bricks.

*"Pure and genuine religion is this:
to take care of orphans and widows
in their suffering and to keep
oneself from being corrupted
by the world."*
James 1:27 (TEV)

CHAPTER 16

After the revolution the living standards of many citizens plummeted. Inflation vaulted to 300 percent per year. More factories closed because they were not profitable in a free market economy. Solvent factories were privatized, and the new owners made handsome profits. They were the lucky ones.

Ironically, it was the poor, backward peasants who stood the best chance of survival. At least they could produce their own food and sell any surplus. Urban dwellers were put in a hopeless crunch as their paychecks failed to keep pace with rocketing prices.

The unemployed could not start their own business because it was impossible to get a loan. There were few banks in Romania. Most larger cities did not have a single bank. Economic crises loomed immanent.

Some ten percent of the population prospered after the revolution. Half maintained their same living standard, that is to say: they could survive with little extra. Forty percent of Romania's families were hurt economically by the revolution. They could not afford sufficient food. Mike felt the "vision" was intended for these people.

Because three or four families often lived in one house, few homeless were seen on the streets. However, the hungry dug through garbage dumpsters. When inflation hits 300 percent a year, putting a single meal on the table becomes difficult. Life became desperate. Meals were limited to one, possibly two a day. Payment of utilities was impossible. Utility companies tried to work with people, but many times were forced to cut off service.

The homeless in Romania are children, mostly boys. When a family cannot buy food, it is the boys who are first put in orphanages. Conditions in orphanages are so poor that boys often run away. If a girl is put in an orphanage, she usually stays put, but not always. Some boys will leave home because they know their parents cannot afford to feed them. These boys spend their days and nights on the streets. To deaden the hunger they sniff rags dampened with gas or solvent.

The need was obvious. Families needed assistance simply to keep their children. Also something had to be done about the homeless children. Mike did not stop to analyze the magnitude of the problem. If he had, he would have been overwhelmed. He believed God wanted him to help, so he had to start somewhere. Of course it appeared futile, but God would cause something to happen. God would have to work miracles. In the meantime Mike tried to figure out ways of making quick money so that he could give it away.

More than once Mike found himself at the top of a high rise apartment. The old communist elevators were slow, and took a long time to arrive. Rather than wait, he took the stairs down nine floors. He saved little time, but at least he was on the move. Likewise he felt he had waited long enough to carry out the vision. It was time to "take the stairs." Through trial and error, he sought a solution.

On an earlier trip to Romania, he had carried several packages of Kool-Aid with him. It was an instant hit, so he tried importing it. People enjoyed this novel drink, and best of all, it was American. Mike imported more Kool-Aid and rented space to store it. He became Romania's Kool-Aid connection. However, when the novelty wore off, sales slumped. Romanians preferred a real fruit juice, naturally sweetened.

Mike made money on his Kool-Aid venture, and was able to help some people with the profits. But it took much time! It seemed he could make more money if he turned his storage space into a small grocery store. Again he was able to help people with the profits, but this too, took much time.

Mike looked for a simple product with a good profit. It had to be something the people needed, something poor people could afford. The picture of pasta production formed in his mind. A pasta factory only needed four things: a pasta machine, flour, eggs, and water. Mike converted the grocery store into a pasta factory.

People liked Mike's affordable pasta and soon he hired full time employees. Within a year the factory was at maximum production, and he was able to expand. In December of '95 he ordered a larger machine, and production increased five fold.

As Mike went about his business, he noticed homeless boys on the street. He thought of his own children, and pictured them homeless. His heart broke. "God!" Mike cried from his soul. "Help these boys. Send someone to help them. This is wrong, just plain wrong. These boys should not be on the streets."

Two days later Mike met a man by the name of Ungur. He was also troubled by the homeless boys' environment. He had little to work with, but he had a heart that loved kids, and he had faith. Ungur spent time with the boys and fed them soda and sandwiches. He told them about the love of Jesus, and the boys listened. Most of the boys were not delinquent, but they were at risk of crossing over and walking the wrong path. Ungur felt any good he did was undone when he had to leave boys on the street at night.

Ungur began to pray. He prayed for a house, a place where the boys could stay, a place of safety. He had no money to buy a place, and he had no plan. So he just prayed for what was needed.

There was a sick woman in the hospital who heard of Ungur. Her name was Mariş, and the doctor told her that she had two months to live. Her lungs were diseased. So in her forties, she prepared to die. Mariş owned a house, and knew she would not need it much longer. She offered Ungur her place if he would use it for the boys.

She felt she had done the right thing when she signed the deed. Then a curious thing happened. Not only did she feel good about giving her house away, she began to feel physically better. The next day the doctor commented that her cough had improved. A few days later the doctors could find nothing wrong with her. She was discharged from the hospital.

Now Mariş did not have a house. She went to Ungur and asked him if he needed someone to cook for the boys. This woman was an answer to the prayers Ungur had yet to pray. He had not thought about cooking.

The house was soon filled with ten boys. They learned what it meant to trust in Jesus, for it was Jesus who supplied their daily needs. Ungur did not have resources and neither did Mariş. If there were no groceries or cash for the electric bill, everyone asked God to solve their problem. Provision always came, usually from unexpected sources. With each small miracle, each little answer, the boys' faith grew.

When Mike met Ungur, he needed a second house for ten more boys. Then, before long, a third house was opened. Yet Ungur had no steady sponsors. Mike offered a portion of the pasta factory's profits to help with monthly expenses. Also he sent the homes all the pasta the boys could eat.

The most important thing these boys learned from Ungur was how to have a personal relationship with Jesus. As one older boy grew in faith, he became concerned for his parents. He was sure they did not know about the love of Christ. He had run away from home in eastern Romania, and feared his parents would grow old and die without knowing Jesus. The boy assured Ungur that he would return, he just needed to talk to his mom and dad.

People in the community were not always happy to have a house full of boys next door. Ungur made many moves, and currently needs a place where he can house all his children.

Ungur with orphaned twin boys.

Mike always responded in childlike amazement when God provided. Yet at the same time he was staggered by the untouched need. He worked so hard that, at times he felt like he was close to "burnout." The desire to live a "normal" life grew inside him.

Ana was busy, too, with seven children and a part time job. Anyone who has met the Olari family is impressed with pleasant and well behaved children. Mike and Ana have a good marriage and enjoy each other's company. There is pain when they are apart.

One night, back in Phoenix, after the kids were in bed, Mike got a chance to relax. Stretched back in his Lazy-boy, Ana saw fatigue in his face. She thought of how the children missed their father. "Mike, are we doing the right thing?"

Mike looked up. "What do you mean?"

"Maybe there is someone else who should be doing this job." Ana paused, "Maybe someone without so many kids — someone who is better qualified."

"Honey, I am sure many can do this job better. Maybe God talked to them, but they just didn't hear. But I heard, and I have to obey."

"I know." Ana looked down momentarily, "But, Mike, you work so hard. You don't rest. Look at you, you have indigestion half the time. I'm afraid it's an ulcer."

Mike knew Ana's concerns were legitimate. He would like to spend more time with the family. They agreed to pray about it. Mike asked God to show him again what he should do. He had no idea how God would communicate. But he had a feeling that God would say something like: "Mike, you have worked hard. I have someone else to take over now."

Mike went to bed that night and dreamed. There are some dreams we need to pay attention to because God speaks to us in dreams. He spoke to people in Bible times through dreams and still does the same today. At the same time, other dreams spring from our subconscious. These may provide insight into our inner workings, but are not words from the Lord. Finally, other dreams come when one has eaten too much pizza before bed. These dreams are bizarre. It would be foolish to put credence in such manifestations.

Usually, when Mike dreamed he only had fuzzy recollections the next morning, except for the rare occasion when God directed. This night Mike would dream not a visual dream, but an auditory dialogue.

"Mike, you are tired, and you want to quit. You have just started what I have for you."

This was not what Mike hoped to hear.

"What has happened up to now has been a lesson for what I have for you. You have worked hard. I want you to let me lead and bless."

Mike remained silent in his sleep.

"I want you to form a non-profit corporation. You will be a connection between churches in the United States and churches in Romania."

"But no one will trust another guy just out raising money." Mike remembered how some TV evangelists misused contributions.

"Each contributor will be able to check where their gifts end up. A contributor will sponsor one family with a pledged amount on a monthly basis. Donors can write the family to see if the money actually arrived. Local pastors will take applications from needy families, and verify their accuracy."

This sounded like it might work.

"I want you to form a board from respected honest people. Include Christian leaders, businessmen, and lay people. They will help you and give you ideas."

For Mike this was a new concept; a whole plan he had never considered. He was excited, but past experience taught him it would be a lot of work. In the morning he told Ana about the dream.

She furrowed her brow and thought for a couple of seconds. "You know, it might work. This is something I have never thought of before. This could be exiting!"

At first Mike was enthusiastic, but he was already too busy. His fatigued body caused him to think how much work this project would require. He wondered if this might only be a common dream, just one he happened to remember very well. Could this idea have popped up from his subconscious?

As Mike went about his work, he tried to put the dream out of his mind. All the time it continually haunted him. Deep inside he knew what had to be done.

Mike let another two weeks pass before he contacted a number of trusted Christian brothers. He asked them to come to a meeting, and nine showed up. Mike presented the plan. All nine were interested, and all wanted to be involved. Mike had his board of directors.

Board members came up with good ideas, like a plan to run the mission on volunteer staff. This cut expenses so more of the contribution could reach its destination. Virtually all aid organizations skim contributions to finance their programs. For the foreseeable future, 100 percent of the gift would reach the targeted family. A volunteer teacher from Phoenix Community College created a computer program. This cut time in bookkeeping and mailing. A volunteer banker took care of government tax-exempt applications, so the organization could have nonprofit status. Now they could issue tax deductible receipts.

The board prioritized who would get the monies. Single parents were high on the list. Those who were completely unemployed due to massive factory shutdowns, had high priority. Those who were employed but could not keep up with inflation were lower on the list. Denominational preference would not be a factor with any funds distributed. Aid to families would not be limited to those in the Christian community. However, pastors and church elders would monitor eligibility and expenditures.* Recipients understood that this was not welfare, but temporary assistance. In turn, when they were able, they were encouraged to help others in need.

Some money would be given to orphanages, but most would be given to families. For if families had enough to eat, then they would not need to put any of their children in an orphanage. Board members decided that a donor should be able to choose to support a pastor or evangelist if they wished.

The board decided not to give addresses of contributors to Romanian families. But all assisted families would give their address to the contributor. The contributor could then contact the family if they wished to check up on funds, or they could become penpals. That would be each contributor's decision. They could write letters in English, as it is not difficult to find a translator in Romania. If Romanians replied in Romanian, volunteers in the American-Romanian community could translate.

The organization was named Family to Family—Outreach Romania. To varying degrees all former Bloc counties suffered from maladies similar to Romania's. It is Family to Family's dream to reach out to these people also. Now assistance is modest—God does not expect us to solve all the world's problems. But He does expect us to reach out in love and do what we can—somewhere.

In 1998 a contribution of fifty American dollars would double a suffering family's monthly income. With this ad-

---

*Board members divised a system to double-check where monies went. Funds were sent to an accountant in Romania, who in turn mailed cash to recipients. (Checks are not yet used in Romania.) Romanian law requires all cash to be sent registered mail. Government receipts indicate the amount received in the form of a signed register tab. The accountant keeps all receipts on file, which can be inspected at anytime.

ditional income, a household has enough to eat and is able to pay utilities. A fifteen or twenty dollar contribution helps most families tremendously. In the summer of 1998, Family to Family helped fewer families than Mike hoped. It assisted just over 300 households, or about 3,000 people. The board and Mike still pray more people will see the vision and help the destitute.*

While Family to Family may help, it is not a long term answer. It is emergency assistance; still an emergency may last for years. If people are going to make a living, the economy must be rebuilt, from the ground up. Assistance is only meant to sustain families in the interim.

Mike knocks on the "door" to deliver assistance, a contribution from someone stateside. Most of this family's children pose.

---

*Readers with an interest in family assistance should contact: Family to Family—Outreach Romania, P.O. Box 2094, Sun City, AZ 85351-2094, USA.

International investment adopted a wait-and-see attitude towards Romania. New jobs have not materialized. Romanians find it impossible to get loans to start small businesses. Banking, as we know it, has just started in a few cities. While the country was debt free at the time of the revolution, it was also dead broke and had no credit.

Under communism, workers did not receive paychecks. They received cash in envelopes. They could not open saving accounts, because they did not exist. Extra cash was stuck in a shoebox, and slipped under the bed. "Shoebox savings" were wiped out with 300 percent inflation.

The government ran something that might be called a bank, but it dealt with government concerns. If, for some unusual reason, a person received a check, they could take it to one of these banks. Maybe they would get their money in three or four weeks.

Staggered by handicaps, some entrepreneurs were still able to forge ahead and start businesses. In the fall of 1996 Romania held elections. The old communists were forced into a runoff,[1] which they lost. Romania had a new president, Emil Constantinescu, a university professor. Power had transferred peacefully. A solidly noncommunist government was in place. The attitude of foreign investors began to shift to a more favorable position.

Economics, new businesses, banks, and factory startups at one time seemed beyond Mike's concern. In 1995, a group of American investors approached Mike. They wanted to employ him as a liaison of sorts. Mike spoke fluent Romanian, knew cultural nuances, and more importantly, he knew a lot of people. The investors wanted to start a bank in Arad and sought Mike's assistance. He was needed to contact officials, buy property, oversee construction, and help open the bank. Experts from the states would manage the actual banking business, and train

Romanians to take over. In the process he met the President and Prime Minister, and worked with important officials in the Ministry of Finance.

In the summer of 1997 some believers asked Mike to help start a Bible college in Arad. The need was obvious—years of repression had bred much ignorance. Mike had seen the problem as a young teen when false teaching was endorsed by well-intentioned people. Under communism, seminaries were allowed to exist in Bucharest, but attendance was severely limited. This mere token gesture allowed the communists to control religious activity more easily. The Pentecostal seminary could only have a dozen or so closely monitored students.

The need for a Bible college becomes more pressing in light of recent government reforms. The law now states that children must attend religious instruction classes of the student's denominational choice. The new government realizes that strong spiritual principles build a strong nation. However, there is a shortage of Bible teachers.

A few Bible schools started after the revolution, and Arad has a couple Christian high schools. More are needed. Mike was busy with the bank and felt he did not have time to be involved in education.

One evening a knock sounded on Mike's apartment door. It was Dr. Moţ Ghiocel, a professor in mathematics. He told Mike how Arad's planned Bible college was to be accredited by the Ministry of Education. He explained their high academic expectations and described a need for English and Bible teachers at the college level. He especially desired to meet the demand for public school religious instruction teachers. He told how a student could attend college for only 100 American dollars a month. Room, board, tuition, and books were included in the price. They planned to start small in the fall of 1997 with fifteen or twenty students, and hoped to have guest instructors from America come for a few weeks or semesters. In time the founders hoped to expand and include other fields of instruction. Naturally Mike was seen as a link to American resources, but Dr. Ghiocel had another concern. He wanted Mike to pray for this endeavor. He wanted Americans to pray in solidarity. He had learned under communism that only God could make an effort prosper.

Shortly after one a.m. Mike gave into Dr. Ghiocel's persuasion. Before the fall semester started, Mike sat on a panel that screened each student applicant and tested their English. Facultatea de Teologie Penticostala "Betania" Arad (Bethany Pentecostal College, Arad) opened in September 1997 with thirty full-time students, and thirty part-time students.* While the college services the Pentecostal community, it is their goal to produce public school teachers who teach from an interdenominational perspective.

An amazing course of events had led Mike to be involved in both the economic and spiritual well being of his countrymen. People's physical needs required attention. He knew that to meet only physical needs is to say people are machines of flesh. If spiritual needs are not nurtured, then the spirit is amputated. This is the most inhuman of mutilations. Yet to preach to a soul and ignore worldly pain is hypocrisy. All human needs had to be addressed, spiritual and physical.

At times Mike's mind wanders back to the days of his childhood, herding sheep and goats for his penniless family. Then he thinks of how God has blessed him, and is amazed. Through different circumstances he was learn-

---

*If the reader desires to sponsor or partially support a student, please contact: Family to Family—Outreach Romania, P.O. Box 2094, Sun City, AZ 85351-2094, USA.

ing the same lesson as St. Paul taught when he said, "I have the strength to face all conditions by the power that Christ gives me."[2] As he looks down the future path, mountainous obstacles loom high. He has no idea how this new path will twist and turn. He knows that mighty governments will continue to fail, and powerful enterprise will come to nothing, but his attention is focused on an ancient Hebrew prophet who was instructed by an angel of the Lord. "You will not succeed by military might or by your own strength, but by my spirit. Obstacles as great as mountains will disappear before you."[3]

THE BEGINNING

ENDNOTES

Chapter Five
[1] "Eminescu, Mihail." Encyclopedia Britannica. 1973 ed.

Chapter Eight
[1] Genesis 24.

Chapter Thirteen
[1] Rosenblum, Mort; David and Peter Turnley. *Moments of Revolution Eastern Europe.* (New York, N.Y.: Workman Publishing, 1990), 28.

[2] Codrescu, Andrei. *The Hole in the Flag. A Romanian Exile's Story of Return and Revolution.* (New York: William Morrow and Company Inc., 1991), 114.

[3] Ibid., 114.

[4] Stanley, David. *Eastern Europe on a Shoestring,* 2nd edition. (Hawthorn, Victoria, Australia: Lonely Planet Publication, 1991), 545.

[5] Ibid., 546.

[6] Codrescu, Andrei. 30.

[7] Rosenblum, Mort; David and Peter Turnley. 24.

[8] Kronenwetter, Michael. *The New Eastern Europe.* (New York: Franklin Watts, 1991), 113, 114.

[9] Lorimer, Lawrence T., Editorial Director. *Lands and Peoples, Special Edition: Life After Communism.* (Grolier Inc., 1993), 58,87.

[10] Ibid., 58.

[11] Codrescu, Andrei. 123.

[12] Ibid., 46.

[13] Ibid., 102.

[14] Kronenwetter, Michael. 114.

[15] Doerner, William. "Vicious Keepers of the Faith." *Time* January 8, 1990. 32,33.

[16] "Fear and Loathing in Bucharest." *U.S. News & World Report,* January 8, 1990. 38,39, and Banta, Kenneth; Mader, William; Wilde, James. "Unfinished Revolution," *Time,* January 8,1990. 32.

[17] Codrescu, Andrei. 39-40.

[18] Ibid., 71.

[19] Abel, Elide. *The Shattered Block, Behind the Upheaval in Eastern Europe.* (Boston: Houghton Mifflin Co., 1990), 148-151.

[20] Lorimer, Lawrence T. 29.

[21] Kronenwetter, Michael. 114.

[22] Lorimer, Lawrence T. 31.

[23] Able, Elide. 150.

[24] Kronenwetter, Michael. 114.

[25] John 7:21-23.

[26] 1 Corinthians 1:12-13, 3:1-9 (TEV).

[27] *Romania After the Revolution,* TVP & Agape Europe, Video cassette, Walter Kast, Switzerland.

[28] Luke 22:42-44; Matthew 26:52-54.

[29] Isaiah 53; John 3:1-21, and 13:34-35; Acts 1:6-11; Romans 3:21-31; 6:23; 10:9-13, 1 John 2:1-2; Revelation 21:1-4.

[30] Lapadat, Claudiu. Personal Interview. Translator- Daniel Musteaţa. August 6, 1996. Timişoara.

[31] Roske Sile. Personal Interview. August 1996. Bucharest.

[32] Greenwald, John. "A Revolution's Unlikely Spark." *Time*, January 1, 1990. 37.

[33] Codrescu, Andrei. 27.

[34] Stanley, David. 546.

[35] Codrescu, Andrei. 27,28.

[36] Mehedinti, Nelu. Personal Interview. July 6,1996. Timişoara.

[37] Peţan, Tudor. Personal Interview. July 6,1996. Timişoara.

[38] Mehedinti, Nelu. Personal Interview. July 6,1996. Timişoara.

[39] Stanley, David. 546.

[40] Codrescu, Andrei. 27.

[41] Mehedinti, Nelu. Personal Interview. July 6,1997. Timişoara.

[42] Codrescu, Andrei. 28-29.

[43] Borrell, John; and Mader, William. "Slaughter in the Streets." *Time*, January 1,1991. 34-37.

[44] Codrescu, Andrei. 28-29.

[45] Borrell, John; and Mader, William. 37.

[46] Musteaţa, Daniel. Personal Interview. August 3,1996. Arad.

[47] Negrea, Traian. Personal Interview. August 12,1996. Arad.

[48] Silaghi, Teodor. Personal Interview, translator- Musteaţa Daniel. August 6.1996. Timişoara.

[49] Lapadat, Claudiu. Personal Interview, translator- Musteaţa Daniel. August 6,1996. Timişoara.

[50] Mehedinti, Nelu. Personal Interview. August 6,1996 Timişoara.

[51] Peţan, Tudor.. Personal Interview. August 6,1996. Timişoara.

[52] Mehedinti, Nelu. Personal interview. August 6,1996.

[53] *Rumänien Nach Der Revolution.* Agape Europe & TVP. Videocassette. Campus für Christus, Switzerland.

[54] Codrescu, Andrei. 30.

[55] Stanley, David. 546.

[56] Friedrich, Otto. "When Tyrants Fall," *Time,* Jan. 8,1990, 26.

[57] Wilde, James. "A Kaleidoscope of Chaos." *Time,* January 8,1990. 35.

[58] Negrea, Traian. Personal interview. August 12,1996. Arad.

[59] Nagorski, Andrew; and Kounalaikis, Markos. "Down With Ceausescu!" *Newsweek,* January 1,1990. 28-32.

Chapter Fourteen

[1] Rosenblum, Mort; David and Peter Turnley. *Moments of Revolution Eastern Europe.* (New York, N.Y.: Workman Publishing, 1990), 25.

[2] Codrescu, Andrei. *The Hole in the Flag. A Romanian Exile's Story of Return and Revolution.* (New York: William Morrow and Company Inc., 1991), 31,32.

[3] Ibid, 33.

[4] Nagorski, Andrew; and Kounalaikis, Markos. "Down With Ceausescu!" *Newsweek,* January 1,1990. 28.

[5] Stanley, David. *Eastern Europe on a Shoestring,* 2nd edition. (Hawthorn, Victoria, Australia: Lonely Planet Publication, 1991), 547.

[6] Codrescu, Andrei. 35.

[7] Stanley, David. 547.

[8] Rosenblum, Mort; David and Peter Turnley. 25.

[9] Borrell, John; and Mader, William. "Slaughter in the Streets." *Time,* January 1,1991. 36.

[10] Stanley, David. 547.

[11] Codrescu, Andrei. 36.

[12] Stanley, David. 547.

[13] Rosenblum, Mort; David and Peter Turnley. 25.

[14] Musteața, Daniel. Personal Interview. August 3,1996. Arad.

[15] Codrescu, Andrei. 37.

[16] Stanley, David. 547.

[17] Negrea, Traian. Personal Interview. August 12,1996. Arad.

[18] Stanley, David. 547.

[19] Rosenblum, Mort; David and Peter Turnley. 26.

[20] Stanley, David. 547-548.

[21] Interview shown on "CNN News," Dec. 21,1989.

[22] Thomas, Ted. Personal Interview. Spring 1996. Phoenix.

[23] Stanley, David. 547-548.

[24] Codrescu, Andrei. 35-36.

[25] Rosenblum, Mort; David and Peter Turnley. 25.

[26] Codrescu, Andrei. 36.

[27] Rosenblum, Mort; David and Peter Turnley. 27.

[28] Codrescu, Andrei. 37.

[29] Nagorski, Andrew; and Kounalaikis Markos. 28-32.

[30] Codrescu, Andrei. 37-39.

[31] Rosenblum, Mort; David and Peter Turnley. 24.

[32] Codrescu, Andrei. 40.

[33] Stanley, David. 584.

[34] Ibid., 548.

[35] Thomas, Ted. Personal Interview. Spring 1996. Phoenix.

[36] Codrescu, Andrei. 40-41.

[37] Stanley, David. 548.

[38] Thomas, Ted. Personal Interview. Spring 1996. Phoenix.

[39] Banta, Kenneth W./Timişoara; Mader, William/London; Wilde, James/Bucharest. "Unfinished Revolution." *Time.* January 8, 1990. 29.

[40] Video tape recorded from T.V.R.L., (TV România Liberă) aired on April 15 or 22, 1990 Timişoara. Translation provided by Mike Olari.

[41] Banta, Kenneth W. 29.

[42] Watson, Russell; with Meyer, Michael; and Breslau, Karen/Bucharest; Nordland, Rod/ Timişoara; and bureau reports. "The Last Days of a Dictator." *Newsweek.* January 8, 1990. 23.

[43] Video tape recorded from T.V.R.L., (TV România Liberă)

[44] Codrescu, Andrei. 25.

Chapter Fifteen

[1] Codrescu, Andrei. *The Hole in the Flag. A Romanian Exile's Story of Return and Revolution.* (New York: William Morrow and Company Inc., 1991), 10.

[2] Watson, Russell; Meyer, Michael; Breslau, Karen; and Nordland, Rod. "The Last Days of a Dictator." *Newsweek.* January 8, 1990. 16-23.

[3] Jones Jr., Landon Y. "Busted by the Baby Boom." *Time*, January 29, 1990, 36.

[4] Echikson, William. *Lighting the Night, Revolution in Eastern Europe.* (New York: William Morrow and Co. Inc.), 193.

[5] Breslau, Karen. "Overplanned Parenthood." *Newsweek,* January 22, 1990, 35.

[6] "AIDS A Sneak Attack on Eastern Europe," *U.S. News and World Report.* February 19, 1990. 11.

[7] Stanley, David. *Eastern Europe on a Shoestring.* 548-549.

Chapter Sixteen

[1] Porubcansky, Mark J. "Voters Send Message in Romania, Bulgaria." *The Arizona Republic:* November 5, 1996.

[2] Philippians 4:13 (TEV).

[3] Zechariah 4:6 (TEV).

Inquiry Form

Family to Family, P.O. Box 2094, Sun City, AZ 85351

Voice Mail and Fax (602) 504-6077

_____**Please send information about sponsoring a Romanian Family.**

_____**Please send information about sponsoring a Romanian Bible college student.**

Name:_____

Address:_____

City:_____ State:_____

Zip:_____

Telephone: (_____) _____

To order a copy of *Hidden Destination*
Call 1-800-931-BOOK (2665)

Postal orders to: ACW Press, 5501 N. 7th Ave., Suite #502
Phoenix, AZ 85013-1755
Include $12.99 for each book plus $4.00 for shipping and handling.
$1.00 for each additional copy.
Arizona residents must include 6.8% sales tax.